S. Edelestin

DR

ʻm W ×

FALSE PRETENCES

An Abbot Agency Mystery

Veronica Heley

Severn House Large Print
London & New York

This first large print edition published 2012
in Great Britain and the USA by
SEVERN HOUSE PUBLISHERS LTD of
9-15 High Street, Sutton, Surrey, SM1 1DF.
First world regular print edition published 2009 by
Severn House Publishers Ltd., London and New York.

British Library Cataloguing in Publication Data

Heley, Veronica.
  False pretences. -- (An Abbot Agency mystery)
  1. Abbot, Bea (Fictitious character)--Fiction. 2. Women
  private detectives--England--London--Fiction.
  3. Detective and mystery stories. 4. Large type books.
  I. Title II. Series
  823.9'14-dc23

ISBN-13: 978-0-7278-9884-5

Severn House Publishers support The Forest Stewardship Council
[FSC], the leading international forest certification organisation. All
our titles that are printed on Greenpeace-approved FSC-certified paper
carry the FSC logo.

MIX
Paper from
responsible sources
FSC® C018575

Printed and bound in Great Britain by the
MPG Books Group, Bodmin, Cornwall.

ACKNOWLEDGEMENTS

Thanks are due to my IT friend Mark, who was kind enough to talk this technically challenged writer through the unusual computer procedures which feature in this book.

ONE

Bea Abbot ran a domestic agency which didn't 'do' murder – except that every now and then she found herself dealing with just that. At sixty years of age, she thought she ought to take it easy and let her two young protégés handle routine cases, but what might be routine to some could be murder to others.

Thursday evening

He told her the moment he got back. Scrambling down from his Range Rover, he confessed the lot, admitted he'd been found out. Perhaps, if she hadn't that minute returned from decimating the rabbit population, she wouldn't have thought of scaring him with the shotgun. But this latest mistake of his, added to his recent shenanigans, was too much.

She aimed at his head.

'No, no! Honoria, no! I was ever so careful, I swear!' A scream. 'No, please! No one knows that it was you who ... Where's my medication?'

He dived into one pocket after another but in his panic only succeeded in scattering keys, cash and the all-important pills on the ground

7

around him.

She booted the pills beyond his reach.

He collapsed, clutching at his heart. Tried to speak. Something about having left messages on his computer?

She lowered the shotgun to watch him die.

A week later, Friday afternoon

Bea couldn't concentrate.

Sometimes she could go for a whole day and not think about Hamilton. For whole weeks at a time, she was able – just – to live with the fact that she'd never see him again. And then, wham! Down she went.

She stared at the email on her computer screen, trying to make sense of it. Her phone was ringing. She could hear it but couldn't make herself respond.

Stop work? Walk away from it all?

No, she couldn't. This was a working day, and if she didn't work, she couldn't pay her two assistants' wages, or keep the house going. So work she must. Only, she couldn't concentrate.

She considered a crying bout and decided against it. Tears didn't help; they only gave her a headache. Friends were no help, either. They said, 'How well you're coping. But of course you've always been strong.'

Aren't strong women occasionally allowed a day off on which to weep?

No tears allowed in working hours. She got up, needing to move, trying to shift the depression that threatened to overwhelm her. She checked the collar of her plain white shirt in the mirror and saw that she was now looking every day of her sixty years. All the care she'd taken to have her ash-blonde hair cut in a becoming style, and her still fine 'eagle' eyes, couldn't disguise the fact that she was over the hill.

The phone stopped ringing. And started again.

She put both hands over her eyes, and then moved them to her ears, trying to block out the sound.

It was no good. She would have to take some time off.

She walked out of her office through French windows into the seclusion of the back garden. Wrestling a reclining chair into the shade under the sycamore tree, she collapsed on to it.

It was very warm. Almost too hot. She told herself there were only so many days in the year when the sun shone in a blue sky, unhindered by cloud, and that she should make an effort to enjoy it. She told herself to count her blessings, and couldn't. In her head she knew that she had much to be thankful for, but in her heart ... ah, that was where the trouble lay.

She wriggled her toes free of her sandals and ordered herself to lie back, close her eyes and let the world go hang itself.

Only, as soon as she cleared her mind of one worry, another leaped into its place. At least there was no rain forecast, which was a blessing since she wasn't at all happy about the guttering at the top of the house. Neither of her live-in assistants had complained about the drip-drip tack-tack noise outside their rooms when it rained, but Bea could hear it in her bedroom immediately below them, and she knew that some time soon the guttering would have to be replaced. At enormous cost, no doubt.

Then she was expecting a phone call from Max, her self-important Member of Parliament son. Had she really promised to go with him to a 'do' that evening? Unfortunately his wife was heavily pregnant, and Max had asked Bea to substitute at some important political function or other. Boring, boring. Bea wasn't looking forward to it.

There wasn't anything much she *did* look forward to nowadays.

An angry exchange of words streamed out of the French windows from her office.

What were the youngsters doing in there, anyway? Computer geek Oliver had his own office beyond Bea's, while Maggie was supposed to be in reception at the front of the house.

A crash. Bea's eyes flew open.

Maggie had dropped something? Maggie could be clumsy and, when upset, she did tend to throw objects as well as words.

Silence.

Bea was not fooled. Something had happened indoors, something that had caused Oliver and Maggie to have a shouting match. Except that eighteen-year-old Oliver did not shout. That wasn't his style.

Prompt on cue, Oliver appeared in the door-

10

way; all bright-eyed intelligence. His hands were raised to his shoulders in apology. 'Sorry, Mrs Abbot. Maggie says you won't want to know, but I said you should decide for yourself.'

Bea's eyes went beyond Oliver to where another man of mixed race stood, holding a large cardboard box. A man perhaps ten years older than Oliver and several inches taller, a handsome man with a warm brown skin. Bea had never met him but knew immediately who he was: Zander, short for Alexander. Trouble.

'Mrs Abbot. I must apologize for intruding without an appointment. Could you spare me ten minutes? I've been responsible for a man's death, and I need help.'

His voice was pure chocolate cream. Maggie had gone overboard for this man last year, and had then taken fright and run away from him as fast as she could. Maggie wouldn't want him in her life again. Zander knew that, of course. So it must be something important which had brought him here today.

Bea closed her eyes, hoping she'd been dreaming. Knew she hadn't been. She pulled herself more or less upright. 'Take a seat,' she said, indicating a folded-up chair nearby. She realized she hadn't anything on her feet and wondered vaguely what had happened to her sandals.

Zander set the box down on the flagstones, pulled up the second chair, opened it out and set it down nearby with a mastery over inanimate objects which Bea was forced to admire.

11

He seemed to have recovered well from the beating which an erstwhile colleague had inflicted on him. And the knifing, too. Maggie had said he was shaven-headed, but he'd allowed his hair to grow since then, possibly to cover his scars?

Oliver shrugged and padded back into the house, while from a first-floor window came the sound of pots and pans being crashed around. Maggie had retreated to the kitchen and was making her displeasure felt.

Her visitor also looked up at the kitchen. He laughed, a little self-conscious, oozing charm. 'I didn't mean to upset Maggie.'

Bea felt and sounded sour. 'But you wouldn't let a little thing like her being upset stand in your way?'

He looked down at his hands. Big hands, well shaped. 'I did consider it, but you are the only person I could think of who might help me. I know Maggie often works out of the office. She might not have been here today. I decided to risk it.'

Her eyes went to the cardboard box. Something picked up from a supermarket? Not new.

He pulled open a flap and withdrew a bronze figurine of a dancer which he placed on the flagstones beside her chair. 'Signed. French. Art deco. Worth a bit.'

She touched it with her fingertip. Smooth and classy, like him. 'Stolen?'

'Now why would you think that?'

They both smiled, for it was his innocent

involvement in some stolen art treasures which had landed him in hospital and his assailant in a coffin.

'No, not stolen. But not mine, either.' He delved into the box again, and one by one he withdrew and placed on the table: a silver photograph frame, a gold pen, a leather diary, a Thermos flask and some other bits and pieces which must have cost someone a small fortune. The collection was the sort of thing which might normally be found on an executive's desk.

Bea's eyebrows rose higher. 'Not yours, and not stolen?'

He sighed. 'I need a witness, someone impartial but with a sharp mind, to go with me when I return these things to the dead man's widow.'

'The man whose death you brought about?'

He winced. From above came a burst of music. Maggie had turned on the radio. And the television too, probably. Maggie liked noise.

'All right, you've earned yourself an interview. Let's adjourn to my office so that I can take some notes. If I can find my sandals.'

He retrieved her sandals, and she eased her feet into them. He packed everything back into the box and followed her into her office, which was shady but still rather too warm on that fine summer's day. She switched on the fan.

Seating herself behind the big desk that had once been her husband's, Bea drew a pad of paper and a pen towards her and waited for him to start.

13

'When I left hospital,' he said, looking out of the window and not at her, 'I found my balance had gone. Not my physical balance – that came back quickly enough – but my ability to live on the surface of life. I looked at myself in the mirror and realized that, though I wore the same clothes, I was no longer the same man.'

Bea nodded. A near-death experience can do that to you.

'Money and sex, that's all my friends talked about. They expected me to join them in the usual round of parties and pub visits. I couldn't. I rang Maggie a couple of times, but she didn't want to know. Oliver intercepted my last call to her. He was kind enough to meet me at the pub and try to explain how she felt. I understood she wasn't ready to see me again yet and left her alone.'

He hadn't understood, of course. His forehead creased when he spoke her name. But this was not the time to try to explain Maggie's complicated love life.

'I'd lost my enthusiasm for my old job, couldn't see the point of updating websites to sell expensive trivia any more. I gave my notice in at work, moved to a room in an elderly lady's house. It's quiet there. Healing. And I can make her life easier by doing odd jobs, mowing the lawn, changing light bulbs, that sort of thing. It seemed to me that if I'd been given my life back again I should try to do something useful with it. Someone at church told me of a temporary job that—'

'Which church? St Mary Abbots?' This was her local church and the one her husband had loved.

'Er, no. That's a bit – elaborate – I suppose you could say. Beautiful but dark. No, I go to St Philip's. Do you know it? It's not so fashionable, of course, but I found it friendly and they've a beautiful garden. Anyway, I applied for the job and got it. It was for the Tudor Trust. Have you ever heard of it? It's a charitable housing trust, very old established, very respectable. They wanted someone to create a website for them. I'd hardly started when the receptionist-cum-office-manager left in a flurry of hissed accusations and red faces. There was no one to answer the phone, so I did, and somehow I slid into taking over most of her work. They were pleased with me and asked if I would stay on till they could reorganize the office. I found out later that that was just an excuse. They hadn't employed anyone of mixed race before, and though some of them thought it was the right thing to do, others took time to come round to it.' His tone was ironic; he'd dealt with slurs about his background before.

'The Trust was set up in the nineteenth century when some well-to-do members of the aristocracy built blocks of flats in the City to house deserving cases. They have an office down there to assess applications, collect rents, deal with everyday maintenance, but the headquarters is in an early-Victorian house overlooking Kensington Gardens and that's where I work. It's all very old-fashioned and upright and well meaning. I liked the feeling that I was working with good people, helping to make other people's lives a bit easier.'

He stopped, his eyes flickering over Bea, into the garden, back to his fingers, and up again.

She prompted him. 'It was your personal Garden of Eden. How long did it take you to realize there was a snake in the undergrowth?'

'Months. I didn't want to see the problems. I soon got to grips with the office manager's job in addition to handling the website, and they made the post permanent. Yes, I was naive, but so were most of the board. Do you know, only one of the directors has ever had any business training, and the only one who has an enquiring mind is the oldest of them all and the frailest? The directors were all born with silver spoons in their mouths. They treat the premises like a club, come in for lunch most days – which does cost a lot, but they regard it as their perk – and only a few actually put in some time for the Trust.

'They don't take a salary; they're entitled to an honorarium and expenses, but not all of them take even that. When one director retires or dies, someone of similar background is suggested to take their place. Noblesse oblige, they said. One of them was kind enough to explain it to me.' A tight smile. He was probably as well educated as any public school boy.

Bea grunted, all disbelief. 'So because they were members of the privileged classes, they did it for love not money? Untrained? Not a sensible way to run a company. What happened? No, let me guess. Somebody from the real world exploded their bubble. Auditors?'

'Yes. A new man. His father had retired, after having done their books for some twenty years or more. The son discovered the Trust was operating at a loss, and being a trust all the directors were liable to make up for the losses. He said they must bring in someone to sort it out immediately. What a tempest that raised! They had never, ever ... couldn't understand, etcetera. Lord Murchison – he's the great granddaddy, the one on the wrong side of ninety – proposed bringing in a grandson of his to retrench, reorganize and resurrect. But this young man – who's in his fifties, by the way – wouldn't come without an appropriate salary. It sounded sensible to me, but the proposal split the directors. They couldn't believe that a man should want to be paid to work for a Trust! Unheard of! Obviously not a pukka wallah.'

Again that tight smile. 'Some of them really do talk like that, you know. Unbelievable. Anyway, the board fragmented, some wanting to bring in their own nominee, some wanting to wind up the Trust, sell the buildings and be done with it. The one thing they all wanted to avoid was publicity. I could see the whole thing dragging on without resolution for months. Meanwhile, we were haemorrhaging money.

'So I started to look at the figures myself. My computer was linked with the one at the office in the City so I could access all the necessary information. The rents were coming in OK and were on a par with similar accommodation in that area. The staff in the offices – that includes those who manage the day-to-day work of collecting rents, the people who go out into the field to inspect the properties, and the ones at head office – are paid at slightly below the going rate, because they've been sold on the idea that it's a privilege to work for a Trust. The Trust owns the Kensington HQ; the rates and utility bills are reasonable. True, if that building were sold and the Trust moved to a smaller place in the suburbs they'd save a mint, but the directors can't imagine locating to a less prestigious venue.

'The biggest outgoing – and it's huge – is on maintenance, but the Director responsible was always saying that they need to do more, because elderly buildings need money spent on them to keep up with today's Health & Safety regulations. Fire doors. Lifts. Heating. Rewiring, and so on.

'I started to look at the cost of maintaining the buildings. For years the Trust had put all its maintenance work out to a building contractor called Corcoran & Sons. Recently Great Granddaddy – Lord Murchison – had suggested diversifying by splitting the work between Corcorans and another firm, in which he had shares. Naturally,' his voice flattened, 'they wouldn't consider using a firm whose directors they didn't know personally.

'As usual the directors had been divided in

their opinion about using a firm new to the Trust, but he'd overridden them to arrange for this second firm to rewire one building while Corcorans rewired another. Both contracts had just been completed and the invoices received. As part of my job I opened the post and took the bills through to the Maintenance Director for checking and payment, and I happened to notice that one bill was for twice the amount of the other. For the same work.

'We are not talking peanuts. The Maintenance Director saw that I'd spotted the discrepancy and remarked that it was always better to use good workmen, even if they were more expensive, rather than those who bodged the job. He sold that idea to the board, who agreed to continue with Corcorans, though they did murmur that perhaps they ought to ask one or two other firms to quote for jobs as well. The figures burned into my brain. I started to go through invoices from Corcorans for the past few months. They'd been charging astronomical sums for changing a couple of light bulbs. The repair of a door hinge would pay a family's gas bill for a quarter.

'There were a number of small maintenance jobs on hand waiting for attention. I arranged for half of these jobs to go to Corcorans as usual, but I asked the firm recommended by Lord Murchison to attend to the rest. Corcorans came in at roughly double what the others would have charged.

'I didn't know what to do. I'd overstepped the
19

mark, I'd gone behind the director's back, and I told myself that if there really had been anything wrong, someone else would have spotted it, and that if they continued to ask for quotes, the scam – if there was a scam – would die a natural death.'

Bea nodded. She could see how tempting it must have been to do nothing.

'Only, the more I played around with the figures, added up a possible overspend here and there, the more I realized that, if someone had been fiddling the books, they might have got away with half a million, maybe more. I assume that Corcorans had either been greedy and been taking the Trust for a ride or, perhaps, that someone in the Trust had been taking a kickback for throwing work their way.'

He braced himself. 'The only person who could have swung such a scam was the director in charge of maintenance, who was on excellent terms with the managing director of Corcorans, even had him in to lunch once a month. This particular director bullied the staff and fawned on the other directors. He referred to me by names that, well, if I'd wanted to make trouble, meant I could have taken him to a race tribunal. I told myself it was a cultural thing, that he'd been brought up to think the British were top dogs, the Empire lives on, public schools rule OK.'

Bea nodded. Oh yes, she could well believe that Zander would bend over backwards to avoid being thought prejudiced. 'Don't tell me;

he was a public school type who wasn't trained for the job but thought the world owed him a good living? Someone with a triple-barrelled name such as Montgomery-Peniston-Farquahar?'

A dimple appeared on Zander's cheek. He really was a most attractive man. 'You've missed something. The title. He's an Honourable, and his wife is a Lady. He told me that, if we ever met, I must call her "Lady Honoria" at first and then "My lady".'

'But in the end you did take your research to the board of directors. And...?'

'I thought I might be laughed out of court, because the evidence was all circumstantial. He put up a brilliant defence. I wondered – I still wonder – if he was more stupid than sly. I can hear him now, saying that good workmanship always costs more but is economic in the long run. He pointed out that he'd given the best years of his life to the Trust and had never taken a penny more than the honorarium and expenses which they were all allowed.'

'What did he live on, if he only took an honorarium from the Trust?'

'Stocks and shares, inherited wealth. He said he'd done his best, had been tearing his hair out trying to make ends meet, and would of course resign if they wished. I could see the board of directors thinking that of course he'd meant well, and if he'd misjudged Corcorans, well, they might have done the same thing. One of them even started to blame himself that he hadn't spotted the problem earlier.'

'They preferred to think him incompetent rather than criminal? Hmm. Ignorance is no defence in law, and usually gets thumped for it.'

'I could see they were going to close ranks against me and that I'd be out on the street in no time. So I chanced everything on one question. I asked if he'd show his bank statements to Lord Murchison, to prove that he'd not received any kickbacks from the builders. He collapsed, and I was sent home.

'I don't know what went on after I left, but that evening he had a heart attack and died. The verdict of heart failure was accepted with some relief by all and sundry, and no one uttered a word about people fiddling the books.

'Unfortunately his widow is a formidable person. She said that we'd driven her husband to his grave. She vowed to sue the Trust for libel, slander and the cost of dry-cleaning the clothes he died in. The Trust couldn't afford to pay her off and couldn't afford to let it be known that one of their directors had been accused of embezzlement. Delegates of directors traipsed out to see his wife, trying to resolve the situation. Eventually they succeeded ... but she's asked for my head on a platter.'

He flicked a finger at the cardboard box. 'These are the personal contents of his office. She's requested that I take them out to her, when I understand she'll decide whether or not I am to keep my job. The directors wipe sweat off their brows. Most of them would be happy to see me go in order to close the books, but one in particular would like to play fair. He advised me to grovel and said that, if I do get the sack, he'll see that I get some kind of pay-off. It's true that I do feel responsible for the Honourable Denzil's death. If I hadn't pointed the finger at him he'd probably still be alive and, even if he was as corrupt as I imagined, I couldn't wish death upon anyone.'

'It's weighing on your mind?'

He lifted his hand and let it fall. Yes, it was. Bea remembered now that this man believed in a loving God, that he attended church and read his Bible. He was a man who tried to do the right thing in a world which didn't much care about right and wrong any more. If it ever had done, which she thought unlikely.

Bea laced her fingers and leaned her chin on them. 'What do you want me to do?'

'I need backup, someone to come with me when I take this stuff back to his wife. I need an impartial observer. I understand that Lady Honoria shared her husband's view of people of mixed race, and to be frank I'm not sure how much more racial abuse I can take. If she starts ... No, I know it's no good losing my temper with her. When I was first advised to grovel to her, I thought that I'd tell her to get lost. But I like the job, and I don't see why she should be able to get me sacked for what I did. Then I thought that, if she tried to sack me, I'd say I'd go to an industrial tribunal and then all her husband's little ways would come out into the open.

23

She wouldn't want that, would she? Oliver's told me a lot about you and the problems you've solved for other people. I thought that if anyone could, you might be able to face her down, point out the law to her.'

And he wasn't averse to seeing Maggie again. Hmm.

He said, 'You don't actually have to pretend to be a solicitor, but a hint of that might help?' He produced a chequebook. 'Your fee? I'm willing to pay in advance.'

Bea swivelled round to look out of the window. If Zander was right, and she rather thought he was, then a large-scale fraud had been perpetrated – and possibly was still continuing – on the people at the Trust.

Fatigue dragged her down. She simply hadn't the energy to help him. In any case, what excuse could she make to accompany him to see the widow, and what difference could she make if she did?

It was his own fault that he'd got himself into such a mess. Such naivety was asking for it.

He exclaimed something, and she turned back to see a slow tide of red climbing up from his throat to his hairline.

Ouch. Had she spoken her thoughts aloud? 'Oh. I'm sorry. I didn't mean—'

'Yes, you did. And you're quite right. I always want to give people the benefit of the doubt until ... No, you're right. Forgive me. I shouldn't have come.'

Bea pressed her fingers to her eyelids. Her

24

dear dead husband had always liked to look for the best in people, too. Although he'd often been disappointed, he'd always gone on hoping. But when he'd come across something nasty, he'd not hesitated to do something about it. So what would he have done in such a case?

She had a sudden vision of Hamilton wrinkling his nose, saying, 'I smell Roquefort!'

Yes, she could smell strong cheese, too.

She said, 'It was a very timely death, wasn't it? What were the circumstances?'

'I don't know. I think he got home and just dropped dead. There's to be a big funeral and then a memorial service.'

She said, 'I don't fancy pretending to be a solicitor, although I do agree that it might be as well for you to have a witness when you see her. I suppose I could carry a briefcase and look professional, but—'

'That's all I need. A witness with a cool head.'

'When do you have to visit her?'

'Tomorrow at eleven.' He stood, smiling. 'The only thing is, can you drive me? I haven't a car.'

Friday evening

Honoria contained her rage with an effort. If only Denzil had been more careful! How often had she told him...! And now look where he'd landed her, having to do battle with the Trust to keep the manor going. Well, she could do it. Of course she could. Hadn't she been the power behind his throne for ever?

The worst of it was, she'd have to find a replacement for Corcorans. Sandy thought they could continue as before. More fool him. On the other hand, it shouldn't be too difficult to find another building firm sympathetic to her point of view, and if Sandy started to be difficult then ... out goes he!

First get the practicalities out of the way. The funeral. No one had queried the death certificate. Dicky heart, natural causes. She must put in another stint on the phone, advising people about the funeral. Tiresome, but necessary. At least no one expected her to act the part of the grieving widow, since Denzil's weakness for young girls had been well known.

Honoria grinned. In due course she was going to take her revenge on the little sluts who'd encouraged him to stray, but first things first. There would be time for pleasure once the business end of things had been tied up.

Tomorrow she'd deal with the coffee-flavoured troublemaker. She didn't anticipate any difficulty. She'd teach him his place, and that would be that.

TWO

Friday evening

Bea climbed the stairs from the agency rooms to the kitchen, pulling herself up by hanging on to the banister. Whatever was the matter with her? She knew, really. Age and grief. Sixty wasn't old, but grief was a killer.

Maggie, tall and gawky, was crashing around the kitchen in a scorching temper. Bea braced herself; she did not feel like taking on Maggie in a tantrum.

Oliver was laying the table for supper but as usual had put the knives and forks the wrong way round, irritating both Bea and Maggie. He hadn't even the excuse that he'd been brought up in a family that ate off its knees in front of the telly, since the first eighteen years of his life had been spent as the adopted son of an English headmaster and his wife. He hadn't fitted in there very well, and on discovering something nasty on his father's laptop, had been thrown out of the house ... only to be rescued and brought to Bea by Maggie, rather as one brings home a stray cat. Since then he'd become Bea's right hand at the agency and was turning into a handsome young man.

Bea failed to understand how Oliver could make a computer juggle statistics but become a cack-handed idiot when faced with domestic chores such as laying the table. Personally, she blamed Maggie for mollycoddling him.

Maggie, on the other hand, could only perform the most basic functions on a computer but had developed into a successful project manager, while at the same time running their four-storey Kensington house with noisy efficiency. And she knew how to lay a table properly.

Winston, their long-haired black cat, made as if to jump up on to the work surface ... and nearly got swiped by Maggie with a pan. Winston knew when it was best to make himself scarce. He plopped out of the cat flap on to the iron staircase that led down into the garden.

Bea wished she could do the same.

Maggie shot evil glances at Oliver as she dished up some of her special meatballs in tomato sauce, with spaghetti and baby courgettes.

'...and I thought I'd made it quite clear that I did not, repeat NOT, want Zander hanging around with his tongue out. I hope you told him I was going out with a rich property developer. Make that the owner of a football club, or better still, a polo-playing South American. What excuse did he make this time?'

Oliver lifted both shoulders as she brandished a pan close to his head.

'He's in trouble,' said Bea, pushing herself to

defend him.

'So why come here?' Maggie thumped a bowl of grated Parmesan on to the table. 'Unless, of course, Oliver told him to. That's it, isn't it, Oliver? You've been sneaking out behind my back to go to the pub with him. Do you think I'm blind and deaf? You make arrangements to see him on your mobile late at night, when I'm trying to get to sleep.'

Oliver rolled his eyes, and held his tongue. Wise lad.

Bea said, 'Zander's been subjected to a lot of racist abuse. He blew the whistle on his boss, who then died. He's got to see the widow tomorrow, and he wants me to drive him there and see fair play. He's afraid he's going to get the sack.'

'If you believe that...!' snorted Maggie, winding spaghetti round her fork as to the manner born. Her make-up was imaginative, her short hair was bright orange this week, and she was wearing a sequinned top, the clashing colours of which made Bea blink. Oh, and scarlet shorts. A sight to terrify ... which was probably her intention. Maggie's pushy mother and ex-husband had made her feel worthless. Was this extreme get-up her way of fighting back?

'I believe he could do with a spot of good luck for a change,' said Bea, forcing small mouthfuls down.

'So do I,' said Oliver, clearing his plate and looking for seconds. 'I like him, I sympathize with what he's had to go through – all the racial slurs and that – and I'd like to help him.'

'Oh, you!' said Maggie, her fury evaporating as fast as it had arisen. Maggie was pretty well colour-blind as far as race was concerned, as was Bea. But they both knew racial prejudice did still crop up in social life and in the workplace.

Bea put down her fork, her food half-eaten. 'Sorry, Maggie. I don't seem hungry.'

Maggie switched from virago to mother hen. 'I thought you were looking a bit off colour. Throat sore? Glands up? There's a lot of it about. Why don't you go to bed early and I'll bring you up some of that stuff which is supposed to stave off colds for twenty-four hours, though what happens after that I've never been able to work out. Does the cold come back again? Or go away for good?'

'I promised Max I'd go with him to some reception or other at the House of Commons.'

Oliver reached for his mobile. 'He won't want you there if you're incubating flu. I'll give him a ring, make your excuses.'

'Yes, but...' The prospect of not having to talk to anyone for a couple of hours was enticing. Let Oliver make her excuses. She wasn't tired, exactly. Just screaming with pain. 'I suppose I could do with an early night, but then tomorrow I've promised to take Zander out to wherever it is, somewhere in the country. Don't let me oversleep.'

'I'll drive you,' said Oliver. 'No problem. Now if only I had a cap and uniform jacket, I could pass as your chauffeur. I'd like to see this famous old house that Lady Honoria owns. Zander says it's been in the family for yonks, should be handed over to the National Trust but Her Ladyship won't let go of it. What price her husband's death turns out to be murder? I do like a good murder.'

'Shut up, you!' said Maggie, tipping Bea's half-eaten plateful of food on to his. 'Can't you see she needs to be quiet for a bit?'

Bea shook her head at him. 'Behave yourself, Oliver. Nobody's hinted at murder.'

'That's what you've said before, and each time you were wrong. Murders mean extra work for us; that means a bonus, and I'm saving for a car.'

Maggie said, 'Lunkhead!' and swiped a hand at his head. He ducked, smiling.

Bea produced a wan smile, too. She knew what they were both thinking. Yes, they were both fond of her in their own way, but they also knew that if she were ill their jobs with the agency would evaporate because she *was* the agency. If they could do something to help her back to her normal self, they would.

She climbed the stairs to her bedroom but was too wound-up to go to bed. She was beginning to wear a track in the carpet from the front windows overlooking the tree-lined Kensington street, to the back window overlooking the garden. At each window she paused, now looking out over the quiet street, and now across the back garden and up through the branches of the sycamore tree to the steeple of St Mary Abbot's church. Hamilton had loved that view. She liked it, too.

Backwards and forwards ... The house was quiet around her. The youngsters went out; she heard the front door bang once and then again. Good. She didn't want them coming in with cups of tea, asking if they could do anything to help. To and fro. The church clock marked the hours, and so did she.

Would she sleep tonight? Perhaps. Perhaps not.

Only, if she didn't, she'd be good for nothing in the morning.

Saturday morning

'Pretty around here,' said Oliver, in the driving seat. 'It's what I think English countryside ought to look like.'

'A painting by Constable?' said Bea. 'Complete with broken-down cottage and poverty-stricken but happy peasants?' She'd slept for a few hours, but her mood was still on the cusp of dangerous.

Oliver grinned. 'Define "peasant".'

'Someone on social security?'

Oliver laughed out loud. 'Come off it. The peasants worked hard and received a wage and a tied cottage in return. By that definition I'm the modern peasant, and you're my tight-fisted employer.'

Zander, sitting in the back, didn't smile. Lost in his own thoughts, he may not even have heard the exchange.

Oliver had bullied Bea into getting a satnav, so he was threading his way through the country lanes without any difficulty. Substantial, brick-built stockbroker type houses flitted past the car windows. Tall beeches almost met shadowed lanes. There were passing places here and there for the occasional car, and horses at pasture. Down an escarpment they went, past an inn which looked popular. Up a steep, curling hill. They hung a sharp left by a church squatting among ancient yew trees and passed along a tree-lined lane to be met by a gate marked 'private'.

Zander would have got out to open the gate, but Oliver insisted it was his job as acting chauffeur. The gate swung open without a sound. The immaculate private drive now branched right and left. To the right you went through an archway which was decorated with a charming blue-faced clock – unfortunately not working – into a stable yard. There were no horses to be seen.

To the left, you swished round to the front of a building which looked as if it might have started in Saxon times as a large farmhouse and thrown out a wing here and a wing there in subsequent generations. The roof had recently been re-tiled, and the lath and plaster walls had been painted white between silvery-grey oak timbers.

There was a stunned silence in the car.

Zander shook his head. 'I thought it would be a small stately home with a portico, perhaps

Georgian.'

'I imagined a Tudor building with barley-sugar chimneys,' said Oliver, peering up at the uneven roofline.

Bea got out of the car, and stretched. 'Manor house, umpteen generations, the owner probably owned all the land around here at one time. I wonder if the doorbell works.'

She told herself she could go through with this, of course she could, and put out her hand to steady herself on the oak front door with its original studs. The door was the genuine thing, accept no substitute.

There was a heavy iron bell pull, which roused the neighbourhood. The sound seemed to echo from the surrounding hills. At that point she realized she had a ladder in her tights and had chosen the wrong shoes for a foray into the country. And of course, it was a bad hair day. Well, there was nothing to be done about her appearance now. And did it matter, anyway?

'No dogs,' said Zander, at her elbow with the cardboard box, 'or they'd be barking like mad.'

The door opened. 'You're late.'

A heavy-set woman with a magnificent torso. She was about Bea's age but carrying far more weight. Thin lips. Pale eyes in a pale face, pale hair cut to chin length, heavy-duty slacks, a man's shirt, boots. You might be fooled into thinking this was a dedicated countrywoman, but Bea noticed that an expert had cut the woman's hair and care had been taken with understated but effective make-up. The woman

34

would probably scrub up well.

'Lady...?' Bea had forgotten the woman's name. How dreadful of her!

'You may call me Lady Honoria.' Her eyes switched from Bea to Zander. 'I was expecting the Chocolate Box, but I didn't expect it to come with an entourage.'

Chocolate box! And she'd referred to Zander as *it*!

Zander reddened, but he didn't lack for courage. 'This is Mrs Abbot, a friend of mine. She was kind enough to give me a lift.'

Eyebrows pencilled in grey rose. 'Really? I relish the unexpected, but this really takes the biscuit. With a chauffeur, no less? Tell him to take the car round to the stable yard but not to expect tea in the kitchen. Are your shoes clean? I don't suppose you're accustomed to visiting important houses such as this one, which was mentioned in the Domesday Book ... if you know what that means, which you probably don't. Don't stand there dawdling; I've no time to waste even if you have.'

Bea nodded to Oliver – who had his own ideas about what to do that morning – and stepped inside after Zander to enter a dimly lit, panelled, flagstoned hall. Would this be the oldest part of the house? It smelt of dog yet no dogs had come to the door to investigate the visitors.

'Put the box there,' said Lady Honoria, indicating a circular mahogany table, probably early Victorian, in the centre of the hall. There was an assortment of dogs' leads and a flat brass

35

dish containing bundles of keys on the table along with newspapers and junk mail. Zander put the box down, pushing some of the dogs' leads aside.

'You were expecting to be met by my husband's Labradors? I've never liked Labradors, so I found them another home. Bull terriers, now; they're more my sort. I'm told your kind are always afraid of dogs,' said Lady Honoria, contempt in her voice.

Zander set his teeth but refused to rise.

Bea jumped in. 'I'm more of a cat person, myself.'

The woman stared at Bea with pale eyes and dismissed her as being of no importance. Turning, she led the way through a doorway slightly too low for Zander's six foot two height.

A vast room, with heavy beams crossing the ceiling. An enormous brick-built fireplace, probably Tudor. A worn carpet of many colours, shabby upholstered chairs of different styles, an empty vase on a piecrust table with a crack across its top. Curtains which looked as if they'd shred at a touch. Dust motes dancing in the air as the sun made its way through latticed windows.

To set against this picture of mild decay, the walls had been painted within recent memory and modern central heating installed. Also, there was a huge, modern plasma screen and state-of-the-art stereo system which must have cost a small fortune. Bea wondered if they were 'his' or 'hers'.

The lady of the house threw herself into an armchair before the empty fireplace. She didn't suggest that they seat themselves but Bea did so, anyway. Zander hovered and then sat as well.

Their hostess sighed. 'I suppose I'd better check that you haven't pinched anything on the way over. Bring the stuff in here, and set it out on the table.'

Zander got up without a word and went to fetch the box, taking everything out of it and placing it on the table beside Lady Honoria.

Bea understood that the woman was intent on breaking Zander down. Fetch this, go there, do that, keep your mouth shut. Oh yes, Lady Honoria knew what she was doing all right. She ignored Bea, who kept quiet and used her eyes.

'Is that a chip off the bronze? I shall hold you responsible for any damage ... No, I suppose it's all right. Put it on the window sill over there ... No, not that window, stupid! The other one. An inch to the right. Now turn it slightly ... Haven't you the sense to see that it should face the room, not the outside world? Do I have to do everything myself?'

Zander was becoming clumsy under these directions. Bea really had to hand it to the woman; she was a bully, but a successful one. The place was clean enough, so presumably she was able to get someone in to do the dirty work for her. Bea hoped the cleaner exacted double pay for putting up with the woman.

Zander returned to his seat, looking pale rather than red.

The lady of the house surveyed him from top to toe, and said, 'Humph. So you're the creature who drove Denzil to his death, eh?'

Zander muttered that he'd had no such intention.

'What? Speak up, don't mumble. I can't be doing with people who swallow their words. Now; did you or did you not, totally without proof, accuse my husband of fraud?'

'I–I asked the directors about a discrepancy which—'

'You had no proof.'

Zander swallowed, his colour receding further. He shook his head. 'But –' he was trying to fight back – 'when I asked if he'd show his bank statements to—'

'How dare you try to justify your actions! You knew any strain might bring on a heart attack—'

'No, I—'

'Don't you dare contradict me. It was common knowledge. You must have known. Everyone did. It was you and you alone who drove him to his death. Admit it!'

Zander bowed his head. 'I did what I thought was right.'

'No, you didn't. You didn't think. I doubt if you are able to. What you saw was an opportunity to embarrass a fine, hard-working man in front of his peers. So without asking him, without giving him any opportunity to explain, you went behind his back in an effort to destroy his reputation, everything that he stood for. Out of

38

envy! Jealousy! Heaven forgive you, for I doubt if I ever shall.'

Zander was silent. Hands twisting, eyes on the carpet. Every word striking him like physical blows.

Bea wanted to intervene but couldn't think what to say. *Dear Lord, she's flaying him alive. Please, give me something to say, to deflect her.* God was silent. Or perhaps she wasn't listening hard enough?

Lady Honoria threw herself back in her chair, and exhaled. 'I suppose you think that if you apologize I'll forgive you, but I'm not made like that. Forgiveness has to be earned, and so far I've seen nothing to persuade me that you are sincerely sorry for what you've done and want to make amends.'

Zander frowned, looking up. 'Amends?'

'Well, I am not one to hold a grudge against a man of poor education and little sense. I don't suppose you've ever been taught the meaning of loyalty, or discretion.'

Zander winced.

'The directors have begged me not to prosecute. At first I was very inclined to ask for my pound of flesh, but they have persuaded me to consider another option. I am to take my husband's place at the Trust, with a proper salary, of course. Three days a week, in charge of maintenance, with a brief to find a cheaper firm than Corcorans for all the maintenance work.'

Zander gave her a steady look, difficult to read. Was this the price the directors were

39

having to pay to hush the death up?

She sighed. 'How I shall miss him, my dear, dear husband. But work, they tell me, is a great help in times of grief. I start next week. So now we have to decide what to do with you, eh? Do I keep you on or let you go?'

Zander frowned. She was playing with him, cat and mouse. If he was kept on to work for her, she'd make his life miserable. Could he bear it? Should he? 'I don't think—'

'You're not required to think. On balance I think you should stay on. How else can you make amends, Sander?' She made the 's' quite clear.

'Zander,' he said. 'With a "z". It's a contraction of my Christian name, Alexander.'

'I shall call you the Sand Boy. Easier to remember. It reminds me of all the work that still needs doing in this old place, sanding down old paintwork, then putting on the primers, the undercoats and finally the top coats. My dear husband never would take more than expenses from the Trust, but now I'm going to work for them, for a proper wage, I'll be able to get some more repairs done. Sander. It suits you. A manual labourer. Well, I think that's all. I shall expect to see you at the office on Monday morning next.'

Zander rose to his feet, clearly torn between throwing the job back at her and remembering how much he'd enjoyed it at first.

Lady H also got to her feet. 'In future you'll leave all decisions about who the Trust employs

40

to me, right? You stick to making the tea and running errands, and I'm sure we'll get on very well.'

He wasn't finished yet. 'I will have to think about this. Perhaps it would be better to make a clean break.'

She put steel into her voice. 'Oh, you owe me, Sander. You owe me big time. And by the way, they're docking your salary to help pay for my services. A very reasonable adjustment, I thought.'

He was dignity itself. 'I will give you my decision after the weekend. Meanwhile, will you sign for your husband's belongings? I made out a list in duplicate.'

She narrowed her eyes at him but signed one copy with a scrawl, before giving it back to him. 'Wait a minute; where's his briefcase?'

Zander frowned. 'It wasn't in his office when we cleared it.'

'It's not in his car. I looked.' Her lips thinned even further. She was not pleased. 'Well, you'd better find it for me on Monday.' She said no more and let them out through the hall into the sunshine.

As the door thudded to behind them, both Bea and Zander let out a sigh of relief. Zander wriggled his shoulders. 'I rather think I've had enough of the aristocracy.'

Oliver had had an errand to run in the village below and had taken the car with him, so Bea and Zander set out to walk down the hill.

Bea said, 'The members of the aristocracy that

41

I've met have perfect manners. She is definitely not typical. EPNS rather than solid silver, perhaps?'

'What?'

'She reminds me of electroplated nickel silver. It looks real but isn't.'

'Ah, yes. My gran had some. The silver wears off eventually, doesn't it?'

Bea was annoyed with herself for wearing the wrong shoes. This particular pair had a nasty habit of rubbing her left big toe, and she had difficulty keeping up with Zander, who was sensibly shod for walking in the country. 'I suggest you let me photocopy the list she signed, just in case. By the way, I thought you kept your temper admirably.'

He rolled his shoulders. 'She's a sadist. She'd take pleasure in destroying me, if I worked for her.' A flicker of a smile. 'I begin to have some sympathy for her husband.'

Bea set her teeth, remembering how the woman had called Zander 'a chocolate box'. And referred to him as 'it'. 'Oliver and I will find you another job.'

He lifted his head, breathing deeply. 'That would be the easiest thing to do. But would it be right? If I went, wouldn't I always wonder...? I do owe her something, when all is said and done.'

They didn't speak again till they reached the car, parked under some trees opposite a pub. No Oliver. Ah, here he came down the road, smiling and clutching a plastic bag full of apples.

Neither Bea nor Zander were smiling. Bea was kicking herself for keeping quiet throughout the interview. Why hadn't she stood up for Zander when he was being used as a football?

'Lighten up, you two,' Oliver said, unlocking the car and putting the apples inside. 'Lunchtime, and the pub's got a decent menu.'

Zander hesitated. 'I'm not sure I fancy any food. I feel as if I've just been handed a black spot – that was the sign that you were marked out for death in *Treasure Island*, wasn't it?'

Oliver grinned. 'Did she make your blood run cold? That's nothing to what the locals say about her. I've been chatting to the lady who was selling these windfalls. Want to hear her take on the Lady of the Manor?'

Bea took Zander's arm. 'Everything will look better after we've eaten. Come on, Zander; Oliver's hungry.'

Saturday noon

Honoria locked and bolted the front door behind her visitors, thinking that the Chocolate Boy wouldn't give her any more trouble. She knew his sort. They needed to be shown who was boss. They might need a twitch on the leash now and then, but when all was done and dusted, he would do as he was told in future.

The nerve of him, asking her to sign a receipt for Denzil's bits and pieces! Although, come to think of it, the statuette was worth a bit. Not that she'd ever cared for it. But maybe, just maybe,

43

she could find another use for it? She smiled. Yes, why not?

Now, back to business. Luckily Denzil had had his electronic notepad in his car when he died. She'd grudged him the money he'd spent on it at the time, but there ... he'd had to have the very latest to show off with, hadn't he?

Had he really thought using a password would stop people accessing his files? What an idiot! She'd known for ever that he used the name of whichever bit of fluff appealed to him at the time. Recently it had been 'Kylie'.

Kylie! The very name of the chit sent her blood pressure up. Well, one of these days she was going to deal with Kylie.

Once into the system, she'd been horrified to find so much soft porn. She hadn't realized just how far he'd gone down that road, downloading pictures of young girls. Disgusting! Delete, delete. The only file she'd kept was the one for his staff records. Knowing the way his mind worked, it hadn't been hard to discover which file contained the home addresses and telephone numbers and hours worked for everyone who worked for the Trust, and she needed those for getting even with people who'd tried to wrong her.

Soon, very soon, she was going to make them pay for it.

THREE

Saturday noon

The pub had a Georgian frontage, but the building behind it was ancient, consisting of a series of small rooms on different levels. An extensive garden at the back boasted a stretch of lawn dotted with picnic tables, each with its own umbrella. All the tables were occupied on this fine summer's day.

Bea found her appetite had returned and enthusiastically ordered a steak and kidney pie with vegetables, but she refused to sit outside in the sun. 'Ants,' she said. 'Wasps. If there are any within fifty miles, they'll make straight for me. No, we'll find ourselves a table inside like civilized people.'

'Cheer up,' said Oliver, handing Zander and Bea halves of bitter. He never drank alcohol when he was driving. 'And listen up, for do I have a tale to tell! There's no shop in the village unfortunately, but down the road I spotted a woman struggling to put up a trestle table outside her front gate. Naturally I went to her assistance, being the kind, courteous soul that I am.'

45

Zander attempted a smile, and Bea did the same.

'She was selling plants and windfall apples, which I helped her to barrow from the garden at the back and to arrange on the table. I bought some of her apples, and she offered me a cuppa. I said she was the light of my life, so she brought me out a mug of some peculiar brew which she claimed was coffee but might have been tea. I couldn't tell which it was but, never mind, I drank it. I told her I was hanging around waiting for my boss to return the Lord of the Manor's effects to his widow. She straightened up like she'd been ramrodded and went all tight-lipped on me. But then curiosity got the better of her, and she unbuttoned.'

'Mixed metaphors,' said Zander, with a better attempt at a smile.

'So what? Did I get the low-down, or did I? My informant has lived in the village all her life, and her father and mother before her down to the twentieth generation, or so she said. Mr Faulks-Pennington – or whatever his name was—'

'Near enough,' said Zander. 'The Honour-able—'

'She said he should have been called "Dis-honourable", but apparently he did have some title or other. He bought the old manor house for his wife some ten years ago. It was a complete wreck, and they've been doing it up ever since. His wife boasts that her family once lived there, though my informant begs leave to doubt that.

46

I'm not sure why. Apparently the Lady of the Manor was married before, perhaps to someone else with a title? However it was, she kept the title when she remarried and insists on being addressed as "Lady Honoria", or "my lady". My informant pulled a sour face when she mentioned this.'

The food came. Delicious. Bea was, indeed, hungry. 'Hold on a minute. She asked us – no, ordered us – to address her as "Lady Honoria" which means she must be the daughter of a duke, a marquess or an earl. Denzil must have been the younger son of a nobleman too, if he claimed to be an Honourable.'

'My informant says that she's Lady Muck, and no one calls her anything else behind her back though to her face they're polite enough. She's pure poison, they say.'

Zander grunted. 'She is that.'

'And, wait for it,' Oliver reached the climax of his story, 'they all think she murdered him.'

'What?' said Bea.

Zander shook his head. 'Oh, come on!'

Bea was indulgent. 'Oliver loves a good murder.'

'No, no!' said Oliver, waving his hands about. 'You haven't heard the rest of it. They say he was a miserable creature, totally under her thumb—'

'I can believe that,' said Zander. 'He threw his weight about at work, but no, he wouldn't have lasted two rounds with her. She's a heavyweight.'

'So he came down here to the pub every night to drown his sorrows. Zander; you might be sitting in the very place he used to occupy, night after night, with the two dogs under his feet.'

Zander's arm jerked, and he looked around as if expecting his old boss to appear and turf him out of his chair.

'And,' said Oliver, 'he was supposed to be having an affair with one of the barmaids here.'

Zander and Bea both craned their heads to see who was serving drinks at the bar. A big, pot-bellied man, and a woman of perhaps forty, dressed like a teenager in an off-the-shoulder, skimpy T-shirt and very tight, low-slung jeans. A lot of lipstick, a lot of eye make-up, and not much chin. A laugh to frighten.

Zander and Oliver both looked at Bea, and she looked back at them. She shook her head. 'Don't even think it. Oliver is letting his imagination run away with him. By all accounts the Honourable Denzil was an unpleasant man to work for, and we've seen today that she's no better. He's dead, rest his soul, and we have to move on. Zander has to make up his mind whether to continue working for her or not—'

'I think not,' said Zander, setting down his empty glass. 'Life's too short.'

Bea reminded him, 'You could get her under the Race Relations Act. I could be your witness.'

He shook his head. 'I might get compensation, but it would mean going through a court case, and I'd still lose my job. One way or another,

48

whistle-blowers lose out.'

Bea got to her feet. 'Well, I'm fresh out of ideas. Suppose we have a coffee, and then make our way back. Order one for me, will you, Oliver, while I go to the loo?'

She felt bleak. Yes, some part of her agreed with Oliver that something was very wrong at the Trust, but there didn't seem to be anything obvious that they could do about it. She agreed with Zander that he ought to get out of there, but ... If only God had given her some idea of what to do or say ... but he hadn't. So she might as well call it a day.

She had to duck her head under a low lintel to get into the ladies, and once there she had to edge her way round a young girl who was hogging the washbasin. And crying, while trying to bathe an eye that was rapidly developing into a shiner.

'Oh, my dear,' said Bea. 'Are you all right? Silly question, of course you're not. Can I fetch someone for you?'

The girl shook her head. Yellow hair all over the place in bird's-nest fashion, pouting lips, too much make-up, too much flesh showing, a pretty bust. Very young.

'Don't fetch no one. He's gone and good riddance. What am I going to do? Me mum'll kill me.'

'I'm sure she won't. Here, let me look.'

One eye painted like a panda, one partially cleaned of make-up, the eyelid reddened and swelling. Bea sat the girl down on a stool and finished bathing the afflicted eye.

'How old are you?'

'Eighteen.'

A lie. Possibly seventeen? Possibly even younger.

The girl sniffed. 'Like, I didn't think he'd go off and leave me. How ever am I to get home now?'

'Perhaps he's waiting for you outside, to apologize.'

'Not him. Went off on the bike, sticking his fingers up.' She looked in the mirror and howled. 'Whatever do I look like? And I haven't got me eyelash curlers with me. I can't face everyone like this, can I? And me mum'll kill me.'

'Best wash the whole lot off, then.' Bea cleaned the girl's face as tenderly as she could. Without make-up the girl looked even younger. 'Where do you live? If it's not too far away, perhaps I could give you a lift home.'

'Over the hill. If I'd known he was going to walk out on me, like, I'd have worn me ballerinas.'

She was wearing four-inch, spiky heeled sandals. Her toes and heels were already chapped and rubbed raw. Her toenails had been painted black, as were her bitten fingernails. All chipped. She was a mess.

Bea said, 'You live up by the manor house? We were there this morning, taking some stuff back belonging to the owner.'

'Like, you're having me on, aren't you? Me mum cleans for the old witch, twice a week.

50

Can't please her, not anyhow. Last week Her Highness wanted to dock Mum's wages, and they had a right old to-do. She says Mum was spying on her, but she was only looking for his cigarettes, which he always used to let her have a couple, but that was before he copped it. Mum reckons she's so tight with money she'd steal the tartar off your teeth, if she could.'

'You knew them both?'

'Everyone knows them. Poor old git! I quite liked him. And if he wanted the odd fumble, then it was only to be expected, like, seeing as they've always slept separate, though I can't say I'd have gone that far with him.'

'Er, no. So you knew him quite well?'

A shrug. 'Randy old goat. Hands up your skirt soon as look at you, breath like a distillery, but give him his due, he always paid his way.'

'How?' Though Bea could guess.

'How d'you think? Like, half an hour's chat and a hand on your knee, and it's a fiver. An hour or so and a cuddle, it's ten. A couple of kisses and a hand up your bra in his car, and it's fifteen. It helped the cash flow, didn't it? He used to come down here every night, twice at weekends. My boyfriend that was, has a part-time job here, helping in the bar, washing up and that, so I often come in on my way home from—'

Was she going to say 'from school'? But she went on with hardly a second's pause.

'Work. A friend lives in the village and gives me a lift here and then I wait for Tony – that's

51

me boyfriend that was – to take me home when he's finished.'

'He didn't mind your flirting with an older man?'

A shrug. 'We shared the takings. Why not? Only today Tony said I should be nice to another old gent that's been eyeing me up, but I couldn't. He stinks, see. Yuk! Tony argued with me, saying he'd promised the old man I'd give him a cuddle, and he took me outside and walloped me one when I wouldn't, and then he got on his bike and went off and left me. And Pat – that's the landlord – he's going to be livid, being left in the lurch like that. And he's going to ban me for being under ... for being Tony's girl, and me mum's going to kill me!'

Bea bit back distaste. Didn't the girl realize she'd been on the slippery path to prostitution? 'Maybe your mum's right, and you could be making better use of your time.'

The girl wriggled, pushing up her bust. 'Homework, you mean? I should be so dodo. I know what assets I got, and they're right here, in front. They're what gets me a coupla drinks and some tips. What have I got to look forward to, otherwise? Sitting at a checkout in a super-market all day? That's what Mum used to do till she got fed up with it and went on to shelf-filling and a couple of cleaning jobs, and if that's all that's coming to me, then I'll take my fun where I can, thank you very much. Now,' she got up, fluffing up her hair in the mirror, 'how about that lift, then?'

'Give me five minutes to drink my coffee, and meet me in the car park.'

When they met up in the car park, the girl looked at the men, who reacted as if they'd been given an electric shock. They recognized what this girl was, far more quickly than Bea had done.

It turned out that Kylie lived not far off their route back to London. Bea suggested that Kylie sit in the back with her. Kylie wasn't too happy about this. She dismissed Oliver after one coquettish glance, but tipped her hip at Zander and moistened her lips, giving him what she thought was a provocative smile. When he failed to respond, she got into the car and slammed the door, saying it was a nice car but not exactly new, was it?

Bea decided to ignored that. 'So, Kylie, what did you think when you heard the old man had upped and died?'

A grimace. 'I was sorry, a bit. Most people thought it was funny like, joking that she'd frightened him to death. Pat, the landlord, he said she could frighten for England. Poor old Dishonourable. Always on about his heart, taking pills, wouldn't walk further than from the car park to the bar, made the dogs run behind his car to give them their exercise, which he shouldn't have done on these roads, it's dangerous, we all said so. But he wasn't going to listen, was he! Not him! Not the Dishonourable.'

'Was his heart that bad?'

Another shrug. 'He was supposed to be having some operation or other, but it got put off for some reason. Money, I expect. She spends every penny she can get on that old wreck of a house.' She pulled a mirror out of her handbag and yelped. 'What on earth do I look like? If I get in before Mum, I can put some more slap on, and maybe she won't notice. She'll kill me when she finds out I've busted up with Tony.'

'Don't tell me; you divide your takings three ways? Tony, your mum, and you?'

'I have to be nice to Pat, as well.' The girl humped a shoulder. 'What's it to you? And you can drop me off here, like it's only just round the corner, and I don't want no questions about why I'm coming home in a big car with no money to show for it. Er, you couldn't spring to a fiver, could you?'

Bea took one of her business cards and a tenner out of her handbag and held it up. 'I'm collecting information about the people at the Manor. If you think of anything more, or your mother has anything to say, would you give me a ring? It will be on a business footing, you understand? Payment by return of post.'

Kylie snatched the money without making any promises and got herself out of the car. All three watched her rump twitching up and down as she minced her way out of sight. Neither man commented. Bea felt like saying a whole lot of stuff about poverty and education and the unnecessarily hopeless view of life taken by some, but got tangled up in so many conflicting

54

thoughts that she kept silent.

Oliver drove smoothly off, taking them back to London by the quickest route.

Saturday evening

Bea paced up and down the garden. Surely she'd soon be tired enough to sleep. Across the back of the house she strode, between the huge pots which Maggie had planted up with Busy Lizzies, petunias and geraniums. Past the ironwork staircase that curled up to the kitchen on the first floor ... along the flagstones to where a garden shed crouched in the shadow of the brick wall ... across the garden to the sycamore, where the folding chairs sat neglected ... and back again to the house.

Again. And again. Like a squirrel in a cage.

Or a hamster, maybe.

The phone rang several times, but she ignored it. The house was silent above her since both the youngsters had gone out for the evening.

She paused mid-stride. Some of these old houses had once had wells in their back gardens. In its growth from prehistoric village to today's megalopolis – if that was the right term – the originally swampy ground had been drained by many small rivers all leading down to the Thames; rivers such as the Fleet which had subsequently been built over and forgotten. Many of the gardens around had once had their own well, used for drinking water as well as everything else. Unsanitary, but pretty.

She liked the idea of a well in her back garden. Something in soft red-brick, built up to hip height, with a lead canopy over it, held up by wrought ironwork. Charming. And of course, offering a neat solution to grief.

That is, if there'd been any water in the bottom of the imaginary well, which there might not have been, in that dry summer.

She pulled her thoughts back from the darkness in which they wanted to dwell and went into her office to switch on her computer.

Zander had decided he couldn't work for Lady Honoria.

Bea sympathized. She wouldn't have liked to work for her, either. On Monday Oliver would see if there was anything suitable for Zander in their books. Probably not, but you never knew. Jobs for office managers were not precisely their field. Bea had volunteered to ask if her busy Member of Parliament son might know of an opening for him.

Something Oliver had said was bothering her.

Over the years the agency had found staff for clients of all sorts and sizes, titled and otherwise. Hamilton had made Bea learn how to address their clients in the manner to which they were accustomed. Granted, they were more likely to be asked to find a butler for one of the embassies that proliferated in Kensington, than to provide staff for a prince in a palace. She'd probably misunderstood what she'd heard. But it did no harm to check, did it? And the longer she occupied her mind with something downstairs, the less time she had to pace up and down her bedroom, sleepless hour after hour.

There were some amusing sites on the Internet, offering to sell you a lordship or a title for peanuts. All scams, of course.

She found the site she was after at last; it was pretty comprehensive, but it didn't entirely answer the question that was hovering at the back of her mind.

Was Honoria really entitled to call herself *Lady* Honoria? Surely only the children of the top echelons of society had that right? Unless, of course, her husband was a knight. But the Honourable Denzil had not been a 'sir', or someone would have mentioned it. Honoria might well be exactly what she claimed to be, the daughter of a duke or an earl, but somehow Bea doubted it.

She had no good reason to doubt it.

Except – Roquefort. Strong cheese.

She sighed, exited the site.

It was still only half past nine. Her eyelids were stiff, her legs were tired, but her brain was going round and round and...

She delved into her handbag. Somewhere she'd kept a business card for a certain Mr Cambridge, the father of a school friend of Oliver's. Oliver had a knack of making friends of all ages, and this Mr Cambridge had not only taught him a whole load of tricks to use on computers – which Bea suspected might not be entirely legal – but had also instituted himself as something of a guru in Oliver's life.

She dialled, hesitated, cut the line. The answer

57

phone light was winking, indicating three missed calls. She ignored them.

Who was Mr Cambridge, exactly? Oliver had said he was an expert called in by the police on occasion. 'Occasion' not specified.

He'd looked old enough to be the grandfather, rather than the father, of Oliver's schoolfriend, but he'd certainly known how to summon the right policeman to sort out a nasty case of murder in which Bea had been involved some time ago.

She'd kept his card, thinking she would never want to use it, but he was the only person she could think of who might be willing to listen to a moan about a bully of a woman, injustice and racial prejudice. He'd said that if ever she wanted to talk over a tricky case, he'd always find time to listen.

She dialled again, and this time let the call go through.

'Mr Cambridge? Bea Abbot here. I wonder if you remember—'

'Most clearly. You unravelled a tangled ball of wool with great skill some time ago. How may I be of assistance?'

She was already regretting the impulse which had led her to call him. 'It's nothing, really. I can't see that anyone can do anything, but...' She tried for a laugh. 'I hate injustice, and I think you do, too.' Should she tell him? He had offered to listen any time she wanted to talk, but had he meant it? Well, she'd try him and see what happened. 'Could you spare me ten minutes while I rant away about something? You don't need to take any action afterwards.'

'I can do better than that. I have a rather good bottle of champagne here. Shall I bring it round? I don't suggest your coming here as my son appears to be having a rave-up downstairs.'

'I can offer a quiet room overlooking a peaceful garden. I would suggest we open the bottle in the garden, but I'm a martyr to midges.'

'Ten minutes.'

She felt better already. She looked down at what she was wearing, thought it was boringly biscuit-coloured, but did nothing about it. She renewed her lipstick and ran a comb through ash-blonde hair, making the fringe lie aslant across her forehead. Checked her make-up, giving a passing regretful thought to young Kylie and her probable descent into prostitution.

She was upstairs, tidying the big sitting room, when he rang the bell. A quiet man, grey and thin, who drifted like smoke into the house and opened the champagne with the minimum of fuss.

She had glasses ready; they sipped, expressed approval, settled into comfortable chairs in the sitting room. The blinds and shutters were closed at the front of the house, the French windows at the back left open to let in the cooler evening air.

He was wearing grey, shirt and trousers. He had grey eyes and a finely cut nose over a long upper lip. A wide mouth, a satisfactorily sharp chin. The skin on his neck was not yet deeply seamed, so he was probably younger than his air of fragility would seem to indicate. About her own age?

He set down his glass. 'So, rant away.'

'A question first. What do you know of the Tudor Trust headed by Lord Murchison?'

He was still for a moment then picked up his glass again, to sip at the champagne. To gain time? 'Why do you ask?'

'Another question; when is a woman entitled to call herself Lady Honoria?'

The faintest of wrinkles on his brow. 'I'm sure you know as much about the peerage as I do.'

'I doubt it.' She put her glass down with a click. 'I'm guessing that you know Lord Murchison socially, and that you would know how to uncover a scandal which he would very much like to keep quiet. Am I right?'

'I think you'd better start ranting. I'm totally in the dark at the moment.'

She didn't think he was. He knew something, she could sense it. His middle name was probably Discretion, or Loyalty. Could she prise him open? Not if he didn't want to be prised, no. But she had a feeling that even if he denied all knowledge of Lord Murchison, even if he told her she was barking mad, he'd not forget what he'd been told and might even do something about it.

If she pitched her tale well enough.

'We start,' she said, 'with an innocent abroad, who happens to be of mixed race but is what my parents would have called one of nature's gentlemen. A man who believes in God, who enjoyed his work helping other people. He suffered some racial abuse but put up with it, until...'

She talked on, while the light faded. He re-filled her glass once, but she refused any more after that. When she'd finished telling him what had happened that day, she said, 'So tell me I'm being stupid. Tell me I can go to bed and forget what's happened, that it's nothing to do with me.'

His eyes had been fixed on her all the time she'd been talking. She suspected that if asked to repeat what she'd said, he'd be able to do it without missing a word.

Now he let his eyes wander round the room. He could probably produce an inventory of her room without taking notes.

He got to his feet and, hands behind his back, walked over to inspect her dear husband's portrait, which hung beside the back window.

'Who did this? It's good.'

'My first husband, the portrait painter. Surprisingly, they were good friends for some years before ... before. Hamilton used to say he smelled Roquefort when something odd like this came up.'

'I met him once. There was some suggestion of putting him in for an honour in the Queen's birthday list. He refused, said he was dying. Cancer, wasn't it? A loss.'

She was not going to cry. No. Where had she left her handbag? Did she have a hankie on her?

Probably not. She sniffed, hard.

He said, 'Do you really think Honoria has invented a title for herself?'

'I don't know.' Sniff. 'She's a detestable woman.'

'That's no grounds for wanting her investigated.'

'No, I don't suppose it is. I told you, I just needed to rant and rave.'

'The racist slurs. You say the man won't prosecute?'

'Would you?'

He resumed his seat, steepled long fingers. 'You've no proof of anything but racial abuse. Tell your client to return to work and make notes of anything else racist which is said to him. Get him to threaten to prosecute, to go to the press. That should stir things up nicely. Meanwhile, I'll get you an interview with Tommy Murchison, whose son was in the army with me. Tommy's no fool. It will be interesting to hear what he thinks about all this. Roquefort, you say?' He lifted his glass to Hamilton's portrait and drained it. 'Roquefort, it is.'

Saturday evening

She'd looked everywhere, been through every drawer in his study, searching for the bank statements. She'd found five empty whisky bottles and thrown them away, plus some pathetic love tokens, presumably from that slut down at the pub though one of them was from

Della's misbegotten niece. No bank statements.

They must be in his briefcase, the briefcase which had not been returned to her as it ought to have been. Should she be worried? No, not really. She'd find it on Monday. Trimmingham was solidly on her side, would never let her down.

She was annoyed that Mr Milk Chocolate had failed to fall in with her plans immediately. Perhaps he needed to be taught a lesson? Hm. Yes. She knew just how to do it. He wasn't a serious problem, and neither was the pale creature he'd brought along with him. Was he her toy boy? Ha! She'd give him some stick about that on Monday. Neither of them posed any kind of threat, did they?

FOUR

Sunday morning

Bea slept well enough. Surprising, really, as the interview with Mr Cambridge had raised more questions than it had answered. For instance, what on earth did he expect to achieve by arranging for her to have an interview with Lord Murchison? And was it really a good idea to urge Zander to go back to work?

She felt flat. And unexcited by the fact that the sun was shining. Hooray for the sun. Lots of people would welcome its appearance. Personally, she didn't. Church bells were ringing; people were waking up to the day of rest and turning over in bed, thinking that they could have a nice long lie-in, and...

And not bother about the phone ringing. There was no sign of Oliver or Maggie so she would have to answer the phone herself.

'Mother, where have you been? That young man of yours said you weren't feeling quite the thing the other night, but you knew it was an important occasion and I do think you might have made an effort to come.'

Ah, her important Member of Parliament son,

Max. Now what did he want?

'Sorry, darling. You know how it is.'

'You're not going down with a depression, are you? That sort of thing gets around, and people don't know how to deal with it. One of Nicole's friends went into a depression, and she was off work for months. How will you cope at the agency if you're off work? You'll have to sell and—'

'Oh, shut up, Max!' Had she really spoken so sharply?

Shocked silence at the other end.

She made an effort to keep her voice down and soft. 'No, Max. I'm perfectly all right. I got overtired, that's all. Haven't been sleeping well.'

'That's one of the symptoms, isn't it? Have you seen the doctor?'

'No, and I don't need to. Really, Max. I'm touched that you care so much, but I'm going to be all right. It's just that I haven't had a holiday for a long time and have been working too hard.'

'Oh. Oh, well; Nicole and I have been thinking about a holiday, but the airlines won't take her at the moment. Too near her time, they say.'

'Yes, well. Perhaps you can find somewhere in Britain?' Nicole was finding the later months of her pregnancy hard going and made sure everyone knew it.

A heavy sigh from Max. 'You wouldn't like to come over and sit with Nicole for a bit, would you? She complains that I'm out almost every evening, but she doesn't want to go out herself because she feels so awful and looks such a sight. And when I try to suggest something, she doesn't want to know. I really can't bear it when she cries.'

Bea set her teeth. 'Perhaps I can give her a ring this afternoon, arrange to see her midweek.'

'It will have to be in the daytime. She's not up to anything by supper time.'

That meant eating into her work hours. Oh well. 'I'll see what I can do.'

'Bless you.' Another heavy sigh. He disconnected.

Rearranging her social life for the following week in her mind, Bea prepared to set aside some time for her daughter-in-law. Summer was a busy time in the agency, because people needed replacements for staff going on holiday. If she saw Nicole one afternoon, she'd have to work late that evening to make up for it.

What did she have on next week? She couldn't think. Ah, she'd promised to go with her infuriating though sometimes helpful first husband Piers to a show at an art gallery one night. Which day? He hadn't said, had he? His latest painting would no doubt be on show at some fantastic price. Piers was doing very well indeed nowadays, thank you.

Seeing Nicole wasn't that important, was it? Hm. Perhaps it was. Max had sounded really worried about her. Bea tried to make herself feel sorry for Nicole and failed. Oh dear. Was she turning into a legendary bad mother-in-law?

Well, tough. Work was more important, wasn't it?

Well, actually; not. She sighed. All right, all right. She'd find time for Nicole somehow.

Downstairs she decided against a cooked breakfast and switched the kettle on.

Oliver padded in, yawning. 'Are we having a full English breakfast today? Maggie's not up yet.'

Bea clicked her fingers. 'I had your guru round here last night, Mr Cambridge. He said there was a rave-up at his place. Were you there?'

'Me, Maggie and a dozen others. Watching a rough cut of a film Chris has been making in Docklands. Weird stuff but brilliant. He was trying out various bits of music for the soundtrack, and we voted on what worked and what didn't.'

Bea opened her eyes very wide. 'You never cease to amaze me. I thought it would be all cans of beer and maybe an illicit smoke.'

'No, no. Serious stuff. Chris never wanted to go to uni but doesn't really know what he does want to do. He shoots film at weekends, holidays. Mr C says Chris can leave uni if he proves he can make a short film which is accepted by some organization or other, I forget their name, something very Establishment.'

Bea was silent. Oliver had been on track to go to university himself, until he'd found pornography on his father's laptop and been thrown out of the house. Another whistle-blower who'd got hurt.

Bea had suggested he reapply for another year, but he'd said he wanted to stand on his own two feet. She hoped he wasn't going to change his mind as she didn't know what they'd do at the agency without him.

'Chris is Mr Cambridge's only son?'

'Mm. Married late, wife died a couple of years back. Shall I grill some bacon, then?' Clearly, he really wanted a cooked breakfast. Bea didn't, particularly, but got out the bacon, anyway. 'Was Zander one of the crowd last night?'

'Not his scene. I'm glad he decided not to go back to work. I'm sure we can find him something better.'

'Mr Cambridge wants him to do so and to report any abuse to the police.'

Oliver poured half a box of cereal into his own large bowl and added milk. 'Zander won't want to. I don't blame him.'

A delicate subject. 'Have you ever experienced abuse?'

'Everyone does. It depends how you deal with it. We had a spot of name-calling at school, but it was all fairly good-natured. You just spat out a few names in return. Scumbag. White-face. That sort of thing. I'm part Asian, which makes a difference. Zander's father was from Africa; Sierra Leone. Africans get more flak than Asians, I think.' He shovelled cereal into his mouth. He was growing fast and beginning to fill out. He ate as much as Maggie and Bea put together.

She wondered, 'Does it really make that much

68

of a difference where your people come from?'
She answered her own question. 'I suppose it
does. I suppose I have an automatic reaction,
thinking that Chinese and Japanese people are
bound to be clever, good at music and maths;
that Asian people make good traders; and that
Afro-Caribbeans are the best at sport.'

'You? You're pretty well colour-blind.' He
chucked his empty bowl and spoon into the sink,
from which it would have to be rescued to go
into the dishwasher. 'Now me, if I see a group of
black youths hanging around a corner I think
drink, drugs and knives – or guns. Which
proves, I suppose, that I'm more racist than
you.'

Bea laughed, for she knew very well that he
treated everyone who came to them for a job
with the same scrupulous courtesy.

Dishing up bacon and eggs, mushrooms,
tomatoes and a slice of fried bread for him, plus
a couple of rashers of bacon for herself, she
wondered if the difference between Oliver and
Zander was not one of racial background, but of
their experience of life.

Looking at Oliver, scoffing food, checking his
watch to see what time it was – where was he
going that day? – dressed in quality casual wear,
she reflected that, despite the trauma of being
thrown out of the house and being disowned by
his family, he was growing up to be remarkably
well balanced. Yet Zander, with a similar mid-
dle-class background, wasn't. But of course you
had to factor in what had happened to Zander

69

recently.

Hmm. She sipped coffee, staring out of the window through the sycamore to the spire of the church. Should she go to church today? She might. Hamilton had gone most Sundays, but he'd said once that every person worshipped God in their own way, and that the ritual which suited one person, turned another off. He'd appreciated the beauty of St Mary Abbot's; he'd often dropped in there during the week to sit in a side chapel to be quiet and pray.

Bea had struggled to do the same, but somehow ... it just hadn't worked for her. Her fault, doubtless.

Dear Lord, I'm doggy-paddling through life, trying to keep afloat, but I'm a poor swimmer and land seems out of sight. I know the fault is in me that I don't listen to you often enough. I couldn't even settle to read the Bible last night, or the night before. Yet, looking back over what's been happening, I see – at least, I think I see – that you've been pushing me into doing something for Zander. Right against might.

I know I was angry with you because you didn't help me defend Zander when that terrible woman was attacking him, but then you put that poor creature Kylie in my way, so that I could learn more about that precious pair. That was your doing, wasn't it, Lord?

So tell me: what do I do next?

Oliver got to his feet to drain the last of the cafetière into his mug, one eye on the clock. 'I'm going out for the day. All right?'

'Before you go, will you ask Zander to come in to see me? Today.'

He didn't like that. 'What do you want to see him for? It's all settled, isn't it?'

'If you can walk by on the other side of the road from an accident and say it's nothing to do with you, I can't.'

'You want him to ... do what?' Oliver was being ultra-protective of his friend.

Bea told herself to take this slowly. 'I want to talk to him, that's all. I want to discuss what steps might be taken to right the wrongs done to the Trust, and also to him personally.'

Oliver still didn't like it. Hesitated. Hovered. Frowned into the middle distance. Finally shrugged. 'All right. It's your funeral ... or maybe I should say it's going to be his?'

'No funerals, by order. I'd like to see him this morning, if he's not going to church somewhere.'

Oliver looked relieved. 'Oh, he will be. And then he helps out at some children's club or other on Sunday afternoons.'

Bea knew when she was up against a blank wall. It was good of Oliver to try to protect Zander, but in the long run was that the best thing for him? No. Toughen up, mate. The world's a sad old place, but if you cast yourself as a victim, then that's what you will become.

'All right. Give me his phone number, and I'll have a word myself.'

'I'll leave it on your desk.'

He wouldn't, of course. She remembered now

that Zander had told her he didn't attend St Mary Abbot's church, but went to another one ... now what was its name? St Philip's? Yes, that was it. Well, she could always catch up with him there. So she smiled at Oliver, said the weather forecast was good, and watched him depart – without leaving her the phone number.

St Philip's was probably not much older than St Mary Abbot's, but it was a completely different type of church. For one thing, it wasn't a national treasure built by Sir Gilbert Scott. It was a routinely pretty, stone-built Victorian church set in a garden at the end of a long road of individual houses built for the upper-middle classes. No busy traffic junction, no crowding in of expensive-looking shops as there was at St Mary Abbot's. No crowds. Peace and quiet. You had to pay big money to buy into this part of Kensington; though not, of course, as much as for Bea's own road, which was early Victorian at its cream stucco and large sash-windowed best.

Bea had decided it was a trifle too far for her to walk to St Philip's in what promised to be another hot day, so had taken the car. There was space for parking around the church. The garden was a haven, surrounded by shrubs and small trees, interspersed with bedding plants.

She'd intended to catch the mid-morning service but had mistimed her arrival to find it was due to finish in a few minutes' time. She wandered into the garden. Plenty of wooden seats, some in shade, some not. What a luxury in this built-up part of London!

She seated herself in the shade, half-listening to the hymn being sung inside the church. The words and tune seemed familiar, but she couldn't place them. She had never been a regular churchgoer, not like Hamilton. She'd caught a glimpse now and then of the extra dimension that belief in God and fellowship with other believers might make to her life. Most of the time she trusted in Him, but there were times – such as now – when her hold on her faith was shaky.

Sitting there in the garden with its evidence of loving care, she wondered if the members of the church cared as much about one another as they did about the church's surroundings.

She started awake as people began to leave the church at the end of the service, chatting to one another, shaking hands with the vicar. Children ran around in circles, chasing one another. A young father lifted a small child to perch on his shoulders. His wife tidied a baby into a pushchair. Older people appeared in clumps, some with walking sticks and two with Zimmer frames, helped along by younger people. There was a good mix of ages, cultures and colours. Well balanced. A knot of young people made arrangements to meet later. Churchgoers gradually spread through the garden and left by the gates on to the road. Some gave Bea a smile in passing; they must be used to people coming in from the road to rest awhile.

Finally the stream dwindled to a trickle, and stopped. No Zander. Bea gathered herself together and went into the church herself. Yes, he was there, stowing away an overhead projector. He took one look at her, and his shoulders slumped.

Aha. You know what I've come for, which means that Oliver told you I was on the warpath. Well, not the warpath, exactly. Or perhaps it was?

She said, 'I thought I could treat you to lunch at a pub. I'm happy to wait till you've finished.'

He nodded, busied himself with this and that. Bea took a seat, looking around her. Yes, she liked this sort of church, light and airy.

Although she had the car and suggested going to a pub in the country, he said he had to be back at church for the afternoon children's club, so they went to a quiet local place nearby. Roast dinner for two. Not as good as Maggie's cooking, but not bad, either.

'I must explain,' said Bea.

'No need. Oliver warned me. Well, I might go back, but only on my terms. You do realize, don't you, that I'm no knight in shining armour?'

That deflated her. 'What happened to make you change your mind?'

'When I got back yesterday I found a letter from Major Buckstone—'

'Is he the director who's been sympathetic towards you?'

'Yes. Just a line or two to say that Lady

74

Honoria would be taking over her husband's duties, and he hoped we'd be able to work together for the good of the Trust. If I had any queries, would I ring him at home. Which I did. I told him I didn't feel I could work for Lady Honoria and would forfeit a month's salary rather than return to the office and work out my notice. More in sorrow than anger, he pointed out that, if I went straight away, I would be putting the Trust in a very difficult position, leaving them without an office manager just when they'd lost their Maintenance Director. He said that of course he understood my position but, for the general good, couldn't I work out my month while they tried to find someone to take my place? He said that if I did so, he personally would see that I received some kind of bonus and an excellent reference. In fact, he thought he might have heard of a job which would suit me, through the old boy network.'

'So you agreed to return.'

'He was talking sense. Surely I can put up with her for a month?'

Bea was indignant. 'He bribed you to stay. Oh yes, he did. Very cleverly. What's more, he did it in a phone conversation and not in a letter, so he can't be held to what he promised you.'

'He's not like that.'

Bea sighed. 'Zander, how you've managed to live to the ripe old age of whatever, I do not know. Why, even Oliver has more street savvy than you.'

'Major Buckstone's a good man.'

'I don't say he isn't sympathetic to your case, but his first allegiance must be to the Trust. Is he the one who normally deals with personnel? Is he the director for Human Resources?'

'He is, and I think he does a good job. He's also the vice-chair, who takes meetings when Lord Murchison isn't well enough to do so.'

'Can you trust him to see that the Trust is run properly in future?'

An uneasy silence. 'I think his heart is in the right place.'

'What about his liver and lights? Sorry. Didn't mean to be frivolous. Zander, let me tell you how I see this next month developing. You return to the office and ensure that it runs smoothly. Everyone is pleased. Lady Honoria is delighted because now she knows that, whatever names she calls you, you won't walk out on her. Are you looking forward to that?'

He hunched his shoulders. 'Maybe someone will have a word with her.'

'Why should they? You've committed yourself to a month's torture.'

'I can always walk out, if she starts on me.'

'But would you? I think not. You'd think of the good of the Trust; you'd grit your teeth and stay.' She realized that she'd started off wanting Zander to stay and fight, and now was urging him not to do so. What on earth was the matter with her, changing her mind every five minutes?

He said, 'What can I do? What would you do?'

Bea shook her head. 'I see the attraction of the

76

job for you, and a month's wages is worth having, but I wouldn't put up with any abuse, and I don't see why you should, either. The law is on your side. May I give you a word of advice? Keep your mobile phone switched on when she's anywhere near you. Record any abuse, and then take it to the police. You might not even have to take it the police. Just the threat to do so should be enough to make her keep a civil tongue in her head.'

'But I couldn't stay on after I'd done that. It would be equivalent to walking out on them.'

'That's their problem, not yours. You have the right to be treated properly.'

Zander pushed his empty plate away. 'It's all very well for you. You don't know what it's like to—'

Bea was sharp. 'Stop being sorry for yourself. You've had a bad time and—'

'I used to think I was immortal, until I got beaten up and knifed. Then I realized I was as vulnerable as any child.'

'Huh! If you go around expecting people to beat you up, it's as if you've inked the word "victim" across your forehead. You cringe even before they lift a hand to strike you.'

He leaped to his feet, reddening.

'Oh, sorry,' she said, one second wishing she could recall the words, and the next deciding that no, they had to be spoken.

He paid the bill for their lunch and stalked out. She followed, grimacing. How awful; she'd allowed her temper to get the better of her. She

77

opened the car up, but he made no move to get in.

He spoke over her head. 'I must get back to the church, prepare for the afternoon.'

'Of course. Let me give you a lift, and of course I'll reimburse you for lunch.'

He still wouldn't meet her eye. 'What you said ... You're right, of course. I hadn't realized just how far this has got to me.'

'Keep your mobile switched on when she's in hailing distance?'

'Maybe.' He saw her safely off into the traffic and walked away.

Bea told herself she was an idiot. Even a child could have handled that better. She'd patronized him. Instead of building up his self-confidence, she'd undermined it further. She hit the steering wheel in frustration. How could she have been such an idiot?

Sunday afternoon

'Is that Major Buckstone? Lady Honoria here.'

'How are you, Honoria? Bearing up, I trust?'

'No use giving way.' It didn't sound likely that she would, but there was a formula for these occasions. 'Funeral's all fixed for a week on Monday. I assume you'll all be there?'

'We will do our best. Tommy might not make it, but I don't suppose you expect—'

'Oh, but I do, Major. I do. A full turnout to honour my poor dear Denzil's memory. I don't think anyone would expect less than that, do

78

you?'

'I'll see what can be done.'

'Of course you will. And as to that other little matter—'

'Zander's promised to stay on, to work out a month's notice. He's really very good, you know. We shall be sorry to lose him.'

'Have you found Denzil's briefcase yet? It's not here.'

'I don't know anything about that.'

'The Chocolate Boy must have taken it. I'll have words with him on Monday.'

It was a threat.

FIVE

Sunday afternoon

Bea got home to find the house as quiet as the grave. So, no Maggie. No Oliver. She relished the peace. She stopped herself wondering what the youngsters were doing. They were old enough to look after themselves. Mostly.

She pottered around, watering the big pots in the garden. The shushing noise of the hosepipe calmed her even more.

Finally she told herself that she couldn't put it off any longer and went indoors to phone her daughter-in-law.

Nicole answered the phone straight away, but didn't sound pleased to hear from Bea. Nicole was seven months pregnant and finding the hot weather difficult. According to Nicole, no one in the world had ever suffered more in pregnancy from the heat, swollen ankles and sickness than she did. Almost ten minutes was taken up by Nicole telling Bea how dreadful she felt, and how appallingly selfish Max was being, not helping to amuse her or rub her back or anything. In fact, he was out now, at that very minute, when she'd asked him specially to find her some green tea, which she thought she might fancy.

Bea listened and made the appropriate noises. She did sympathize with Nicole because being pregnant in hot weather was no joke, but she also had a sneaking sympathy with Max, who might perhaps be finding Nicole's complaints a trifle tedious – particularly since all suggestions to make her life easier were turned down out of hand.

A nasty, cold thought slid into the back of Bea's mind. Max loved Nicole; of course he did. But he was a not unappealing man, being tall, dark and handsome. True, he was running a trifle to seed, but he was still photogenic. He also had a soft heart, which meant he was not good at managing women. His wife would be the first to agree about that.

Perhaps, thought Bea, that was her fault? No, she didn't see how it could be. She'd always tried to support him in everything he decided to do. The alternative was to recall that his father was not only a portrait painter at the top of his profession, but also a ladykiller who could charm the pants off women without even thinking about it. Max hadn't inherited much of Piers' charm, but perhaps something in his genes made him super-attractive to the opposite sex?

To his wife's much younger and not pregnant sister, for instance?

Bea killed that thought. Surely he had more sense than to tangle with someone else while his

81

wife was pregnant?

'So where's Max today?' Bea asked, interrupting Nicole's sighing complaints.

'How should I know? He said he'd be back at three, and it's a quarter past already.'

'Wouldn't it be easier for you if you went back home to the constituency for a while? I'm sure it's not as warm up there as it is in central London, and your parents would be around to help.'

'I would, but Max is on some important committee or other which means he has to be here throughout the summer. It's a great honour to be asked of course, but—'

Which reminded Bea. 'You don't happen to have come across a Lady Honoria, do you?'

'Lady Honoria what? What's her husband's name?'

'Not sure. She calls herself Lady Honoria, recently widowed, manor house in Bucks. A squareish woman with a hard face.'

'Daughter of who?'

'Unknown. She might legitimately be calling herself "Lady Honoria". I don't know.'

Nicole was almost interested. 'You think she's trying it on?'

'Mm. Maybe. She's not a woman to tangle with unnecessarily. If you remember, could you ask Max when he comes in?'

That set Nicole off again. Bea arranged to see her later in the week and put the phone down.

She was restless. Although she didn't usually work on Sundays, Bea decided to go down to

her office and record everything she could remember of her visit to the manor house, of the
gossip Oliver had extracted from the woman
selling apples and plants, and finally, what she'd
learned from young Kylie.

Something was bothering her. The front doorbell. Someone was leaning on it. Now who...?
Ah. Piers, her ex. He did sometimes pop round
on a Sunday when he was in town, but he usually telephoned first. Of course – here she shot a
guilty look at the winking light on the answerphone – she hadn't picked up her messages
recently, had she?

It was indeed Piers, his shock of dark but
greying hair a trifle too long, his over-thin body
dressed in expensive casual clothing. Piers,
dancing with energy. He gave her a hug and a
kiss on her cheek, and she laughed out loud. He
nearly always had that effect on her.

Sometimes she wondered how they'd ever got
together, the up and coming young artist and the
naive girl straight out of school. They'd married
young and produced Max, but Piers' tomcat
ways had finally made Bea face the fact that
he'd never keep his marriage vows. And so
she'd divorced him, even though she didn't in
theory agree with the practice. Still didn't. Still
felt slightly guilty about it.

As a single parent, life had not been easy. Piers
had not then been earning enough to support her,
and she'd worked all hours at all sorts of jobs
until at last she'd met and married Hamilton.
Her dear second husband had adopted Max and

given them both stability, and a deep, abiding love.

After Hamilton's early death, Piers had re-appeared in her life. Apparently Hamilton had made Piers promise to keep an eye on her! An idea which made her laugh and shake her head. She didn't believe Piers could be trusted to look after her now, any more than he had ever been. However, now she'd accepted that he'd never change, they'd become friends of a sort.

'Was I expecting you?'

'No, no. At least, I did phone and ask if you were going to be free tonight. Thought we might go out into the country somewhere for a bite to eat.'

She thought of Kylie, wondered how she was getting on and whether she'd accepted another sugar daddy yet. 'Twice in one weekend? I had a pub lunch in the country yesterday. Would you mind if we went somewhere local?'

She looked around for her handbag. Where had she left it? 'Piers, you mix in the very best society. You haven't come across someone call-ing herself Lady Honoria, have you?'

'Not the Graves-Bentley woman?'

'Dunno. Manor house in Buckinghamshire. Husband died recently.'

'A square head on top of a square body, on top of thick legs? Single-minded and ferocious. Reminds me of a pit bull. I believe she used to breed them at one time. They say owners get to look like their dogs. Or perhaps it's the other way round and owners choose dogs which look like them?'

'That's her. So her name's Graves-Bentley?'

'Something like that. I met her at some "do" or other. Fixated on her ancestral home. Husband made noises about having his portrait painted but she put a stop to that, saying that if anyone was to have their portrait done it would be her, because it was her family home, not his. An odd argument. Fortunately she didn't want to pay my prices. I try not to prejudge when asked to paint the notoriously nasty, but in this case I was happy she didn't want me. I heard the husband had died. Not that I knew him at all. Not my type.'

'If you don't want to go out to eat, I could rustle up something here. The youngsters are both out.' Normally he could sit down and relax with her, but today he seemed jumpy, avoiding her eye.

'What?' He'd gone to look down into the garden. 'Oh. Just as you like. Somewhere local, fine.'

'So, what was Lady Honoria's husband like?'

Piers was clearly worrying about something but not yet ready to tell her about it. 'The husband? A nonentity trying to make out he was important. Well connected in a younger son sort of way, not that that counts for much nowadays. Hadn't made much of a mark for himself in the world; worked for a small Trust somewhere. I don't think I know anyone who's going to the funeral.'

'Lord Murchison?'

85

'What? Yes, I know him. Painted him some years ago. What do you want to know about him?' He focused on her. 'Bea, don't tell me you've got into another fine mess?'

'Sit down, and I'll tell you. I'd be grateful for any gossip or insights you can give me...'

She told him what had been going on, and he concentrated, pulling a face at the end.

'Bea, my gut feeling is: keep out of Lady H's way. Tommy Murchison's all right but ancient, might pop his clogs at any minute. Did some good in the House of Lords in his day, a clear brain, one of the best of the old school. Major ... Buckstone? Don't know him. Most of them drop the title when they leave the army.'

'But you've met the Lady Honoria.'

He frowned, made as if to say something, changed his mind.

'Out with it. Is she, or is she not, entitled to call herself Lady Honoria, rather than Lady Graves-Bentley?'

'Or whatever his name was. Fact is, I know some people are sticklers about titles, get all upset if they're addressed wrongly. In my line of business I have to try to remember who's who, but after the first introduction very few people insist on the formalities. I mean, it's the person behind the title that you're dealing with, not the handle itself. I think – looking back – I think there were one or two well-concealed sniggers when she informed me that she was Lady Honoria.'

Bea picked up her handbag and checked to see

what the weather was doing outside. Still fine and bright. There was no breeze moving the leaves of the tree outside, so it was probably safe to go without a jacket. 'Well, I probably won't ever meet her again. Shall we go?'

'Er, yes.' Now he was back to worrying again. 'Fact is, I know I've been a bad father, hardly took any notice of Max till he was grown up, and of course we do meet occasionally now, and I'm pleased to hear he's so well regarded. Hard-working, painstaking, trustworthy, and all that.'

Ouch. She'd already guessed what was coming.

'There's been some talk. Nicole's pregnant, isn't she? Of course people don't expect her to accompany him all the time when she's not feeling well, but a couple of times recently he's been seen with a piece of arm candy whom I'm told is Nicole's younger sister. I wouldn't normally say anything, but I understand the bimbo's been acting as if she owns him. Max, I mean. Is there anything in it?'

'Letitia,' said Bea, making it sound like a curse. 'Letitia the Limpet. And yes, she's a threat. She tried to get him to leave Nicole last year, and only stopped when Nicole got pregnant. The idiot! No wonder Nicole's upset.'

'Mm. The thing is, with my track record, I can hardly warn him to be careful, can I? I wondered if you might.'

The last thing Bea wanted to do was interfere, but she saw that she might have to. What a bore.

'The thing is, Max seems unable to say "no" to the scheming little minx.'

She caught Piers' sceptical eye and laughed at herself. 'All right, he finds it difficult to fend her off.'

'Humph!' said Piers, eyebrows working overtime.

Bea went pink. 'Yes, yes. He's inherited your genes and will probably always have a problem in that direction. Yet he does love Nicole, and he's thrilled at the idea of becoming a father.'

'The reality,' said Piers in a gravelly voice, 'doesn't always live up to the promise. How will he cope with nappies and sleepless nights?'

'How will Nicole?'

They contemplated this picture of unhappy parenthood in silence.

Bea nerved herself to look on the bright side. 'I'm sure they'll both be enchanted by the baby when he comes and turn into parents who can't talk about anything else.'

Piers snorted. 'I know I didn't.'

'True. But she could have a day nanny for the first couple of months, so she doesn't get too tired. You and I couldn't afford it when Max was a baby, and I know his wailing in the night drove you crazy, but Max is in a much stronger position financially than we were then, although he has many other expenses and ... I'm not sure exactly how they are fixed, come to think of it. Maybe I'll have to pay for a nanny. Oh dear. As if there weren't enough calls on my purse. The guttering at the back of the house needs replacing and it means scaffolding and I keep putting off doing anything about it.'

'Want a handout? I was never able to give you a proper amount of maintenance in the old days. I didn't earn enough then. I remember feeling guilty because you had to go out to work even before Max went to school.'

'I ended up working for Hamilton and look how well that turned out.'

'Yes, but scaffolding and workmen, they need paying with real money.'

'I'll manage.' She thought back over her recent conversation with Max. 'I wonder if Max was trying to ask for help when he rang me. He talked all around the subject of Nicole but didn't mention Letitia. Well, I'm seeing Nicole in the week, but if you could just let Max know that gossip is circulating, it might do some good. Children!'

'Lucky we only had the one.'

She gave him a dark look. 'If only he'd inherited the streak of toughness you hide under your famous charm.'

'He did get your good looks, my dear.' He smiled down at her, and although she knew he was deliberately exercising charm, she allowed herself to smile back. He was not going to change, was he?

She set the alarm and let them out of the front door. 'So tell me; who are you due to paint next?'

As Bea and Piers let themselves back into the house she heard the phone ringing. She managed to kill the alarm and pick it up just as it switched into answerphone mode.

'Is that Mrs Abbot? Lord Murchison here. A friend has suggested we might meet. Are you free tomorrow lunchtime, by any chance?' A clear-cut voice, good BBC intonation.

'I could be,' said Bea, thinking that Mr Cambridge had wasted no time in arranging this meeting. 'Where do you suggest?'

He gave her an address in Kensington, and she wrote it down.

'Would twelve o'clock be too early for you? Time for a sherry before lunch, not that I have much of an appetite nowadays.'

'I'm sorry to hear it – the lack of appetite, I mean. A good meal is still one of the great pleasures of life.' Now wasn't that a trite thing to say?

'Indeed. I look forward to seeing you there.' He cut the call.

She put the phone down and reached for her A to Z. A prestigious address, not far away. Overlooking Kensington Gardens?

Piers was interested. 'A lunch invitation? Anywhere decent?'

She looked it up. 'I think it's at the Kensington headquarters of Lord Murchison's Trust, though he didn't say.'

'Well, that'll be interesting, won't it?'

Indeed it would. Particularly if there were going to be fireworks between Zander and Lady H next day.

Monday morning

Bea dressed with care. She hadn't bothered about her appearance when she'd gone with Zander to see Lady Honoria in the country, but now she picked out first one outfit and then another, trying them up against her. The morning sun slanted in through the window overlooking the road. Another hot day? The sky was cloudless.

Eventually she decided to wear a sage-green silk dress with a lowish neckline, and matching low-heeled shoes – not the ones she'd worn on her trip to the country. She didn't wear high heels nowadays for two reasons. First, she was a tall woman and didn't want to tower over her customers, and second, high heels could cause problems. If you ricked an ankle over the age of sixty, you might have to spend time in trainers, which were definitely not her type of shoe.

She fastened a thin gold chain round her neck, donned gold stud earrings. To complete the outfit she picked out a handbag that was a shade darker than her dress, but it was useful because it was big enough to take her notebook along with reading glasses, make-up, purse, keys and all the other bits and pieces she might need. And her mobile phone.

After some thought, she added a small tape

recorder. What other precautions could she take? Indigestion tablets? Pepper spray? A Colt .45? Not that she owned one of those. Would anything less than a .45 stop Honoria in her tracks?

Down in the agency offices, she brought Oliver up to date about Zander and his decision to return to work. Oliver threw up his hands and said there was none so strange as folk, and what were the odds that Zander would last the course? Oliver wanted to drive Bea to the rendezvous, but she said she didn't think she'd be kidnapped by white slave traders within walking distance of home.

Maggie thudded down the stairs, mobile clamped to ear, screaming with laughter to one of her friends. Declaring she didn't need any breakfast, and with papers flapping under her arm, Maggie went off, slamming the front door behind her. She was project managing the modernization of a flat locally and was, of course, late for her first appointment of the day.

Miss Brook, their elderly but efficient accountant, had had a few days holiday but was now back at work in reception. So the agency could be left to run itself for a while.

Bea considered it was too hot to walk, and she didn't want to take the car because it was so difficult to park in that area. Instead, she hailed a taxi.

Tudor Trust occupied an imposing residence, probably Georgian; George II rather than George VI. It was bow-fronted, five storeys high if you included the basement. Stucco, cream-painted. Old glass in the windows; Bea could tell it was old glass because it had a slightly greenish tinge to it. Six steps from pavement to glossy front door. Brass door furniture, nicely polished. A plate on the wall advertising the Trust; everything in good taste. Georgette Heyer would have approved of it as the background for one of her Regency romances. The family home of an earl, perhaps?

'No Parking' signs were everywhere. Did the directors also come by taxi, or did they use public transport?

A gleaming Bentley drew up and the chauffeur helped an elderly gentleman out and handed him a silver-knobbed cane. So that was how it was done. With money and a chauffeur. The elderly gentleman mounted the steps, ramrod upright, a full head of silver hair gleaming in the sun. A superb silk suit. A forceful personality.

'Mrs Abbot? Delighted to meet you.'

'Lord Murchison.' It couldn't be anyone else.

He flourished a key, and the door opened. He waved her inside, courtesy itself. He'd probably bow the Queen inside in the same way. Centuries of breeding, decades of having his own way. Aged eighty or ninety, she could see why he was still chairman.

Inside the hall, a black and white tiled floor was interrupted only by a staircase gently winding to the floors above. A lantern in the roof flooded the place with light. Gilt-framed pictures and rococo side tables along the walls. A

93

stately home in miniature. They should charge entry fees.

A door to the right was marked 'Reception', but Lord Murchison ushered her up the stairs to the first floor – he held on to the banisters all the way – and into a panelled room which shrieked of privilege and looked like the library of a gentleman's club – which in essence was what it was. The room was empty of people but full of leather armchairs and glass-fronted book-shelves, all shining with evidence of tender loving care. A huge bow window overlooked Kensington Gardens.

Thermos flasks of coffee were laid out on a side table together with silver jugs of cream and bowls of cube sugar. On a matching side table was a silver tray burdened with decanters and cut-glass tumblers, all twinkling away.

Bea made an informed guess as to how much they paid a housekeeper or cleaning company to keep the place in such good condition. Hm. Zander hadn't mentioned that expense.

'You'll stay for lunch, of course? Something light. One's appetite fades as we advance in years, doesn't it? Sherry; medium or dry? I won't insult you by suggesting you like it sweet.'

'Thank you. A small dry.'

Abandoning his stick against the arm of a leather chair by the fireplace, he handed her a glass of sherry rather larger than she would have taken if she'd poured it out for herself. Gesturing that she take a seat opposite him, he sank into his chair with what she could see was an effort to hide pain. Or perhaps he was putting it on? His smile appeared to be friendly, pale blue eyes appraising her and apparently appreciating the sight. She reminded herself not to be taken in by his charm.

He said, 'I expect you've been wondering how a charitable concern can afford this rather wonderful old house. Grade I listed, of course. Well, my grandfather gave it to the Trust after his wife died and he retired to the country. I have a small flat nearby which I use during the week, but I still think of this dear old place as mine. Totally wrong of me, I know.'

Oozing charm. Sharp eyes watched to see how far he'd succeeded in disarming her.

'Understandable,' said Bea, sipping the excellent sherry. 'A wonderful house.'

'When I go, it will be up to the board of directors what they do with it. Turn it into an art gallery, or rent it out to the offices of an airline, I shouldn't wonder.'

He sighed. A theatrical sigh, but probably genuine. 'Ah well, we have to move with the times, however painful it may be. No room for sentiment, nowadays. Hard business practice. You must have found that in your line, Mrs Abbot? I understand you had to take over the agency when your husband died. And your only son is a Member of Parliament? How very satisfactory for you.' He indicated the drinks tray. 'May I top you up?'

She shook her head. 'Thank you, no. To complete my CV, my first husband was Piers—'

'The portrait painter. Yes. I only made the connection yesterday. He was kind enough to paint me and my wife some years ago, when she was still with us. I've always admired his work. I must get him round sometime, ask him to quote for a group portrait of the current board of directors. It's something of a tradition here, and one I've neglected, I'm ashamed to say. Are you fond of tradition, Mrs Abbot, or do you think it should be booted out of the window?'

She sipped, smiled in what she hoped was an enigmatic way, and waited for him to come to the point.

'Ah yes, tradition. You probably think more of reputation than tradition, whereas I have to consider both: the long tradition of service to others, which is the hallmark of our Trust, and our reputation. If someone questions the reputation of a Trust, then they're in trouble. Wouldn't you agree?'

'It depends, perhaps, on how widely the question is known.'

'We are in agreement so far.' He lifted the sherry decanter towards her, but she covered her glass with her hand and shook her head. He said, 'I knew I could rely on your discretion. My friend Cambridge promised me that.'

Bea understood that she'd been hooked into agreeing something she wasn't all that sure about. 'You expect me to keep quiet about something I've heard which reflects badly upon your Trust.'

96

A half smile. Old he might be, but he still enjoyed a good clash of minds. 'Dear me. That was rather baldly put. And really not all that accurate. I am deeply perturbed that we allowed one of our directors to outrun his budget, and I was horrified to hear that the worry this caused him may have been a contributory factor in his untimely death. It reflects badly on us that we didn't pick up on the matter sooner. We are all agreed that in future we must be careful to lay out our funds better, perhaps not always employing the very best in the business, but doing the best we can with what we have. You understand, of course. This sort of ... over-enthusiasm is something charities need to watch out for. We failed. We must do better.'

'Mm. It's a good defence.' She set down her glass, still half full. 'And the racial abuse?'

His eyebrows rose, but he didn't act surprised. 'I've heard of none. I asked my fellow directors. They hadn't heard any, either. Zander has been an exemplary employee, and we are truly sorry that he feels he must move on. We had hoped he'd remain with us for some years, but perhaps – if he doesn't feel that a life working for others is quite what he wants – it is better that he goes.'

Bea grimaced. 'What happened to moving with the times? Taking in the stranger at your gate? Adapting to a multicultural society?'

'We tried, Mrs Abbot. We did our best. Sometimes – haven't you found this out yourself? – sometimes people can be, ah, prickly, shall we say? When no slight is intended.'

97

'My friend Mr Cambridge has advised that Zander go to the police to report the abuse he's been subjected to.'

He spread his hands. Very white, beautifully manicured, long-fingered hands. 'And who would he name in his complaint? A dead man.'

'And, perhaps, a live lady?'

'Ah.' He leaned back in his chair and was silent for a long moment. Finally he roused himself, his tone sharpening. 'You understand our dilemma?'

'Oh yes. I've met her. By the way, is she really Lady Honoria? I became confused, trying to work out whose daughter she was.'

He covered his mouth with one hand, his eyes dancing. 'Now you've touched on a tricky subject. She's adamant that she is entitled to be called "Lady Honoria", and it's true that she is descended from an ancient family though perhaps not by the straightest of lines? On the other hand, how would you deal with her, yourself?' Again he spread his hands, inviting her to sympathize with him.

Bea nodded. 'I see your problem, and I see Zander's. Can you protect him from her while he works out his notice?'

'I will see what I can do. Meanwhile, I have your word that our reputation remains solid?'

Bea wasn't sure he could deliver what he'd promised, but she nodded. 'It's worth a try.'

The door opened and Lady Honoria stalked in. As Bea had surmised, Honoria scrubbed up well. She was wearing a black trouser suit and just enough make-up to give her the appearance of a businesswoman, rather than a country housewife.

'Lady Honoria.' Lord Murchison struggled to his feet.

'Fetch the police!'

Behind Lady Honoria came the startled faces of Zander and a couple of middle-aged to elderly gentlemen. Other members of the board?

'I want the Milky Way boy arrested, now!'

'What?'

She brandished the bronze statuette which Zander had delivered to her on Saturday. 'When I came to check over the list of Denzil's effects, I saw this was missing. And his briefcase, too! So this morning I sent the Chocolate Boy out of the office and went through his desk. And there was the statuette, though still no briefcase! He's responsible. He stole it! So, what are you waiting for; fetch the police!'

Bea gaped. 'He gave the statuette to you on Saturday, with the rest of your husband's things. I was there when you told him to put it in the window. You signed for it.'

'You? I heard you were coming in. I suppose you feel you have to defend him, seeing as he's your toy boy!'

Monday at noon

It was always better to attack than wait to be attacked. In this case it was easy to see how to punish the man and neutralize the woman.

99

Of course he was her toy boy! You only had to look at them to realize it was the attraction of opposites; one pale-faced widow, and one hunky black man. Perfect! A match made in heaven. If you believed in heaven, which she personally didn't.

Mud sticks. So let's throw it. In spades.

SIX

Monday noon

'No!' said Lord Murchison, his breathing uneven. 'No police.'

'I insist!' Lady Honoria's mouth curved in triumph.

Zander's mouth was open in shock. A couple of elderly gentlemen grasped his upper arms, though he'd made no move to escape.

Bea recovered some of her wits from the pit into which they'd fallen. Producing her tape recorder from her handbag, she switched it on and held it up. 'Perhaps you'd care to repeat that accusation?'

'What?' The woman didn't like that. 'Put that away, you stupid woman.'

Lord Murchison had fallen back into his chair, his colour poor. 'No police!'

Zander tried to reassemble his own wits. 'You signed for the bronze! I have a copy.'

'That item was crossed out on my copy,' said Lady H, not giving ground at all.

Zander shook his head to clear it. 'Not on mine. And Mrs Abbot is not ... Really she's not ... Mrs Abbot, I'm so sorry.'

101

Bea kept her recorder on. 'What he means, gentlemen, is that I am not the object of his affections. My much younger assistant is far more to his taste, and I can't say I blame him.'

'So you say!' sneered Lady H, and such was the power of her personality that the men holding Zander were unsure who to believe.

Lord Murchison felt in his pocket for a pillbox, extracted a tablet and popped it into his mouth. He lay back in his chair, eyes closed. Stalemate.

'On the other hand,' said Bea, resuming her seat. 'Perhaps we're wrong to let this boil fester.'

Lady H bridled. 'Are you calling me a boil?'

'Certainly not,' said Bea, in a limpid voice. 'I am referring to your insinuations. Perhaps we should explore them, get the poison out into the open. Lord Murchison, I implore you; call the police and get this sorted out. Zander has the copy of the release which you signed—'

'Correction!' said Lady Honoria, flourishing a piece of paper. 'I found his copy in his desk and I have it here. As you will see, the bronze has been crossed out and the crossing-out initialled by me.'

'How very interesting,' said Bea, 'since I took a photocopy of the release after you'd signed it and kept it for my records. The bronze is not crossed out on that. So I assume that the paper you are now holding has been tampered with since I made the copy?'

Silence while this sank in. The two men holding Zander released him and stepped back. One of them muttered an apology.

Lady Honoria hissed, 'I suppose you know how to remove ink marks from documents. Have you had much practice faking them?'

Bea laughed. She held up her recorder. 'Do carry on. You accused Zander of stealing a valuable bronze. I've proved this to be untrue. Slander can be expensive – for you.'

Lord Murchison struggled to his feet, his breathing still laboured but under control. 'No police. Honoria, it appears you jumped to false conclusions, grief and so on, most understandable. Perhaps it would be best if you apologized to all those concerned and we draw a line under it, right?'

'If there has been any misunderstanding, then I apologize,' said Lady H, lemon juice in her voice. 'In return I expect Mrs Abbot to erase the recording she made; quite illegally made, I might add. And let that be that.'

'Of course,' said Bea, with a sweet smile. She pressed buttons and returned the recorder to her handbag.

'Splendid,' said Lord Murchison, reaching for his cane. 'So now, in a spirit of charity, I suggest we adjourn for lunch. Zander, you may return to work without a stain on your character. Major, will you escort Honoria? And it will be my pleasure to take Mrs Abbot in.'

Luncheon was served in another panelled room, this time overlooking not Kensington Gardens but a small garden at the back of the house. More mahogany, more silver, more cut glass, more gilt-framed portraits on the walls.

Lord Murchison sat at the head of a long mahogany dining table, and he waved the others to sit on either side of him. The chairs were Hepplewhite, with brocade-covered seats.

A bony woman in black waitress uniform served a chilled clear soup, followed by a selection of cold meats and salad. Bea sat on Lord Murchison's right, and Lady H on his left. There was no sign of Zander. Did the lowly help eat sandwiches at their desks?

'Forgive me, Mrs Abbot,' said Lord Murchison, all courtesy. 'I have been much remiss in not introducing our board of directors to you. Honoria, I believe you are already acquainted with...? Yes, of course you are. Mrs Abbot, may I introduce Sir Cecil Waite, sitting on your immediate right. Cecil is the man who sees to our finances.' Sir Cecil was a shrimp of a man with a pronounced dowager's hump and an overlarge head. Slightly misshapen, but with a lively eye. Bea got the impression that he fancied her, which she thought rather amusing.

'Major Buckstone is sitting next to Honoria. He has the responsibility for looking after our staff, both here and at our offices in the city. He is also responsible for the smooth running of these premises.' A tidy, well-brushed, white-haired man in his sixties; presumably this was the major who'd been courteous in his dealings with Zander?

'Lastly – how selfish of me to keep you two

104

ladies all to myself at this end of the table – Mr Trimmingham and Lord Lacey, who have the onerous tasks of keeping us on the right side of the law and of fund-raising for the Trust.' Two plump men with identical sharp noses poking out from fleshy cheeks; brothers, perhaps? No, perhaps not, for one was around twenty years older than the other. Possibly related, though.

'Delighted,' said Bea.

'There are a number of other directors, of course,' said Lord Murchison, whose breathing still seemed erratic. Asthma? 'But on a Monday, and at short notice ... These are the core, so to speak, of our fellowship.'

Some fellowship! thought Bea, not much liking their looks.

'They all have offices here, of course,' continued His Lordship, 'and avail themselves of the talents of our secretarial staff. They used to call it a typing pool, but I gather nowadays they have some modern title that eludes me, all being computer trained and so on. What do you call your staff, Mrs Abbot?'

He was being deliberately obtuse, playing the part of a bumbling dodderer, out of touch with reality. In truth, he was probably sharper than most people whom Bea had to deal with. 'My assistants? I call them by their Christian names. One is a project manager, another is our accountant, and the third – what do you call a computer expert who can do everything?'

Bea jumped as a warm hand was placed on her knee. Sir Cecil was smiling into the distance,

105

but it was definitely his hand which was now working its way up her thigh. Bea put her knife on her plate and dropped her right hand below the table. Locating the back of Sir Cecil's hand, she took a nip of his skin and twisted it. Now it was his turn to jump. And to remove his hand. There was a flush of red on his cheeks which hadn't been there before.

She picked up her knife again and smiled angelically – well, perhaps not too angelically, come to think of it – at Lord Murchison, who had probably registered everything but wasn't going to say so.

Lady Honoria was tearing a bread roll into pieces, with vicious strength. 'Are you a "Miss" or a "Ms" Abbot?' Trying to put Bea down, of course.

'Twice married, once divorced. My ex is still living; my dear husband of thirty-odd years died last summer, cancer. So we are both widows, you and I.'

'I am sure,' said Lord Murchison, waving a dessert of fresh fruit away, 'that you have much in common.'

Bea wanted to laugh at this but managed to restrain herself. She had to admire the chairman's ability to pour fire-extinguishing foam over boiling oil. Perhaps his enforced peace would last out the meal? Coffee was served in fragile, translucent cups, hand-painted, with gilt rims. Bea only just managed to stop herself upending the saucer to check if they were Royal Worcester. She was pretty sure they were.

'Would you care to bring your coffee into the library, Mrs Abbot?'

Lady H rose to her feet. 'I'll bring mine, too.'

His Lordship was equal to the occasion. 'I wouldn't dream of taking you away from the men, Honoria. Please stay and enjoy their company. I'm afraid my advanced age requires me to have an afternoon nap, but I want to show Mrs Abbot our first editions before she leaves.'

Bea picked up her cup of excellent coffee and followed His Lordship back to the library, where he subsided into the chair by the fireplace again. 'You handle yourself well, Mrs Abbot.' A nicely graded compliment, with only a touch of patronage.

She inclined her head.

'My friend Cambridge tells me your agency has occasionally been involved in – ah – crime solving.'

'We are a domestic agency. We don't do murder.'

He was startled. 'Who's talking about murder?'

'Sorry. One of my assistants has an overactive imagination.'

Perturbed, he said, 'Denzil had a heart attack.'

'Did he jump, or was he pushed? Local gossip says he was pushed.'

'Local gossip!' He spread his hands, dismissing it.

'Forgive me, but did you follow up Zander's suggestion and demand to see the bank statements?'

'Yes. Denzil said he'd fetch them, but before he could do so, he was taken ill. Under the circumstances we couldn't insist, and of course we expected him to return the following day, when we'd agreed to go into the matter further. I wanted to send him home with my chauffeur as I didn't think he was fit to travel, but he insisted on driving himself. He never returned.'

'At that point you arranged for his office to be searched, with a view to unearthing evidence?'

A tinge of colour. 'Yes, I did. No statements were found.'

'Yet your understanding was that the statements were in his office, and not at home? Surely, bank statements usually go to one's home?'

'The bank statements came here. I checked with the office staff. I suppose he may not have wanted Honoria to see them.'

'Meaning that she didn't know he was taking backhanders?' She frowned. 'I can't believe she didn't know.'

'Well, we can't do anything about it now. We have to draw a line under it and move forward. Honoria threatened to sue us. The major and Mr Trimmingham have been backwards and forwards, trying to avoid publicity, and finally ... Well, you've seen that we had to agree to her terms. What I want to know is, can you get rid of her for us?'

'What? Why me?'

'We've failed. My friend Cambridge thought you might be able to come up with something.'

108

Bea got to her feet. She thought better on her feet. She paced the room, thinking hard. 'I don't see how I can help. As an outsider ... Well, there is one thing. It struck me she didn't want the police any more than you do.'

'She was insistent—'

'She tugged at your chain, and you responded. She now knows that she can throw a hissy fit any time she wants, and you'll agree to her terms. In effect, she's blackmailing you, not for money, but for power.'

'Power?' he echoed, long fingers rasping his chin.

'If she'd sued for compensation to cover her husband's death, however little you wanted publicity, you'd have been forced to defend yourselves by disclosing the circumstances which led to his heart attack. His suspect – if not actually fraudulent – dealings would have been front-page news. Yes, the Trust would have suffered, but her suit against you for contributing to his demise would have been laughed out of court.

'This way, she's happily ensconced in her husband's place with sole responsibility for granting contracts, and therefore for receiving kickbacks. As I see it, you've handed her a licence to print money, and you've assured her that she can be as obnoxious as she pleases because you won't risk going to the police.'

He shook his head. 'We've insisted she uses different firms, not Corcorans.'

'What sort of contract does she have with

you?'

'Trimmingham settled all that. Her contract will be ratified at a board meeting later this week.'

'Trimmingham is the lawyer, right? He has your best interests at heart?'

A bland look. 'He's a legal eagle, highly recommended by Denzil, after my cousin retired from the job.'

She faced him across the room, putting her hands on her hips. What a way to run a business!

'Say it,' he said.

'What on earth were you doing, to let her take over the Trust like this? From my own observations, and from what I've heard about Honoria and Denzil, she was the dominant partner. She's been spending money to restore the ancestral home. And I mean, what she's been doing costs real money. Do you know if she has any income of her own?'

'I don't think so. She was running a business with her first husband, I believe, but it failed when he died. Then she married Denzil, who bought the manor for her. He got it cheap because it was a total wreck. Since then she's concentrated on restoring the house.'

'Denzil was only paid an honorarium and expenses here, right? That's not enough to account for what they've been spending. It seems to me unlikely that she didn't know what was going on here. She probably instigated it.'

'Then why were his bank statements sent here and not home?'

110

Bea thought of his payments to Kylie. Small beer, but probably something he'd like to keep from his wife's knowledge. 'I suspect he was creaming off a percentage which he could keep for his own personal use. He conveniently dies on the day his fraud is exposed. So Honoria, who is determined not to lose her source of income, sets out to threaten and cajole you into replacing him.

'The major seems a decent sort but hardly up to her weight. Trimmingham – he was brought in by Denzil, and we can deduce from the fact that he's giving her what she wants that he's on her side – and possibly on the take as well. She knows you fear publicity and, using that fear, she's blackmailing you into accepting her terms. The next thing you know, she'll be suggesting you step down as chair, so that she can take your place.'

Bea didn't know where that last idea had come from, but it fitted. 'And you are going to sit there and let her, right?'

'No, my dear. Wrong. I admit I have been remiss of late. My health is not good and, since my dear wife died, I have spent a lot of time at my house in Antigua.'

Bea threw up her hands. 'What a way to run a business!'

'True. And that's where you come in. Reasonable or otherwise, I'm prepared to pay you to get rid of her.'

'What? How? You must be joking!' She looked at her watch, noted the time, picked up her handbag, and checked to see that she had everything. 'Thank you for lunch. It was most entertaining.'

'Ah, that reminds me; your tape recorder. You didn't erase Honoria's accusations this morning when you turned it off, did you?'

'No, of course I didn't.' Bea was getting cross. 'I kept them because I felt sorry for Zander, though of all the weak-willed ... and you, too, as well! One look at you lot, and Honoria realized she could do whatever she liked with you. Well, I can't be expected to help people who won't help themselves. I'll see myself out.'

She stormed down the staircase. It seemed to her that the portraits on the walls bent over to watch her pass by. She paused in the hall, debating whether to put her head round the door marked 'Reception' to say goodbye to Zander. She heard a phone ringing and someone answering it. She wondered what lay behind the other doors off the hall: office staff, kitchens? No, the kitchens would be in the basement, wouldn't they? With a butler's lift to carry food up to the dining room?

She went out into the fresh air. Busy street, Kensington Gardens opposite, splendid views. People everywhere. Noise.

There hadn't been much noise inside the Trust building. Except for Honoria.

'Humph!' Bea twitched her neckline straight and headed for home.

112

Someone rang the front doorbell. Bea, Oliver and Maggie had finished supper, but no one was expecting visitors. Oliver went to see who it was, and returned with Zander, who was carrying a stunning white orchid in a pot.

Maggie shrieked, 'What's he doing here?'

'Calm down,' said Oliver.

Maggie slammed plates into the dishwasher. 'Isn't there anywhere I can be safe from him?'

Zander blinked, and took half a step back. 'I'm sorry. I didn't mean—'

Oliver glared at Maggie. 'Grow up, girl. He's not here to see you.'

Bea took the plant off Zander. 'For me? How thoughtful. It's quite beautiful. It needs to be kept out of the sun, right? Come into the sitting room, and we'll find a place for it.'

Zander sent an enigmatic look in Maggie's direction and followed Bea into the sitting room. Bea put the orchid on the coffee table and waved him to a chair. 'I'm not taking any money from you, Zander, and it wasn't necessary for you to buy me a plant, though I must say it is delightful.'

'If you hadn't been there this morning, I'd be in a police cell by now.'

'No, you wouldn't. She doesn't want the police in. She's using that as a threat to make everyone do as she wants. She's poison. Get out while you can, even if you have to lose a month's money or whatever.'

113

'I thought you wanted me to stay and fight.'

'I've changed my mind about that. She fights dirty. You don't. So you can't win.'

'Maybe not. But let me tell you what happened this afternoon. The major came down to see me. He apologized for the, er, misunderstanding about the bronze. He said he quite understood that I wouldn't wish to stay on now, but begged me to see the month out. He said he'd put it in writing. He promised me a bonus. He also promised me that I wouldn't have to have anything more to do with Lady Honoria. He said that if she tried to order me about I was to let him know, and he'd sort it. He said he'd arranged with her to use one of the girls in the office instead. I suggested someone who's been there for ever, is as tough as old boots and looks rather like one, too. She's seen everything in her time and won't put up with any nonsense from Her Highness.'

Bea sighed. Zander had been got at, hadn't he?

Zander said, 'The major's been on to an agency for office staff already, and he's lined up a couple of people for interviews to take over the office manager's job, although they won't be able to deal with the website, of course. He said he was arranging some interviews for me with other firms at an increased salary. I thought about it and accepted his offer.'

Bea threw up her hands. 'My instinct is that you should run, not just walk, away from that building and anything to do with her.'

'Mine, too. But I thought about that trick of

114

yours with the tape recorder, and on the way home I bought one that I can hang on a cord round my neck. Something visible, that I can switch on whenever she comes anywhere near me. That way I should be safe.'

Bea was silent. He was taking sensible precautions. But. 'Zander, you believe in a loving God, don't you? Do you have a special prayer you can say for protection? I know my husband had one.'

He stood up, smiling. 'Yes, Mrs Abbot. I do know one, I do use it, and I will ask protection for you and yours as well. Believe me, I am grateful.'

As she walked him to the door, he said, 'By the way, you'll be amused to hear she's tearing the place apart looking for his briefcase, which has gone missing, and also for some paperwork which she insists her husband used to keep at the office. Would that be the tell-tale bank statements, do you think?'

They both smiled. Bea said, 'Ah well, it's out of my hands now.'

The house was quiet around them, which meant Maggie had gone out. At the front door Bea hesitated, not knowing whether to mention the girl's rudeness to him or not. 'I don't know how much Maggie told you about her past?'

'Very little. We only went out a couple of times before the sky fell on me and I ended up in hospital. Oliver told me she'd had a bad experience a couple of years ago and it had made her wary of men.'

115

'You are still attracted to her, though?'

He shrugged. 'I had hoped the attraction was mutual. It appears not. I'm sorry to have upset her. I won't come here again.'

'Thank you for being so understanding, Zander. Maggie had an overbearing mother who pushed her into an unsuitable marriage with a man who was on the rebound from an affair with a minor media celebrity. He ditched Maggie as soon as his old love showed signs of wanting him back. Between the two of them, bullying mother and cheating husband, they've undermined Maggie's self-confidence to the point that she feels incapable of inspiring love. She's fighting it now she has a good job, but in matters of the heart, she's still unsure of herself.

'She tends to fancy men who can't or won't respond to her, and if they do she runs for the hills before they can hurt her again. Oliver helps by taking her out and about as a friend, but I fear it's going to be a long, slow process to rebuild her sense of self-worth.'

'Ah. Poor girl. I am sorry. Perhaps, some day? I'm afraid I'm not one to chop and change.'

'Time...'

'Perhaps.' He gave her a little bow, and marched off into the sunset. Yes, there really was a rather splendid sunset, with a red sky.

Bea hoped it was a good omen.

Now, what next? She lifted the phone, intending to ring through to Nicole, and her front doorbell rang. Bother. She'd have to answer it, since the others were out.

116

Mr Cambridge stood on the doorstep, holding another bottle of champagne, and behind him came Lord Murchison, leaning on his stick to help him up the steps.

Bea was not inclined to let them in. 'You should have phoned for an appointment.'

'Would you have agreed to see us, if we had? I gambled that you wouldn't turn Tommy away after he's climbed your steps so painfully.'

Lord Murchison stopped on the last step from the top, breathing hard. He was very pale. Was he putting it on? Bea threw up her hands and let them in. 'I don't want any champagne, though.'

'You think it's a bribe? I assure you, it's for medicinal purposes, for Tommy and for me. You may join us if you wish, but it's not essential.'

Bea set her teeth. She had a suspicion that Mr Cambridge was capable of running rings round her, and she didn't like it. She fetched glasses from the kitchen. By the time she returned, Lord Murchison had found himself a seat in what used to be Hamilton's chair with the high back, and Mr Cambridge was easing the cork out of the champagne bottle.

She declined the proffered champagne and took a seat herself. 'I thought I'd made my position clear.'

'Eminently so,' said Lord Murchison, regaining some colour in his cheeks with his first glass of champagne. 'But we thought you might change your mind if you knew the reason why we shun publicity.'

Bea shrugged. A glass of champagne appeared

at her elbow. She felt like smashing it into the fireplace, but she refrained because she knew very well who'd have to clear up the mess afterwards. Besides, these glasses were antiques, which Hamilton had carefully collected one by one, and she couldn't bear to break them.

Lord Murchison held out his own glass for a refill. 'May I have your assurance that you will treat what I tell you in confidence?'

'Discretion is our watchword. But not if the police come into it.'

He winced. 'It's the attention of the police that we particularly wish to avoid.'

Bea laughed, hard and short. 'What have you been up to? Not paying your parking tickets?'

Monday evening

Where was his briefcase? And above all, what had he done with those bank statements? If Tommy Murchison found them, he'd have her guts for garters, and there'd be no chance of milking the Trust for any more money.

Tomorrow she'd tear the office apart. If necessary, she'd set fire to the place to destroy the evidence. She would not be beaten! As for that Chocolate Biscuit, she'd teach him to sneer at her. There were several ways of getting back at him. Hmm. Give it time, and she'd come up with something good.

Then there was Sandy Corcoran; who did he think he was, trying to blackmail her into continuing their special relationship? 'Special relationship', my foot! He hadn't the sense he was born with. Couldn't he see it was impossible for them to continue with their old arrangement? But no, he was crying into his whisky, saying he was going to the wall if he lost their contracts. Well, tough titties! The world had moved on, and if he didn't want to move with it, then someone would have to move him on regardless. And she was the very person to do it.

119

SEVEN

Monday evening

Lord Murchison said, 'Dutch courage,' and downed his second glass. 'My wife's brother is one of my oldest friends. He's very frail now and pretty well alone in the world, but he's always adored his two granddaughters, the eldest of whom – Juliana – happens to be one of my godchildren. While she was still at school she started to go out with Denzil, who is another of my godchildren although I can't say I've ever cared for him very much. But you can't tell how children will turn out when you agree to stand godfather, can you?

'Anyway, Denzil and Juliana had known one another, off and on, since they were children, and when they decided to get married everyone was pleased, though they did think she was rather young to tie herself down. Her grand-father, in particular, grieved that Juliana would-n't be taking up the place she'd been offered at university. Denzil had inherited enough money from an aunt to buy them a flat in a good part of town, and he had a job working in PR for an uncle who was something in the City.

'It was a big wedding. Juliana looked a mere child but so happy. She was besotted with him. When they got back from honeymoon, she got a job in a dress shop. She looked forward to getting pregnant and having children. Six months later she found Denzil in bed with her younger sister Amy, who was fifteen at the time.'

Bea jerked to attention. So Denzil liked them young, did he? Had he picked on Kylie because she was still a schoolgirl?

Lord Murchison said, 'The last thing her parents wanted was a court case, so Amy was packed off first to boarding school and then to university. She's now happily married and the mother of twin boys. Juliana divorced Denzil, but she never really got over the shock. She's had several bouts of depression, even hospitalization, and can't hold down a job for more than a few months at a time.

'Opinions in the family are divided; some think Juliana's frailty gave Denzil an excuse for straying from the marital bed. They point out that Amy was and is something of a handful and might well have led him on. Others swear he's the devil incarnate. His uncle restructured the company and eased him out. In other words, gave him the sack.'

Bea sipped champagne. Shades of Nicole and her younger sister? 'And you thought...?'

'I thought Amy was a little minx. Denzil expressed deep sorrow and regret, said she'd led him on, swore that it was a momentary lapse on his part, that if we'd only give him a second

121

chance, etcetera. He said he'd realized very early on in the marriage that Juliana's mental health was fragile, that Amy had tempted him, being so much more robust than her sister, that he was deeply ashamed of himself, etcetera. Oh, he was charming, persuasive.'

'And he was your godson, and the grandson of one of your oldest friends. So you found a job for him, and Denzil congratulated himself on having got away with it?'

He grimaced. 'I think he meant everything he said, at the time. To give him his due, Denzil worked hard for us for years. We started by letting him handle the interviews for prospective tenants in the Trust. Later he moved over into maintenance, and finally we invited him to become a director with an office in our Kensington headquarters. Ten years after he joined us, he married Honoria. She was a widow of forthright disposition, with an equally good if not altogether straightforward bloodline, though too old to have children by that time.'

Bea was fascinated. He still thought bloodlines important? Well, well. Of course, so did the Queen. Good breeding and bloodlines would always be a matter of consideration to some people when it came to mating horses, dogs and people.

He said, 'We thought we understood how it was that Denzil and Honoria were attracted to one another; not in the usual way that the male dominates the female, but the other way round. We thought he'd made a wise choice, that she would keep him on the straight and narrow. A mother figure, you know?'

Bea took another sip of champagne, thinking, Ah, but you don't know about his dalliance with young Kylie. Granted, the girl appeared to have been willing enough, and he didn't get as far as bedding her...

He cleared his throat. 'There was a rumour a couple of years ago, that he'd been pestering another under-age girl, but it came to nothing. We thought, Give a dog a bad name. We trusted him not to rock the boat, you see.'

Bea said, 'Get to the bit where you began to suspect he was milking the cow that provided the Trust with cream.'

'Ah. Yes. As I said, I haven't been feeling too bright this last couple of years, and I've spent a lot of time abroad. When I got back in harness, although everything seemed fine on the surface ... Well, one has antennae, don't you know? Denzil had brought Trimmingham in, and he was not quite what ... And there was the behaviour of a young girl in the office. She was a school holidays temp with baby-blue eyes and no sense at all. It occurred to me to wonder if Denzil's old, er, proclivities might be starting up again. The office manageress was sure nothing was amiss, but it turned out that the young girl was a niece of hers, and I began to wonder who was deceiving themselves. Luckily she was found with her hand in the till and got the sack. But still, the accounts didn't seem to be too healthy. I've never liked the man from

Corcorans, and it struck me that perhaps an alternative builder might be cheaper.'

'Then the auditors arrived—'

'And your young friend Zander waltzed right into the middle of this delicate situation, and everything blew up in our faces.'

'So you gave thanks that Denzil had dropped dead and generally tried to keep the lid on everything in sight.'

'Until Honoria stated her terms. Yes.'

Bea considered what he'd said and not said. 'You are assuming that Denzil told Honoria everything and that she was his partner in crime? You can't prove anything against either of them unless you find some evidence, and I can't see that you'd gain much by revealing "all" about his private life. I agree with you that if she starts throwing mud at the Trust, some of it would stick.'

'I have to think of Juliana, as well. She is, as I said, fragile. For her sake, too, I'd like to keep this secret. I agree with you that Honoria would prefer to get her own way without involving the police, but my reading of the woman leads me to believe that if she doesn't get her own way she might blow the house down, and all of us with it. So now, Mrs Abbot, you know the whole truth and I ask you once again: will you help us get rid of Honoria?'

'I don't see how. Surely all you've got to do is find the bank statements, or get duplicates from the bank, which would prove what he'd been up to ... And then I suppose you'd need hers, to show that she herself had profited by his dealings.' She hesitated, frowning. 'I suppose it may be difficult for you to obtain copies of his statements from the bank. Confidentiality, and all that.'

He smiled, a gentle, crocodile-type smile. 'Precisely, Mrs Abbot. Now, my good friend here tells me I have been using the wrong arguments to persuade you to help us. My instinct tells me that you could, if you wished, defeat Honoria in straight sets, but I'm advised that I've been overlooking your expertise. You've been running a domestic agency for years. I assume you know better than anyone how a room should be cleaned. Will you come back with us now and search for the missing documents?'

'What?' She saw how neatly she'd been manoeuvred into helping him and had to laugh. A glance at the clock showed her it was after eight in the evening, but there was still plenty of daylight in the sky. 'You don't mean now, this minute, do you?'

'Honoria's proposing to start work again early tomorrow morning. She has her husband's keys to the front door and to his office. Once in, she can ransack the place. The major's office is never locked, and I can borrow his set of keys which will give us access to every room. My chauffeur will take us there and bring you back later. Do you need any special equipment?'

'Who searched her office before?'

'Zander and the major. There was only one

locked drawer in Denzil's room, which the major was able to open as he keeps duplicate keys of everything in his office. There was nothing there but some photographs of young girls and a bottle of whisky. They've scrutinized every piece of paper in the place. No bank statements.'

'So he hid them. Well, he would, wouldn't he? Humph. Would either of the men know where and how to look for something that's been hidden? No, probably not.' Bea got to her feet, reaching for her handbag. 'When are the offices cleaned? In the morning or evenings?'

'We have a couple of women who do the whole house after hours. We've used them for years. Does it matter?'

'Some people clean better than others. I didn't get the impression that Honoria would enjoy cleaning, so it may well be that she's no expert at it. If so, she probably doesn't know the usual hiding places, which might be overlooked by those who are paid by the hour to make the place look all right, but who never get round to deep-cleaning.'

Lord Murchison heaved himself to his feet with some difficulty. 'I imagine you know what you're talking about, Mrs Abbot. So lead us on.'

As soon as Lord Murchison let them into the hall at the Trust, Bea could see that the cleaners were still on the premises, since an industrial-style vacuum cleaner had been abandoned in the middle of the black and white tiled floor. A thickset woman appeared from a door under the

126

stairs and informed them that the offices were closed, and then did a double take.

'Oh, Your Lordship. Haven't seen you for a while. How's the leg?'

'Not too bad, Violet. It is Violet, isn't it? I hope we're not going to get in your way. We've just called to pick up a couple of things.'

As this amounted to an order, although delivered in the mildest of voices, Violet flushed and said she was sure they did their best, though it was difficult to get through everything in the time, and they were a bit behindhand, so if they'd excuse her? She removed herself and the vacuum cleaner.

Bea interpreted this as meaning the woman was either looking for more money or had been scamping what she was supposed to do.

Looking around with a critical eye, Bea gave the place a more thorough inspection than she'd been able to do on her earlier visit. Yes, the hall floor had been properly cleaned. The trick was to look for dust on chair legs, and yes, there was some though not much. The picture frames had been dusted or, more probably, vacuumed clean. Probably anything that could be done with a machine had been properly done, but hand dusting had not been given a high priority.

'This way.' His Lordship emerged from an unobtrusive door on the left holding a large bunch of keys, each one clearly labelled. Crossing the hall, he unlocked a door just beyond the one marked 'Reception'.

Walking into the Honourable Denzil's room

gave Bea the impression of having been dropped back into the nineteenth century. Quite possibly it hadn't been touched since he'd inherited it from his predecessor in the job, who in turn probably hadn't dared change anything. The wallpaper was William Morris in style and might even have been original.

There was an enormous mahogany desk, its surface clear but for a couple of telephones, the famous bronze statuette, and some empty filing trays. Bea could imagine how impressive Denzil would have looked, sitting behind that massive piece of furniture.

In one corner of the room, looking flimsy and a little ashamed of itself by contrast, there was a modern computer desk, on which sat an up-to-date PC, plus a printer and photocopier.

Bea pointed. 'What about the computer?'

Mr Cambridge said, 'I've given it a quick once-over, but it's password protected, and we don't know what that is. I may have to take it home and have a thorough look.'

'Did you look in the usual places? His diary, for instance? Most people keep a record of their passwords somewhere, in case they forget what they are. You've tried "Honoria", I suppose.' She pulled open the top drawer of the desk to disclose the usual muddle of pens, notepads, staplers, biros, etc. Pulling the drawer right out, she peered inside. A Post-it note had been stuck to the back of the drawer, with a series of names on it, all but one crossed out. The last one was 'Kylie'. Ah, the schoolgirl in the pub.

'Try "Kylie",' said Bea. 'That's the name of his latest.'

Mr Cambridge huffed out a laugh. 'Clever girl.'

Bea did not like being patronized. 'Had he no laptop or other notebook? In his position, I'd have expected him to flourish both, and that they'd be the very latest models.'

His Lordship seated himself with a grunt. Was his leg hurting? He wasn't going to complain about it, though. 'He had one of those dinky little notebooks, small enough to stick in his coat pocket, but we can't find it. We assume it went home with him.' His Lordship probably had the very latest gear himself, and he might have been as fast with it as any professional, until his fingers began to gnarl up with arthritis.

Bea turned her attention to the rest of the room. There was an old-fashioned metal filing cabinet behind the desk. She put a hand on it and looked her question at the men.

Lord Murchison shook his head. 'Nothing helpful in it. They checked.'

The chair behind the desk was a giant swivel upholstered in black leather, and there were two other smaller chairs for visitors. A hatstand stood by the window, bare of the normal clutter of overcoats and umbrellas. A large bookcase completed the furniture. There was an old-style Venetian blind at the window and a Turkish-style carpet on the floor, which left about a foot of gleaming wooden floorboards all around it. The pendant light fitment was brass, solid and

129

heavy. The shade was of etched glass. The light looked as if it had been installed when electricity was introduced to replace earlier gas mantels.

Mr Cambridge closed the door upon hearing the noise of a vacuum cleaner, which had started up somewhere nearby, and took a seat by the door.

His Lordship said, 'The major went through every single book in the bookcase, and every drawer in the desk and filing cabinet. Nothing. Afterwards, Zander took all the outstanding paperwork through to his office and dealt with it. No bank statements.'

Bea tried moving the bookcase, but it was too heavy to shift and flush against the wall. It had probably been built into the building a hundred years ago and redecorating had been done around it.

She ran a fingertip across the top of the bookcase. Clean.

She checked the Venetian blind. The cords still worked. The slats were clean, too. 'Your cleaning company is doing a reasonably good job.' She could hear a second vacuum cleaner whining away upstairs.

'There's nothing you can think of...?'

She sat in Denzil's big chair behind the desk, and gave it a twirl. 'Oh yes. It's obvious where he put them. Easy to retrieve. My mother used to press flowers that way. Was he right-handed?'

'I imagine so. Yes, I believe he was.'

'In that case, he'd have put them on this side.'

She went to the corner of the carpet on the right-hand side of the desk and flipped it up and over. It was a heavy carpet, hardly worn despite its great age. Up came the underlay, a soft brown felt. Between that and the floorboards were several large sheets of brown paper. She lifted up the top sheet and there, neatly laid out in rows, were a number of bank statements.

Lord Murchison tried to stand up, but even helping himself with his stick, he tottered and would have fallen if Mr Cambridge and Bea had not sprung to his rescue.

They restored the old man to his seat.

Bea patted his arm. 'Let me. I'm still able to touch the floor with my fingertips.' Click. She could feel both men accessing the date of her birth in their memory banks, and she realized they'd done their homework on her background. So they knew how old she was. So what?

She got down on her hands and knees, and picked up the statements one by one. 'A joint current account, covering the past year only.' She scanned the sheets quickly.

'Allow me,' said Mr Cambridge, removing them from her hands and taking them over to Lord Murchison. 'Ah. Fifteen thousand pounds in here ... Another twenty the previous month ... Ten thousand five hundred here and—'

Lord Murchison snatched them. 'Some months the totals are much bigger than others. Look at this. Fifty thousand in March.'

Mr Cambridge took the last statement from Bea. 'Most of it goes out straight away, paid by cheque. The statement gives us the cheque numbers but no indication of who he paid the money to.'

Bea sat back on her heels, ignoring a twinge in her back. She was not going to let the men see that her position was causing her distress. 'You are forgetting something. It was a joint account, which I suppose has now been frozen pending probate. Either he or she could have taken money out. Money deposited means they were being paid for something, and we can guess what, but bank statements don't tell us who paid it in, and we need his chequebook to find out who he paid money out to.'

She inched her way to the other side of the desk and bent the carpet back again. More bank statements; this time for the previous year. She picked them up and slapped them down on to the desk top. Mr Cambridge took them straight over to His Lordship.

Bea grimaced. Her knees were beginning to play up. Couldn't Mr Cambridge join in the fun and investigate the other two corners of the carpet? Apparently not.

She pulled herself upright by hanging on to the desk and straightened the kinks out of her knees and lower back. Perhaps she could lift up the other corners without getting down on her hands and knees? She threw Mr Cambridge a dark look, which he ignored. She bent over to lift more corners. This time she drew blanks. 'That's it.'

His Lordship was disappointed. 'It's not

enough. Unless we can prove that the monies concerned came in the form of kickbacks, we're stymied.'

'So where's his chequebook?' said Mr Cambridge.

'Briefcase?'

The men looked at one another. Lord Murchison said, 'Yes, where is his briefcase? He had one, of course. Initialled. My old friend gave it him for his twenty-first, and he always carried it with him. I suppose Zander sent it back to Honoria when he and the major cleared the room.'

Bea shook her head. 'No, no briefcase. Zander's an honest man. He said he hadn't seen it, and he wouldn't lie. Honoria seems to think it's still here. Where did he keep it? By the side of his desk?'

'Yes. Always. On his right.'

Bea thought about it. 'How old did you say it was? Twenty-odd years, perhaps? Did he look after his things properly, or was he one of those whose belongings are always getting scratched and torn?'

Mr Cambridge looked bewildered, but Lord Murchison replied, 'Somewhat battered, I seem to recall.'

Bea sighed. Couldn't they see what was under their noses? She went out into the hall and looked around her. Someone was vacuuming upstairs, but the door to Reception was open, and someone was vacuuming away in there, too.

The heavy-set cleaner – what was her name? –

133

looked up as Bea tapped on the door. 'Yes?' Not particularly friendly.

'So sorry to interrupt,' said Bea. 'Particularly since I think you're doing a really good job here. These old houses are a lot of work, aren't they? I'm in the domestic agency business myself, and I know a good job when I see it.'

'We do our best. No one can't say otherwise.' Folded lips, brass-bright hair, wedding ring sunk into a fleshy finger.

'The thing is, you know one of the directors died recently? Well, his widow's going spare, trying to find his wretched old briefcase. Fit for nothing but the dustbin, I know, but there were some papers in it which she needs. I hoped you might have come across it?'

'Oh, that old thing.' There was a flicker of intelligence in her eyes which Bea recognized. The woman knew what had happened to it, had probably taken it herself. 'Broken strap. No good to man or beast. When we was cleaning the room, we asked Mr Trimmingham what to do about it, him poking around like he does...'

'Mr Trimmingham was in Mr Denzil's room?'

A nod. 'Poking around. "What's this, who's that, what are you going to do with that?" Sir Cecil, too. And then he gets a mite too close to Ruby and, well, you know. Nasty habits some gents have, don't they?'

'They do,' said Bea, remembering the hand on her thigh at lunch. 'So he told you to give it to him?'

The woman bridled. 'We knew better than

134

that, didn't we? It's not his to say what should be done with it. There were papers in it and all. So we said we'd lock it away safely till the widow could say what she wanted done with it.'

'Quite right, Violet. Absolutely on the ball,' said Lord Murchison, appearing in the doorway. 'Your finding the briefcase quite rejuvenates me.'

She laughed, as he intended she should.

'Paperwork.' He shook his head. 'When someone dies, the paperwork seems to multiply. And when one of our directors goes...' He sighed. 'The minutes of the last board meeting. We've looked everywhere. Do you think they could have been in his briefcase?'

Violet almost stepped on her own feet in her willingness to oblige. 'I'll fetch it for you, my lord, and then you can see for yourself. Tell the truth, I'll be happier in my mind to get rid of it. I was hoping to see Lady Honoria myself, but she was just leaving when we arrived and couldn't spare the time to talk to me.'

Thank God for small mercies.

Violet disappeared to her cubbyhole across the hall, only to return minutes later carrying a battered-looking briefcase with Denzil's initials on it.

'Thank you very much,' said Lord Murchison, taking the briefcase and pressing a twenty-pound note into her hand as he did so. 'I'll ring Honoria tonight and tell her it's been found. Good work. Yes, very good work. Thank you, Violet.'

Talking still, he backed away and returned to Denzil's office.

'Trimmingham again,' said Mr Cambridge, who'd been listening, of course. 'And Sir Cecil.'

'Cecil's all right in his way, but Trimmingham is a nuisance,' said Lord Murchison, upending the contents of the briefcase on Denzil's desk. 'Trimmingham can be circumvented, I think. Ah. One chequebook, hardly started. One chequebook, stubs only. Luckily he's filled out the stubs. I do hate it when people fail to do that. They think they'll remember what they've done, but they never do.'

Bea went through the rest of the papers in the briefcase as the two men compared cheque stubs with bank statements.

'The writing on the stubs is all in his hand,' said Mr Cambridge, 'so presumably this was his chequebook and she had another. None of these cheques tally with the amounts withdrawn from his account, and he didn't fill in the paying-in slips. Do you think he had a separate paying-in book that we haven't found? Either that, or someone else paid the money into the account direct.'

'There are no cheques covering those amounts in this book, either,' said His Lordship. 'It follows that if he didn't withdraw those large amounts, then Honoria must have done so. I suppose she put them into another bank account which he had no access to, or perhaps she put the money into another bank or a building society. I think we've enough to make her back

136

away from us.'

Mr Cambridge was frowning. 'We really need the bank statements from her own personal account before we can prove that.'

'We've got enough to prove that he was receiving large sums of money from sources unknown.'

'He or she. She might have a source of income that we don't know about.'

'Then let her prove it,' said His Lordship, collapsing into Denzil's chair. 'My leg's playing up again. Old age is no joke.'

'I wonder,' said Bea, in her most angelic voice, 'if the income tax people know about these dodgy payments. I agree that you've probably got enough to make her back off, but if that fails, you could always mention the words "Inland Revenue" and see what happens.'

'Mrs Abbot, I love you dearly,' said His Lordship. 'Why didn't I meet up with you when I was in my prime?'

She laughed. 'I was happily married then. Were you?'

'Adequately so,' he said. 'Is there anything else of interest in that pile of papers?'

She shuffled them together. 'No minutes of meetings, surprise, surprise. A memo pad with lists of things to do. Photocopies of correspondence with Corcorans which you might like to look through. I don't know enough to say what's important and what's not.'

'Put it all back in the briefcase. I'll lock it up in my office now and ring Honoria, tell her not to bother to come in tomorrow and ask her to return her husband's keys as soon as possible. And then I'll run you both home.'

Mr Cambridge helped His Lordship to his feet, looking worried. 'You ought to see the quack again, you know.'

'What good does he do? No, I'm as worn out as that old briefcase, but I'll see this through, God willing. After that, who knows?'

Monday evening

She answered the phone, to hear Tommy killing all her plans for the future. The bank statements showing Corcoran's payments into the joint account had turned up at the office. Tommy had said that, unless she could prove these payments had been legitimately made, he must sorrowfully, and in some distress, assume, etcetera. He said it would be best if she didn't go into the office tomorrow. Someone would return Denzil's briefcase and anything else that belonged to her in the next few days, and collect his keys.

With apologies for having broken into her evening.

She set the phone down with care.

No way was she going to accept this turn of events quietly. Rage took hold of her, making her tremble.

The Chocolate Boy! That's who must have found the briefcase and taken it to the old man. She could just see him gloating over her downfall.

Well, two could play at that game, and she'd have his hide for this.

She booted up Denzil's mini-notebook. The staff addresses? Ah, here they were. Now, where did the Chocolate Boy live? Got it! Now, how should she go about getting even with him?

EIGHT

Tuesday breakfast

'So that's that,' said Bea, sweeping the cat Winston off the central work surface and dishing out toast and tea to her two assistants next morning. 'Zander's job is safe, the baddies have been exposed, and I think we can trust Lord Murchison to mop up any other problems which may arise.' She listened to herself. Was she being too emphatic? It was all over, wasn't it?

Maggie had coloured her hair pink today, and she had outlined her eyes with thick black lines. Bare legs, criss-cross thongs on high-heeled sandals, and a psychedelic top. Colourful.

Maggie said, 'You told him I wasn't interested?'

'Zander? Yes, I told him.'

Oliver grabbed the last two pieces of toast and, with his other hand, pushed his empty mug towards Bea for a refill. 'I like Zander.'

'Yes,' said Bea, 'but Maggie's not ready for a grown-up relationship.'

Oliver said, 'Ouch!' giving Maggie a sideways glance. 'That's a bit thick.'

Maggie filled her mouth with toast and shrugged. If Bea's words hurt her, she didn't show it.

Oliver finished off the last of the honey. 'I'd like to have a go at the Dishonourable's computer. It would be interesting to see what I could find on it.'

Bea waved her hands in dismissal of the affair. 'As far as we're concerned, the matter's finished. I suppose we could invoice Lord Murchison for finding the bank statements and unearthing the briefcase, but on the whole I think not. Zander will probably want to pay us something for saving his job. Keep it low, Oliver. I don't suppose he can afford that much.'

Maggie ignored this. 'I may be late tonight. There's a problem at the flat I'm doing up that I want to check out, but the plumber can't get back there till after he's finished another job. So if someone else can get something in for supper? I propose that Oliver takes a turn at putting something on the table.'

Oliver raised his eyebrows and ignored the suggestion.

'Point taken,' said Bea. 'I'll do it. It's time I filled the freezer up again, too. I need to see my daughter-in-law sometime, otherwise it's business as usual.'

Oliver slid his dishes into the sink instead of the dishwasher. 'Lady Honoria ought to go to prison for what she and her husband have done.'

'Are alleged to have done,' said Bea. 'There's no proof, and no point proceeding with it, now her husband's is dead. The Crown Prosecution Service wouldn't look at it.'

Maggie retrieved Oliver's dishes from the sink, rinsed them and put them in the dishwasher. 'Will you never learn?'

Oliver shook his head, frowning to himself. He went off to start work as the cat Winston leaped back on to the table to see what he might be able to lick up. Maggie aimed a slap at him, then picked him up to give him a cuddle, which he endured knowing full well that she was the likeliest person to give him titbits.

In a voice muffled by fur, Maggie said, 'The thing is, I didn't go off Zander because his looks took a bashing, though I expect that's what you think. No, it's not that. I mean, I do think he's all right in his way, and you can hardly see the scars nowadays. It isn't about looks. It's about him being a loser. I know all about being a loser. I'm a champion loser. I can't team up with another loser or I'll always be at the bottom of the heap.'

Bea blinked. So that was it? Tread with care. 'I agree that you had a bad time. Both you and Oliver. Some people sit down under misfortune for ever, while others get up and get on with it. Some people need a helping hand to get going again. You gave Oliver a helping hand, didn't you? Even though you'd been through a bad time yourself, you picked him up, dusted him down and set him back on his feet. And look at him now. He's bobbed up again nicely, don't you think? You couldn't call him a loser now.'

Maggie put Winston down. He fluffed himself up and applied his tongue to the place where she'd huffed into his fur. 'I suppose.'

'Look at you now. Our clients say you're the best at project management. You have a flair for it, you work hard, stand no nonsense from your workmen, and in a short time you could launch out on your own, if you wished to do so.'

'I wouldn't know how to cope on my own. You aren't going to throw me out, are you?'

Bea gave the girl a hug. 'Of course not. But one day, perhaps, you'll want to fly the nest.'

'When I'm fifty, say? Can you put up with me till I'm fifty?'

'I might be in my grave myself, by then.'

Maggie twitched a smile. 'You're nice. I wish you'd been my mother, instead of ... But we can't choose our parents, can we? I take your point about Oliver, but me? I'm still a mess inside.'

'Give it time. Just don't call yourself a loser in my hearing again. Right?'

Maggie hitched her multicoloured top up over one shoulder and shrugged. But she looked a lot perkier as she went off to work.

Bea stared out into the garden. It was going to be another hot day, by the look of it. She enquired within, so to speak. How did she feel today? The answer was that although her grief for Hamilton had temporarily receded into its cave – sometimes she thought of it as a leopard, biding its time to pounce on her and drag her down – she didn't feel satisfied with herself. Oliver's words about crime and punishment had unsettled her. Perhaps he was right. Honoria should not have done what they believed she had done, and she should not have got away with it.

Bea seemed to remember her husband saying something about letting God do the judging. Sure. Of course. Fine. But human beings wanted justice to be seen to be done, and she felt very human that morning. And, yes, dissatisfied with the outcome of the case. Not that there ever really had been a case, of course.

Oh well. To work. She must ring Nicole, find out how she was doing in this heat. Probably not too well. Brace yourself, Bea, for a difficult visit.

Tuesday afternoon

Bea rang the bell at her son's flat and waited for Nicole to let her in. She'd phoned earlier and been told that if she wanted to come over she could, but not to expect anything by way of tea and sympathy since Max would be out and Nicole wasn't up to it.

She rang the bell again, and this time Nicole's voice, sounding blurred, enquired who was there. Had she forgotten that Bea was coming over?

Once Bea was let in, she understood the reason for the delay in Nicole's answering the entry phone. The curtains were still drawn though it was mid-afternoon, and there were dirty dishes and clothes everywhere.

'I'm in bed.' A weak voice led Bea to the master bedroom, which smelt stale. Dirty mugs and half-eaten plates of food littered the floor, along with a trail of nightclothes which needed to be put in the washing machine.

Bea hadn't seen Nicole recently. The girl was by now some seven months pregnant and looked terrible. Gone was the ultra-smart trophy wife, all blonde hair, high heels, gold chains and bracelets. Here was a grey-faced, stringy-haired, drab-looking female with a bloated stomach. Ouch.

If this was what Max faced every day, then Bea wasn't surprised he'd allowed Nicole's beautiful harpy of a younger sister to be seen out with him. Nicole was nobody's idea of an asset at the moment.

Bea told herself not to gape at the change in her daughter-in-law, who was lying back in crumpled sheets, sweat beading her forehead, eyes closed.

'Are you still feeling sick?'

No reply. Bea knew Nicole had gone on being sick till her fifth month, but hopefully she was past that stage now. In reply, Nicole lifted one hand from the bed and let it fall again. Tears stood out at the corners of her eyes.

Bea remembered her words to Zander about people allowing themselves to become victims. Here was a perfect example. Mind you, it never did any good telling people to pull themselves together, did it? Though those were exactly the words running through Bea's mind. For two pins, Bea would have turned on her heel and walked away.

145

She could imagine exactly what was going to happen next. Nicole would go on whining, Max would get even more fed up with her, Lettice would offer herself to him on a plate and wham, bam, ma'am, Max gets divorced, he and Lettice get married, Nicole becomes an unhappy single mother and the baby loses out. So, of course, would Max, because to Bea's mind Lettice only cared for herself. So in the end that marriage would break up, too.

Bea could see nothing but misery stretching ahead of them down the years.

Dear Lord, do I stand back and let it happen? No, of course not. Marriages may need a bit of a boost now and then but shouldn't fall apart for the want of a kick in the pants, or whatever it is that's needed here. Help required. Right?

She shook herself into action. 'You poor thing. Let's see what we can do to make you feel better.'

The flat had two bedrooms, both en suite. Bea inspected the second bedroom and saw evidence that Max had been sleeping there. She threw back the curtains and opened the windows, scooped up all the bedding, plus Max's discarded shirts and underpants, and carried them through to the washing machine in the utility room. Iced lemon tea didn't take long to make as there were plenty of ice cubes – and not much else – in the fridge. She took that and a towel soaked in ice water through to Nicole, and she cajoled her into sipping water and washing her face and hands. Weakly, Nicole tried to smile.

146

'Let's have you in the shower, and then you can move into the spare bedroom, all nice and fresh.'

Nicole protested, but Bea took no notice. 'Wash your hair while you're at it, and find yourself something clean to wear.' Before Nicole had dried herself, Bea had made up the spare room bed with fresh linen.

'But this is where Max sleeps.'

'We'll have him back where he belongs in a trice. Now get some more of that iced tea down you, and think about what you could fancy to eat while I strip the other bed and clean up a bit.'

There were some benefits to running a domestic agency, and one of them was knowing how to create order out of disorder and dirt. Didn't Nicole have a cleaner nowadays? She'd been proud of herself and her flat in the old days.

'Toast?' Bea offered it, and Nicole took it. There was even a shade of returning pride in her appearance as she ran a brush through her hair as it dried.

'I've been so miserable.'

'You should have called me.'

'I know you've never liked me.'

Bea summoned up her most robust tones. 'Of course I like you. You're the smartest, prettiest wife in the whole of London, and Max adores you.'

'Not at the moment, he doesn't.'

Had Nicole heard the rumours about her younger sister? 'Some men are at their worst in

147

the sickroom.'

'I really have been sick, haven't I? He thought I was putting it on, he didn't understand what it's like to feel sick all the time. No man could. And I couldn't eat anything. I know I look a wreck.'

'You'll pick up quickly now you've stopped being sick. After a couple of visits to the beauty salon and the purchase of some glamorous outfits, he won't recognize you. You are such an example to us all, managing to look stylish when you're pregnant.'

'Me? Go to a beauty salon? Looking like this?'

'Of course not. Do you think you could look out something suitable for you to wear when we go shopping? If you could do that, I'll get busy on the phone, booking you appointments, hairdressers, masseuse, manicurist, you name it.'

'I don't think I've anything that will fit,' said Nicole, languidly making her way to the master bedroom and throwing open fitted wardrobe doors. 'I was so small at first, and then I ballooned out. And Max will throw a fit if I say I want to buy some more clothes.'

'You've got such beautiful shoulders. Have you something with a low neckline?'

'This...? Or perhaps this?' Black or black. Smart, of course, but not suitable for a woman with greenish shadows under her eyes. She was so washed out at the moment that she looked like a ghost.

The house phone rang, and Nicole swooped on it. 'Oh, Max, I can't talk now. Your mother's here and wants to take me shopping. She thinks I should buy things to show off my beautiful shoulders. What do you think? I mean, I know we've spent far too much this year already, but I really do have nothing to wear ... Yes, I'm feeling a whole lot better, really. I mean, but a whole lot better.' Almost, she giggled.

Bea rolled her eyes, gathered up another load of washing for the utility room, and returned with a tray for the dirty dishes. She transferred the first load of washing to the drier. Put the dirty dishes in the dishwasher. Nicole chattered on and on. Once Max was off the phone, she rang one of her friends, to tell her that Max had told her to go out and buy a complete new wardrobe because she'd outgrown all her old clothes. The suggestion that she should buy new clothes had acted on her like a tonic.

Bea sent up an arrow prayer. *Lord, I think I know how to save this marriage, but it involves Piers and I'm not sure that he's going to agree. He's so busy, and he doesn't paint society beauties – if that's what you'd call Nicole – and altogether I'm at my wits' end, so ... please?*

She made some more toast, poached an egg and took it in to Nicole, who was still on the phone but had managed to crawl into some jeans and a white top which didn't look too bad. In fact, the girl was gradually transforming herself from grim-looking waif back to an approximation of the stylish woman that she had once been.

Dear Lord, please make it all right. And while you're about it, you know how fidgety I feel about that other case. I know I have to leave it to you to judge, but ... it bugs me, as much as it bugs Oliver, that Honoria has got away with it. All right, I know. None of my business. I do worry about things which are none of my business, don't I? It's just that I feel, I don't know, as if I've missed a trick. Oh, I give up. Forget it. I intend to.

Summoning a taxi, Bea took Nicole on a shopping expedition which left Nicole bubbling over with excitement ... and Bea exhausted. The cost of the shopping expedition was not mentioned, but Bea had a horrid feeling that she would in due course have to offer Max a sub. Classy clothes don't come cheap.

When Bea finally crawled back to the office, she found Oliver working like an octopus, manning several telephones and his computer all at once. Also the phone was ringing unattended in reception. No sign of Maggie; well, she wasn't in the office today, was she? No sign of the invaluable Miss Brook, either. Now that was unusual.

Oliver took one phone away from his ear long enough to say, 'Miss Brook's got an emergency dentist's appointment, and there's a snarl-up over someone missing a plane in the Middle East and ... Yes, I'm still here.' He went back to the job.

Bea plunged into the fray, answering the

phone, pacifying one client and making another appointment for the other. The phones kept ringing.

When she surfaced, she felt hot, tired and thirsty. Also, she realized with a shock that she'd intended to refill the freezer and organize supper and hadn't done it. But whatever else she had to do, she must first ring Piers.

Oliver went to run his head under the cold tap, and he helped himself to a drink from the fridge. 'Phew! What's for supper?'

Bea sent him a Look and pulled the phone towards her again. This couldn't wait.

'Piers, glad to have caught up with you. Listen, there's a bit of a crisis.' She explained what a wreck Nicole had looked that day, and although a shopping expedition had restored some life to the girl, Bea feared it wouldn't last.

'Then, I had an idea which might transform their marriage.' She took a deep breath. 'Now, don't kill me, I know you're fully booked, but would you consider painting Nicole's portrait? Not Max's, but Nicole's.'

Piers was silent.

Bea bit her lip and flexed her back. Wondered if he'd give her a curt 'no' or think up some good excuse for not doing it.

Piers sighed. 'You think you can blackmail me into painting her because I owe you and Max something?'

Now it was Bea's turn to be silent. Piers had once said he'd like to paint *her* but had never fulfilled his promise. He'd probably forgotten

151

all about it, though she hadn't. Not that she was going to remind him about it. Definitely not.

He said, 'You say she's heavily pregnant. Blonde, ripe and ready for it? I don't do that sort of chocolate box stuff.'

'No, I know you don't.'

'Of course, it's highly commercial. Would she strip, do you think?'

'What? Piers, I didn't hear you suggest that! What would Max say?'

'Hm. I forgot; he's too strait-laced to be true, nowadays. Except when it comes to other young blondes.'

'You wouldn't want to paint Lettice though, would you?'

'As a harpy, perhaps. But Nicole ... I mean, what does Max see in her?'

'You've often told me that you don't always know what you're going to reveal in a person when you start to paint them. Just for once, couldn't you flatter her?'

'I don't flatter. Did you say she's got grey-green shadows under her eyes, and her hair is lifeless? I could paint her as a victim of her pregnancy.'

There was that word 'victim' again. Ouch. Bea winced. 'If you could produce a chocolate box picture, it might save their marriage, give Max a different view of her, and supply her with the courage she needs to carry on being his wife.'

'Until next time.'

Bea was silent. Piers was right. There probably would be a next time. If Piers was anything

152

to go by, Max would still be attracting women in his sixties. Why, she herself had sometimes wondered what would happen if Piers were to suggest a little light dalliance with his ex-wife, but ... No. NO! Kill that thought. She was not going to go down that road.

Piers said, 'Tell you what. I'm due to start another portrait tomorrow. Maybe I'll make some preliminary sketches of my next subject – distinguished scientist and all that – or, better still, take some photos and ask her to send them on to her husband, who's in Australia at the moment, if I remember rightly. She can ask his opinion which pose to use. That would give me some time to paint Nicole, on one condition. That you let me paint you sometime, too.'

She didn't know whether to be flattered that he still wanted to paint her or annoyed that he'd forgotten he'd already asked her. Both. 'At sixty plus? And beginning to look it?'

'Mm. Every line showing and promise me, no Botox. Now *that* portrait I could submit to the Royal Academy next year. So, it's a deal?'

'You're mad.'

'No, I'm a materialistic bum. If I do one chocolate box picture, I'll be inundated with requests from pretty women with nothing between the ears, to paint them, too. I shall double my prices and clean up. And then I'll be able to pay for your guttering to be replaced.'

'Idiot!' said Bea, laughing. 'Give me a couple of days to get her prettied up again. Right?'

'Get her into something soft, lavender or blue-

153

grey or lilac. Plain, but with a low neckline. I'll paint her as a mature beauty wearing her pregnancy with style and grace.'

'And when you paint me?'

'I don't care what you wear. You'll be looking straight at me, through me. Eyes following me round the room. A strong woman and a good one. Now say goodnight, Bea. I've got to get busy rearranging my schedule.'

She put down the phone thinking, *Thank you, Lord.*

Oliver appeared in the doorway, preoccupied, fiddling with his tie. 'Something came up and I'm going out, right? I'll grab a bite to eat later. Shouldn't be too late, though.'

'Uh-huh.' One down and one to go. Perhaps she'd take Maggie out for a meal. Oliver banged the front door as he left. Or perhaps that was Maggie returning? She sighed, rubbed her back. Shopping with Nicole had been a tiring business.

Later Tuesday evening

Well, that was a job well done, wasn't it!

Her preparations had paid off. She'd rung the Chocolate Boy at work that afternoon, pretending to be their disgraced Office Manageress. She'd asked him to call on her that evening, as she had something important to tell him. The fool had sounded excited, agreed to meet her. Fine, so that was him out of the way with no alibi.

Then she'd driven in to check where he lived. She was surprised to find it was such a good address. She'd found a parking space almost opposite. A good omen. A quiet backwater of a street, but with darkened glass windows on the Range Rover, no one could see in. A phone call to his landline produced a quavery voice saying he'd gone out for the evening. An old woman. Housekeeper? House owner?

She said, 'He left his mobile phone at work. I said I'd drop it in for him on my way home, but I'll need a signature if you don't mind.'

'Of course. How long will you be? I'm just cooking supper.'

'It won't take a minute.'

And it didn't. She rang the doorbell, pushed inside. She saw an elderly lady, easy to shove off balance. There was a thin scream as the woman went down, then a thud or two. She'd brought the hammer with her, was wearing plastic gloves. Overalls absorbed the blood.

She opened doors till she found the Chocolate Boy's bed-sitting room, gathered his laptop, briefcase, and leather jacket together and left them in the centre of the room. Then she went upstairs to the old woman's bedroom, easily spotted, the only one on the first floor in current use. She rummaged for jewellery, found some in the top drawer of the chest of drawers. Back down the stairs. She tucked some into the Chocolate Boy's toilet bag and some under the mattress of his bed. She counted to ten. Stood still. Stilled her breathing. Looked around.

Checked she'd done everything she'd meant to do. Something was boiling over in the kitchen.

The kitchen. Fitments way out of date. There were blue and white gingham curtains at the windows, believe it or not. The back door had been propped ajar because of the heat. On an old-fashioned stove, potatoes were boiling dry. She didn't touch it. With any luck, it might start a fire.

That was an idea. There was a box of matches beside the stove. The stove was so ancient it probably didn't even have a pilot light. She struck a match and set the kitchen curtains afire. Took off her overalls in the hall, put them with the hammer into a plastic bag she'd stowed in her trouser pocket earlier. A nice draught drifted through the house as she opened the front door to let herself out. She picked up a stone from the garden and used it to prop the door open. That would give the fire a chance to get going.

Smiling, she returned to her car, stripping off the rubber gloves as she went.

Yes, a good job, well done.

Tuesday evening to Wednesday morning

Bea had a takeaway for supper and spent a few quiet hours catching up on work since both her assistants were out for the evening.

At nine she shut down her computer, deciding to put her feet up and watch telly for a bit. Turned the telly on. Turned it off again. Picked up a book, something light. Yawned. Watered the pots in the garden. Went early to bed.

She couldn't sleep properly till both children were safely back under her roof.

Maggie came in at half eleven, letting the front door bang to behind her. She always tried to be quiet, and she never succeeded.

Oliver? Bea woke at three, looked at the clock. Shrugged. Hoped he was in. She went back to sleep, or tried to. Woke at four. Worried about this and that, as one does at four in the morning. The birds were waking up, dawn was breaking; another day, another set of problems.

At seven in the morning she woke from a light sleep when someone knocked on her door.

It was Maggie. 'May I come in? Are you awake? The thing is, Oliver didn't come home last night, and I'm a bit worried. I'm sure something's happened to him.'

NINE

Wednesday morning

Bea fumbled herself awake. 'What was that?'

Maggie came into the room. Her hair was rumpled; there was a red mark on one cheek where she had slept on a crease in her pillow. She was wearing a pink and red nightshirt, but she hadn't bothered to put her bunny slippers on her feet before coming down to wake Bea. 'I'm so afraid something awful has happened. He told me he wouldn't be late last night because we're so short-handed in the office, what with Miss Brook having the toothache and me being out all day yesterday and again today.'

Bea threw back the bedclothes and felt for her bedroom slippers. She didn't feel happy about it, either, but... 'He's nearly nineteen. I'm told that teenagers often spend the night out.'

Maggie wrung her hands. 'He told me he was seeing Zander. They'd got some ploy or other on together. He was all mysterious about it. They usually go to the health club, listen to music, or go to the pub for a drink or two, though neither of them drinks much. Oliver didn't say anything about a party, and who goes to a party on a Tues-

158

day night, anyway? Parties are for Friday nights and weekends when you can sleep in the next morning.'

Maggie's face, without make-up, looked pale and peaky. Her eyes were bright with tears.

'Ring his mobile,' said Bea.

'It's switched off.'

'Ring Zander's.'

'I tried that, too. Also switched off.'

Bea stumbled into her bathroom and splashed water on her face. Maggie's concern was catching. Bea looked at herself in the mirror; without eye make-up and lipstick, she looked pale, too.

Maggie fidgeted. 'Shall I ring the police? The hospitals?'

'Let me think.' Bea would have thought more clearly with a cup of tea inside her, but Maggie was in no state to provide early morning cuppas at that moment.

Bea snapped her fingers. 'Got it. You say Oliver had got some sort of ploy on that involved Zander? I bet I know what it was. The temptation was too much for them to resist, and they went to see what they could get out of Denzil's computer. As office manager, Zander has keys to let them into the building.'

Maggie clasped her arms round her thin body, holding herself together. 'But they wouldn't be there all night, would they?' She took a deep breath. 'I'm not going to go to pieces. I'm not. Anyone would be worried if their best friend went missing, wouldn't they?'

Especially, thought Bea, since something like

159

this had happened before. A year ago Zander had failed to turn up to work, only to be found the next day with severe head injuries.

'They probably got locked in and couldn't get out again,' said Bea, not believing it for a minute.

Maggie gave her a Look, which Bea felt she deserved. 'All right. We ring the Trust at half past nine, see if they're still there. But he'll probably waltz in any minute now, with some tale of derring-do.'

'I'm ringing the police if he doesn't turn up by half past nine.'

'Yes, do that. Meanwhile, we'd better get ourselves dressed.'

They fidgeted around the house, looking at the clock every few minutes. Neither could eat breakfast. Bea made out a shopping list; Maggie checked that she had everything she needed for work that day. The phone rang and they both jumped, but it was Miss Brook saying that she'd be in a little late as she had to get some antibiotics from the chemist on her way in. She'd had an emergency dental appointment the day before, remember?

Bea began to worry how they'd keep the office going that day if Oliver didn't turn up, Maggie was out on a job, and Miss Brook late. Did they need to take on someone else to help them out at the moment? Could she afford to pay another permanent post?

She dithered. The agency was doing well. Who did they have on their books who might come in for a day? No particular name jumped into her head. She looked at the clock. Again. Had it stopped? She went close to listen to its tick. No, it hadn't stopped.

She tried to read the newspapers, made some coffee as if this were a normal day. But it wasn't normal, was it? She ought to go downstairs and start work. Instead, she began to pace the floor.

Dear Lord, something's wrong, isn't it? This isn't like Oliver. If Maggie's right ... oh, I do hope she isn't, but will you please look after him for us? Please?

At nine o'clock Maggie cracked and rang the Trust. No reply. Open from nine thirty. Leave a message.

'I ought to be meeting the electrician in fifteen minutes,' said Maggie. 'But I can't leave till I know. I'm going to start ringing the hospitals.'

Bea looked at the clock for the hundredth time and nodded. It was better than doing nothing.

The landline rang. Maggie was nearest the phone and snatched it up. She listened, put her hand to her forehead. She said, 'Yes,' and handed the phone to Bea.

'Is that Mrs Abbot? This is CID, Kensington police station. We are holding an Oliver Ingram here. He says he's eighteen years old and that you are his next of kin.'

'Police?' said Bea, trying to keep her head. 'What's happened? We've been worried sick. Has there been an accident? Is Oliver all right?'

'Do you confirm that he's eighteen and that you are his next of kin?'

161

She sat down with a bump 'Well, yes. Of course. At least ... Yes to both. But what's going on? What's happened?'

Maggie was crying, both hands over her mouth, eyes imploring Bea to say that this wasn't really happening.

'There was a fire at a house in North Kensington last night and a fatality, which we are currently investigating.'

'Not Zander! Tell me Zander's not dead!'

'You know him as well, do you? No, it's not him. A Mrs Parrot.'

'Perrot. Her husband was French. That's Zander's landlady. He's very fond of her. Oh dear, he must be devastated. He's not hurt, is he?'

'No, he's not hurt. This call is just to inform you that we are holding Oliver Ingram, who will be interviewed in the presence of a duty solicitor this morning. Since he is only eighteen, you may wish to be present.'

'I don't understand. What's he supposed to have done?'

'He maintains he was with his friend all evening, which may make him an accomplice to murder. Do you know where to find us?'

'What? That's ridiculous!' She tried to think straight. 'I'll be there.'

The phone went dead. Bea stared at the receiver in her hand and only put it down when Maggie shook her arm. 'What's happening? That was the police? Why?'

'Zander appears to be suspected of some

crime or other. Oliver says they were together all evening, so he's implicated in whatever it is that's happened.'

'That's stupid!'

'Yes, of course it is.' Bea suddenly woke to consciousness of telephones ringing downstairs in the agency rooms ... and was that the front doorbell as well?

'Maggie, can you ring your electrician, put him off? And then cope downstairs for a bit?'

'I'm coming with you to the police station.'

'Don't be an idiot.' Bea picked up her handbag and delved into each pocket in turn. Where had she put it? Ah, here it was. Mr Cambridge's card. She dialled his number. It was a landline number, not a mobile. There was no reply. It switched to an answering service. She put the phone down.

'Maggie; electrician! Phones downstairs!'

Maggie gave a little wail, but obeyed.

Bea dialled the number of the Trust, and this time got through. 'Is it possible to speak to Lord Murchison?'

A breathless voice replied, 'Sorry. We're not expecting him in today.' Thames Valley intonation, lacking consonants. Not accepted BBC pronunciation.

'Major Buckstone?'

'I really don't know. He might come in, he might not. Sorry, I'm afraid I really can't help you. Could you ring back later when our office manager gets in?'

Ah, but Zander wasn't coming in, was he? Not

163

that Bea was going to say so. Think, Bea! Think! 'It's really important that I speak to Lord Murchison. My name is Mrs Abbot. I had lunch with the directors on Monday at Lord Murchison's request and returned with him and his friend Mr Cambridge later in the evening. I'm trying to contact him or his friend, and it's rather urgent. Could you perhaps give me Lord Murchison's telephone number?'

'So sorry. I'm not allowed to do that.'

Bea held on to her patience. 'I understand. But, it is rather urgent that I speak with him. Could you perhaps ring him yourself and ask him to contact me? That would be all right, wouldn't it?'

'What's your number?'

Bea gave it, and her mobile number. Then repeated it. Then corrected the girl, who'd got one digit wrong. Put the phone down. Rubbed both eyes.

The phone had stopped downstairs, and now it started up again. Then stopped.

Maggie erupted back into the room, breathless. 'Miss Brook's arrived. She looks awful, but she says she can cope. Did you get through?'

'Yes and no. Maggie, you've got a phone number for Mr Cambridge's son, haven't you? Oliver said you spent some time in that house. Wake up, girl. Oliver's friend.'

Maggie nodded like a Mandarin. 'Of course, of course. Chris. He's a bit weird but nice. They were at school together and now Chris is at uni, but wants to study film-making. I haven't got

164

his mobile number, though, because he's only interested in blondes.'

'Would Oliver have his mobile number somewhere? Has he a personal address book, either a real one or one on his computer? After all, he's been to their house often enough.'

'How will that help?'

Bea set her teeth. 'No one's answering the landline at Mr Cambridge's house; it's switched through to an answerphone. If we can get someone in that household to answer, we may be able to get through to Mr Cambridge. Right?'

'I'll look, I'll look.' Maggie dithered. 'Upstairs in his room, do you think? Or down in his office.'

'You take upstairs, I'll take down.'

Maggie thundered up the stairs, while Bea went down to the agency rooms. Miss Brook was there, with a swollen face but a straight back. The phone was clamped to her ear, and she was busy at her computer. Bea smiled and waved, mimed a 'sorry' about the toothache, and went through into Oliver's den. She switched his computer on, hoping he hadn't put in so many safeguards that she wouldn't be able to access any information. Ah, yes. He had. Access code required. She typed in the one she used herself and was rewarded by being let in to the system.

She went into email, looked at the address list. She'd never bothered to fill in all the details on her address book in email, but Oliver was the meticulous sort who probably updated his every week.

Yes, there it was. Chris Cambridge, mobile and landline number. And also ... hurray, an entry for someone called CJ Cambridge. Chris's father? Only a landline number. The landline number was the same as for Chris.

Bea dialled the mobile number for Chris Cambridge. And waited. The phone rang and rang. Pick up, man!

'Yes?' A hoarse voice. A clearing of the throat.

'Chris Cambridge? This is Bea Abbot here.'

'Who?'

'Oliver's employer and next of kin, apparently.'

'Next of kin?' Chris's tone sharpened. 'What's happened? He's not dead, is he?'

'Far from it. But he is in trouble. I've been trying to ring your father but—'

'Oh, he never answers the phone nowadays because it's always for me.'

'And you don't pick up because...?'

'Because anyone important would know my mobile number. What do you want him for?'

'Oliver's been detained by the police, and they want me to go down there while they interview him. I know your father has some influence—'

'What? Not pluperfect Oliver. I don't believe it. Anyway, Dad doesn't fix parking tickets.'

'No, of course not. But, if you could put me through to him? I need his advice.'

'Oh. Oh, all right. What a laugh! What have they got him for? I can't see old Oliver doing drugs or anything.'

166

'Neither can I.'

From subsequent noises, it sounded as if Chris were on the move. Bea hoped his father was up and about and hadn't gone out of the house already. Maggie came storming back down the stairs, shaking her head. 'Nothing there.'

Bea put her finger to her lips and whispered, 'It's all right, I've got through to Chris.'

'What was that?' Chris had overheard and wanted to know.

'Nothing. Your father is in, isn't he?'

'Far as I know.' His voice retreated. 'Hey, Dad. That bird you fancied is on the phone.'

Bea shot upright. What was that Chris said? That Mr Cambridge fancied her? She didn't know whether to laugh or cry, but she had no time to do either.

'Mrs Abbot?' Mr Cambridge, sounding surprised to hear from her.

'Sorry, sorry, but I couldn't think who else to call for advice. Oliver's been held overnight by the Kensington police, and they're talking about his being an accomplice to murder. It seems Zander's landlady has been killed and ... You do remember who Zander is, don't you? The Trust's office manager.'

'The whistle-blower. Yes.'

Bea wanted to panic, to scream and run around like a headless chicken. She forced herself to keep to the point. 'If I've understood correctly, the police suspect Zander killed his landlady and set fire to the place. Oliver is saying he was with Zander all evening, so they believe he was an accomplice to her murder.'

'When was all this supposed to happen?'

'Last night sometime? I don't know when. I know Oliver went out to meet Zander, and I thought they wanted to have another look at Denzil's computer, but now ... I don't know what to think. They want me to go down to the station, to be present when he's questioned. Of course I'm going, but I've no experience of these things. Could you advise me?'

Silence.

Bea grimaced. Avoided Maggie's pleading eyes. 'I'm sorry,' she said. 'I realize this is asking a lot of you. I had no right to ask. I'll get down there and see what's going on.'

'What appallingly bad luck. I promised Tommy there'd be no repercussions, so this is going to be the devil to unsnarl. The boys were sworn to secrecy. Do you think they'll stand firm under questioning? We really don't want this coming out.'

'You mean you got them to look at the computer, but it's important to the Trust that whatever they found is not going to be leaked to the press? Well, it may be important to the Trust, but if they're not able to give an alibi, I'm not sure how long they ought to keep quiet, and I shall tell them so if I get a chance.'

'How will Oliver stand up to questioning? He's only a boy.'

'But an unusual one, wouldn't you say? I think he'll stand firm – if he knows you're going to come to his rescue.'

168

A sigh. 'Well, Mrs Abbot, I'll see what I can do, but in the meantime get down there and tell the boy I'm working on it.' He put down the phone, and so did Bea.

Maggie had crouched down by her side, trying to hear what was said on the phone. 'Well? He's going to help, isn't he?'

Bea told herself to keep calm, took a deep breath. 'He says I've got to get down to the police station and tell Oliver that he's working on it. So that's what I'd better do.' She felt tears threaten. 'Maggie, he's given my name as next of kin.'

'So he should. I would too, if I were in a fix.'

Bea cast her eyes around the office. Her answerphone light was blinking. There were emails piling up on the computer. But, she must go to Oliver. 'Maggie; Lord Murchison will probably ring to speak to me. Will you tell him what's happened? Meanwhile, can you and Miss Brook keep the agency going?'

'You can't expect me to work while this is going on!'

'Yes, Maggie. I do expect it. Because if it turns out we have to pay for solicitors to defend Oliver, then we're going to need lots of money. And poor Miss Brook; she didn't look fit to be at work. I must have a word with her, see if we can arrange to get someone in to help. And then I'll go down to the station.'

The desk sergeant sniffed. He wasn't sniffing at Bea particularly. The sniff might be a habit he'd

169

fallen into, or it might be that he was going down with, or had just got over, a bad cold. Either way, it drove Bea crazy.

'You say you're his next of kin?'

'Yes.' Look him in the eye, dare him to point out the difference in skin colour. She'd discussed adopting Oliver some time ago, anyway. Not that he'd been keen, then.

'Proof of identity?'

She produced driving licence, bank cards.

'And he's still only eighteen?'

'Nineteen in August.'

'Address?'

She gave it.

Sniff. 'If you'll wait over there.'

A hard chair. She took out her mobile phone to check how Maggie was doing, and the desk sergeant pointed to a sign, which said 'No Mobile Phones'. And sniffed.

She waited. And prayed as hard as she could. *Dear Lord above.* And didn't know what other words to use. *Dear Lord, help.* She repeated the words over and over.

Time passed.

'Mrs Abbot? If you'll come this way.' She was led to a square room without any windows, dimly lit, furnished with a basic table and four chairs. Plus recording equipment. A chunkily built man in plain clothes introduced himself as DI Deltoid – at least that was what it sounded like, though surely she'd heard wrongly.

The door opened and in came Oliver. He'd lost his tie and hadn't shaved. She held out her arms,

170

and he wrapped his around her. They'd never hugged so closely before. 'Let's look at you,' she said, registering that he'd lost weight since the day before. He looked fierce, proud, bewildered and – yes, at the bottom there was fear. She said, 'Your guru has been alerted and said to tell you he was working on it.'

Oliver's face softened, and he nodded.

The policeman said, 'And this is the duty solicitor who will represent Mr Ingram.' A brown man with a brown briefcase. They all sat down, Bea next to Oliver and with her hand fast over one of his. The policeman switched on the recording equipment and recited the names of those present, with time and date of interview.

The solicitor said, 'My client has already made a full statement with regard to his movements yesterday evening. He denies all involvement in the murder of Mrs Perrot, and there is nothing to link him to those events. However, he is anxious to help the police solve the murder and has agreed to answer questions.'

Oliver said, 'I don't know what I can add to the statement I made last night. I met Zander yesterday about seven, we had a pizza in the High Street, and I was with him all evening, working on a computer problem until about ten fifteen. At that time we took a taxi to Zander's place. I was going to take the taxi on home, but when we saw the fire engines and the police, we both got out. And that's it.'

The policeman sighed. 'Let's start again. Where did you go to work on this computer, and can you prove it?'

'I was asked to be discreet about the where and why. It should be sufficient that we were together all evening.'

'No break for coffee or going to the loo?'

'Yes. We stopped for ten minutes, made some coffee, had it together. Time? About nine, I suppose. Talked over what we'd done. Planned what to do next. Didn't leave the office.'

'And you won't tell me where this was?'

'No. We were asked not to, and we won't.'

'Zander says he works for a Trust but won't say which one, or where it is. Do you know where he works?'

Oliver's fingers twitched beneath Bea's, but he shook his head. The policeman insisted. 'You must see that we need to know. Were you involved in some dicey activity last night, perhaps? That's the only reason I can think of why you'd need to hide your whereabouts.'

Oliver thought about that. 'One of the directors of the Trust had died, leaving his business affairs in some disorder. The Managing Director knew I had a gift with computers. He asked me to see what I could rescue from the dead man's records. He arranged for us to be on the premises and asked us not to talk about it. We promised we wouldn't, and unless he gives permission, I won't break that promise.'

'Name of firm? Name of Managing Director? Location of premises? You must see we need to know, so that we can check your story out. No? Let's talk about you and Zander. You are

172

eighteen, and Zander is a good deal older. What is your relationship to him?'

The solicitor frowned, but Oliver answered straight away. 'You can't mean what I think you are implying. Neither of us is that way inclined. I met him when he was going out with a great friend of mine. They subsequently drifted apart, but Zander and I discovered we had a lot in common, kept in touch.'

'But you don't come from – ah – his part of Africa.'

Oliver didn't deign to reply, but rolled his eyes.

Bea pressed his hand gently. She said, 'Oliver was born here in Britain and adopted at birth. He doesn't know who his parents were. I don't know where Zander's people came from, do you, Oliver?'

'His father was a doctor. He was originally from Sierra Leone but practised in a hospital over here, quite legally. He married a British woman, and they produced Zander. But he made the mistake – Zander's father, I mean – of going back home, was caught up in the troubles, and killed.'

'Two lads with chips on their shoulders, eh?'

'No,' said Oliver. 'Is that all you see when you look at us? The colour of our skins? I'd thought better of the police nowadays.'

'It's still odd, though, don't you think, that a schoolboy should be friends with a man so much older?'

Oliver grinned. 'The man I spend most of my

173

leisure time with is in his sixties.'

'So what do you and this man of sixty have in common?'

'Computers. As for Zander, he knows a lot about jazz and I've begun to get interested in it. I go to a pub with him sometimes where they have live jazz. And of course, we're both into computers.'

'So he taught you a lot?'

Oliver shrugged. 'About jazz, yes.'

'You'd say then, that he was the dominant character in the relationship? That, as an older man, you looked up to him?'

Oliver stared at him. 'Fifty-fifty. I know more about computers than he does. He knows more about jazz. So what?'

'I'm trying to work out how he got you into this mess. I can see that a schoolboy would be flattered by the attentions of an older man and willingly allow himself to be drawn into things he wouldn't otherwise consider.'

Oliver frowned. 'Are you trying to make out that I'd happily commit a crime if Zander wanted me to? Rubbish.'

'What I'm trying to say is that you're only a lad, who seems to have been led into crime by an older man. I'm sure the courts would see it that way.'

'Untrue,' said Oliver.

'I can see how easy it would have been to give your friend an alibi for the evening when he asked you to do so.'

'We were together all evening, until we got out

of the cab outside his place and were told what had happened.'

The policeman sighed. 'You're making this difficult for yourself, lad. Why can't you see that lying for your friend is only going to get you into worse trouble?'

'I'm not lying. Check where we had supper. I gave you the bill. Check with the taxi driver who took us back to Zander's place.'

'Oh, we will. Of course we will. Now, let's turn to another aspect of this case. It is distressing, isn't it, when an elderly lady is bludgeoned to death and set on fire?'

Oliver's hand contracted within Bea's. 'Is that what happened to her?'

'It worries you to think about it? Yes, of course it does. I have some photographs here.' He pushed some photographs across the table.

Oliver looked at them, turned his head away. 'Yes, that's distressing. She was a nice lady.'

'She was older than your mother here. Perhaps you can imagine the same thing happening to her?'

Oliver smiled at Bea. 'If anything like that happened to you, I'd hunt down whoever did it.'

'But you're not bothered about who might have hurt another old lady? Because you know it was your so-called friend who did it?'

'It wasn't him, that I do know. I suppose it was some passing thief, an opportunist burglar whom she surprised on the job.' Oliver narrowed his eyes, looked at Bea, looked down at the table. Was he too thinking of Lady Honoria? If

175

so, he was not prepared to say so.

The detective sighed. 'Well, now. Let's look at your friend, Zander. What do you think of him?'

Oliver shrugged. 'I like him. I'm sorry for him—'

'Oh. May I ask why?'

'He's in love with one of my friends, but at the moment she won't look at him. Also, he found a job he really liked but suffered some racial abuse from one of his employers. He may have to look for something else.'

'So he's short of money?'

Oliver shrugged. 'We've never discussed money.'

'Do you pay for the meal when you two go out together?'

'No, we go Dutch.'

'You've just left school but can afford to go Dutch with a man so much older than you?'

'I'm well paid for what I do.'

'By your, er, next of kin?'

The solicitor spoke up. 'I don't think we need to go down that road.'

Bea said, 'Oliver is my chief assistant and the main reason why my agency is so successful. He's worth every penny he gets.'

The detective gave her a dark look. 'Very well. Now, you've been to Zander's house, how many times?'

'Twice, I think. Yes. Twice. The first time he needed someone to hold the ladder for him while he dealt with a wasps' nest at the back of the house. Mrs Perrot couldn't climb ladders, so

I held one steady while Zander went up to deal with the wasps. The second time I called for him before we went to a concert.'

'You went into the house on both occasions?'

'Yes. The first time Zander took me through the house and out into the garden to get the ladder. The second time I stepped into the hall to wait for him.'

'So you know where his room is?'

'He opened the door to his room on the ground floor to show me where he lived. A big room, very nice. I didn't go in.'

'He showed you where the old lady slept?'

Oliver shrugged. 'She slept upstairs, I suppose. He said she was thinking of getting a stairlift.'

'He didn't show you where she slept? Wasn't there some little job she asked you to do for her upstairs?'

'Zander did all her odd jobs.'

'What I'm getting at here is that your so-called friend is using you. He was short of money, about to lose his job, knew where she kept her jewellery– because she trusted him, didn't she? – and was stealing it bit by bit. When she found out and confronted him, he hit her too hard, perhaps not meaning to kill her, and she died. He panicked, started a fire to cover his crime, and phoned you to give him an alibi ... unless, of course, you were there with him all the time.'

'I wasn't,' said Oliver. 'And he didn't.'

'You can't have it both ways, lad. Either you were in it with him, in which case you can say goodbye to the outside world for a good few years, or he gulled you into giving him an alibi. Now think about it. If you confess that he made you give him an alibi, you can walk out of here in a little while, go back home, get back to your job. You're causing your mother a lot of grief by being locked up here. So how about telling the truth for once?'

Oliver stared into space, considering the alternatives.

Wednesday at noon

She treated herself to a vodka and lime. She didn't often indulge, but this was a celebration. She'd put the Chocolate Box in prison where he belonged. He'd have no alibi because she'd sent him on a wild goose chase out into the suburbs last night. She didn't suppose the arson charge would be insisted upon, but the murder should guarantee him a good few years inside, during which he could reflect on the unwisdom of challenging her.

It had all gone without a hitch though she'd been prepared for the worst if he'd come back early. But he hadn't.

She put her feet up, going over and over it again.

No, she hadn't left any loopholes, had she?

Next on the list was Sandy Corcoran, who was being really obtuse about the situation. She had hoped to deal with Della and her stupid little schoolgirl niece this week, but Sandy had

178

promoted himself to the Urgent category. So now, how should he be dealt with?

Shotgun would be easiest. Make an appointment to meet him at his office after hours. His headquarters were in a quiet cul de sac, bustling with people during the day, but deserted at night.

Should she wear her overalls again? They'd been through the washing machine, looked all right now. And buy another pair of rubber gloves. The ones she'd used on the Chocolate Boy's landlady had been thrown into the nearest litter bin when she'd left the house. Yes, another pair of gloves. Overalls. Carry the gun in behind her back. She pointed her forefinger at the television set and said, 'Bang, bang! You're dead!' And so he would be.

She sipped her drink, making it last. She couldn't turn up at Sandy's dressed in overalls and carrying a shotgun openly. So, how to disguise them both?

TEN

Wednesday afternoon

Oliver looked round the interview room, taking his time. Then he turned to Bea. 'I'm really sorry to let you down like this. You'll have to get someone else in to help you.' To the detective. 'Of course I want to be out of here, but I'm not going to lie for you or anyone. I was with Zander from about seven o'clock till about ten thirty.'

Bea squeezed his hand and smiled at him.

He twitched a smile back. His eyes were anxious, but his mouth was firm. He said to her, 'Can you manage without me for a bit?'

'It won't be long. Your sixty-year-old computer expert is on the case.'

He nodded. 'Discretion's the watchword, right?'

He meant that she hadn't mentioned Mr Cambridge's name, and she nodded.

'What's that you said?' asked the detective.

The solicitor got to his feet. 'I really think that's it. Under the circumstances, unless you are prepared to charge my client with something, we're finished here.'

'We've got enough to hold him on giving a false alibi. We can charge him with being an accessory to murder.'

'First you have to prove that Zander did it,' said Oliver. 'As he didn't, you're wasting time. You should be looking elsewhere.'

'Oh, we'll be able to prove he did it all right. I'm not letting you go – yet. We'll have a break now and resume this afternoon.'

Oliver's mouth tightened. 'You're going to get very bored hearing repetitions of my story, I'm afraid.'

A tap on the door, and a policeman in plain clothes entered. 'A word, guv?'

'Interview suspended at ... two fifteen.' The detective switched off the machine and left the room.

The solicitor looked at his watch. 'You don't have to answer any more questions if you don't wish to. Just say "no comment".'

'I can do that,' said Oliver, and they believed him.

The solicitor yawned, stood up. 'I must catch a bite to eat. Be back in time for the next session.'

He went out and left Bea with Oliver.

'I'm hungry,' said Bea, trying to lighten the atmosphere. 'And Maggie'll be going spare. Can I use my mobile in here, do you think?'

'Is she all right?' Oliver, also trying to pretend this was a normal day. 'I've been worrying about work. Miss Brook—'

'Returned this morning, looking awful but

coping. Maggie's cancelled her appointments and stayed in to help.'

Oliver took a deep breath. 'If they hold me—'

'You're doing very well.'

'Yes, but if they hold me for long, you'll have to get someone else in.'

'A temp, do you mean?' She shook her head. 'My money's on your guru.'

A faint frown. 'Yes, but he swore us to silence.'

'That was before Mrs Perrot was killed.'

'What we did last night can't have any bearing on this, can it?' He didn't sound too sure of it.

Neither was Bea. 'I'll get hold of him as soon as I leave here.'

'You'll stay for a while?' Anxiety showing? He'd done well so far, but he was only eighteen years old and had never come up against the law before. The temptation to give in must be great.

'I'm staying as long as you need me,' said Bea.

He gave her a lopsided grin. 'We'd better see about formalizing our family arrangements.' So, although he'd rejected the idea of adoption when she'd raised it before, he was now prepared to go along with it.

Bea said, 'You're eighteen now, so I can't adopt you formally, but you could change your name to mine. Would you like that?'

He nodded. 'I wonder if Maggie will want it now, as well?'

The door opened and the detective returned, thunderclouds hovering over his head. 'Right.

182

You may go, for now. Stay at the address you've given me, and don't leave it. I shall need to see you again soon.'

Oliver slowly got to his feet.

Bea picked up her handbag. 'At last, some sense. What about Zander?'

The detective firmed his jaw. Was he grinding his teeth? 'I'm letting him go, too. For the time being. There will be more questions. Understood?'

Bully for the guru!

There were some formalities, of course. But soon enough Oliver and Bea were standing in the open air, blinking at the brilliance of the day.

'Well, well! And who's been blotting his copybook, eh?' A lad of Oliver's age, with a narrow head, chestnut hair and clever eyes. He punched Oliver's arm, grinning.

'Chris!' Oliver looked dazed. 'But how ... Who? I didn't expect—'

'Dad said I was to collect you from the police station and take you back home with me. I've got a taxi waiting on the corner. Where's Zander?'

'I don't know. Still inside, I suppose.' Oliver took a deep breath, hesitated, but finally said, 'I'd better rescue him.' Although it must be the last thing he wanted to do, he returned to the police station. Bea trailed after him. Zander was there, arguing with someone about an address where he could be found that night, since it was clear he couldn't go back to his digs.

'He's staying with us,' said Bea, crossing her

183

fingers and beginning to worry about how Maggie would take the news. She gave her address again, and Zander was free. He looked all right, a bit rumpled, but not in bad shape.

Outside, Chris was fretting. 'The taxi's waiting. Debriefing. Important, Dad said. Do you want to come too, Mrs Abbot?'

'I think not,' said Bea, letting all her submerged worries about Maggie, the office, Max and Nicole rise to the surface. 'Work, and so on. Oliver, give me a ring when you're on your way home. Let me know about supper.'

She flagged down a passing taxi for herself, wondering how to break the news to Maggie that Zander was going to invade her territory. Again. But what else could she have done?

In the taxi Bea tried to relax. She was so tense that the muscles of her neck ached. She made herself breathe long and deep. She knew she ought to be giving thanks for the latest turn of events, but she was too wound up to think of anything other than the other problems that would be waiting for her back at home.

She found herself praying, *Please, Lord. I'm not sure I can cope. Oh, and thanks, of course. Many, many thanks. Keep on looking out for us, will you?*

And yes, back at home, it was bedlam. Before she went into her own part of the house, Bea went down the steps to the agency rooms to see what was happening there.

She found that Miss Brook had abandoned her station to take painkillers with a cup of coffee, that Maggie was flying from one phone to the other, getting more and more excitable and less able to remember what she was supposed to be doing from one minute to the next ... and, even as Bea opened her mouth to tell them Oliver was free, Bea's important Member of Parliament son Max came pounding down the stairs to the agency rooms.

'Mother!' A couple of years ago Max could have been described as dreamily good-looking, but he was inclined to put on weight nowadays. Today he was also red-faced, and he was working himself up into a temper of classical proportions.

'Oh, Mrs Abbot! No Oliver?' said Maggie, winding one long leg round the other, ready to cry from frustration and anxiety. The phones kept ringing.

'I'm so sorry to let you down,' said Miss Brook, on the verge of tears for a different reason, 'but I really think I must go home and rest.'

'Of course you must,' said Bea, seeing how drawn and tired Miss Brook looked. 'It was good of you to come in. I suspect you ought to have stayed in bed all day. Now don't you worry about a thing here. Go home and get yourself better. The answerphones will take messages, and we'll deal with them one at a time. Maggie, relax! Oliver's all right and will be home shortly.'

How on earth were they going to manage? Well, she'd think of something – in a minute.

'Mother,' said Max, 'this cannot wait!'

'Oh yes, it can, dear,' said Bea. 'I've spent the morning in a state of high anxiety at the police station, and it puts everything else into perspective. Now, Maggie; did you cancel your electrician?'

The phones went on ringing. Maggie sank on to the nearest chair and howled with relief to hear that Oliver was all right, while at the same time shaking her head ... Which might or might not mean she'd contacted the electrician.

Bea rolled her eyes, helped Miss Brook into her summer coat, and coaxed her up the stairs. 'Take a taxi home; I'll pay. And don't come back till you're fit.'

'Come rain or shine, I'll be in tomorrow.' Miss Brook disappeared.

What next?

A client was waiting for attention in reception. A fortyish woman with well-cut dark-blonde hair and sharp eyes. 'Mrs Abbot? I don't suppose you remember me, but your husband saved my life a couple of years ago. I came to thank him for what he did for me, but I understand he's passed on. I'm so sorry. He was a lovely man.'

Max made a noise like a steaming kettle. 'Mother, I insist!'

'Max, one minute. Business first, pleasure afterwards.' She pushed Max away, trying to concentrate. 'Cynthia, isn't it? Of course I remember you. Hamilton found you an office job in a big corporation in Dubai, didn't he? Not our

186

usual field of business, but he happened to know someone who knew of a vacancy. You did well, I believe. He would have been so pleased to see you again.'

'I finished there last week and came back with a nice little nest egg. Before taking on another job, I wanted to thank Mr Abbot. If it hadn't been for him, I don't know what would have happened to me. And you, too. I've never forgotten your kindness. I can see you're up to your neck at the moment. Is there anything I can do to help you for a change? Perhaps I could man the phones here for a couple of hours? Just to take messages.'

Although Cynthia now looked capable of dealing with an armed mutiny, four years ago she'd been fleeing a drunken, abusive partner who had subsequently gone on to kill himself and two others in a car smash. Every Christmas since her departure for warmer climes, Cynthia had sent cards to the agency, saying how well she was getting on and thanking Hamilton for his help.

Bea wondered if this was what the Bible meant about casting your bread upon the waters and finding it again later. Or was it just another answer to prayer, because He had known what she was going to need before she did?

'Cynthia, you're an angel. If you could? You can see we're in a bit of a state.'

'Will do.' Cynthia seated herself at Maggie's desk and picked up the phone. 'Abbot Agency. How may I help you?'

Max planted himself solidly in front of Bea. 'Now, Mother!'

'In a minute. Maggie, dry your eyes, blow your nose and make me a cuppa and something to eat. I'm dying of thirst and haven't eaten anything today. Then you can help Cynthia, can't you? Show her the systems?'

Maggie snuffled her way up the stairs to the first floor. Bea followed, with Max in tow. The sitting room was too warm, the sun streaming in and baking the furniture. Bea unlocked the grilles over the windows and threw them open. Then drew the blinds halfway down. A breeze tentatively played over her ankles.

Blessed relief.

'Now, Max.'

'Where have you been? That halfwit Maggie said you were at the police station, which was obviously a lie.'

'No lie. Oliver was asked to help the police with their enquiries into a murder and subsequent arson—'

'What!? Mother, this comes of your taking in all sorts of riff-raff. It's a wonder you haven't been murdered in your bed.'

'Oh, come off it, Max. Oliver keeps this agency going, and well you know it. If it wasn't for his expertise, we'd have to close down tomorrow, and he was certainly not involved in the murder. He just happened to drop his friend off at the house where a murder had been discovered. And before you ask, no, I don't know who did it, though surely the police will find out.'

'You are far too trusting. Look at the way you've let that woman take over your phones when she'd just walked in off the street.'

'Cynthia is well known to the agency. Be grateful that she was here, or I wouldn't be able to sit down and talk to you now.' She patted the settee beside her. 'Now, sit down and tell me what's got you into such a state.'

Maggie brought in a tray on which sat a large mug of tea and a plate of ham sandwiches. The tea had slopped on to the tray, and the bread of the sandwiches had been cut unevenly. Maggie was not her usual competent self. She sniffed, richly. Bea restrained herself from telling the girl to blow her nose.

Instead, 'Thank you, Maggie. I should think we might expect Oliver back in about an hour. I told him to bring Zander with him as he can't return to his old digs yet. Oh, and can you manage supper for us all?'

Maggie muttered something about not putting up with Zander, which Bea pretended not to hear, and stamped out.

'Really, Mother. That girl is impossible!'

'Ah, that reminds me. Nicole seems to be without a cleaner at the moment. Shall I ask Maggie to find you one?'

'It's about Nicole that I needed to talk to you. Your interference yesterday has put me in the most intolerable position.' He stood in front of the fireplace, assuming the position of all dominant males through the ages. 'Intolerable,' he

189

repeated the word, rolling it around his tongue. 'As if I hadn't enough to put up with at the moment.'

Bea considered throwing her mug of tea over him. The tea was scalding hot. It would probably do him no end of damage. On the other hand, someone would have to clean the mess up afterwards, take him to hospital, get the rug cleaned, and so on. And she knew who that would be. Reluctantly, she abandoned the idea.

He was still talking, of course. It took a lot to stop Max in his tracks once he got on his feet. She felt considerable sympathy for Members of Parliament who absented themselves during boring debates. She wondered which member could empty the chamber fastest. Would there be an unofficial prize for such a man – or woman? For after all, women could be as boring as men when they put their minds to it.

He'd gone puce again. Oh dear.

'Mother, you might at least listen to me when I'm talking.'

'Sorry, dear. A lot on my mind. I went to visit Nicole yesterday. She was in quite a state, poor dear.'

'She does nothing but complain. I try to be sympathetic, but really, she might make an effort. Lettice says—'

'Watch your blood pressure, dear. Lettice really is poison, isn't she? Pretty, of course, if you like that sort of thing.' Bea crossed her fingers. 'I thought she'd got her hooks into someone in the Cabinet nowadays.'

'What? Where did you hear that? I didn't think anyone knew that ... nonsense, Mother. Lettice is ambitious, of course. Any intelligent woman would want to get on, wouldn't they? And yes, it's true that I did introduce her to ... No, I won't say his name. But it turned out that he wasn't ... well, interested.'

'Gay, was he?'

'That is neither here nor there. The fact of the matter is that you encouraged Nicole to go out and spend money that we haven't got.'

'I thought you agreed—'

'A little dress or two, of course. But when I got home last night, the flat was littered with expensive—'

'Of course, Piers might want her to wear something entirely different.'

'What?'

'Piers. Your father, the portrait painter. When he paints her.'

'WHAT!'

'Mm.' Bea sipped her tea, now cooled enough to drink. 'I don't know whether he'll want to paint her at your place or in his studio. The light in your flat might not be good enough. But you can arrange all that with him, can't you?'

He gaped, beyond words.

Bea sighed, reached for a sandwich, bit into it.

'But Piers doesn't ... I mean, he charges the earth.'

'That's all right. It's all in the family, after all.'

Max took a turn around the room. Stopped in front of the portrait Piers had done of Hamilton,

191

his adopted father. It was a good portrait, for Piers had captured Hamilton's strength, humour and goodness. The eyes followed you around the room.

Automatically, Max's hands went to straighten his tie. 'I did think, one day, that Piers might want to paint me, but when I broached the subject he said he only painted elderly, ugly and super-rich people. So why Nicole?'

'Because he promised to pay for the guttering at the back of the house here to be replaced, and he can do this if he paints a few beautiful women on the side, so to speak. It's a commercial proposition for him. He wants a sort of Mother-Earth-cum-Juno look. All ripeness and blonde beauty. I don't think Nicole needs her hair colour lightened, but perhaps eyelash dyeing? I'm told it does wonders for a girl's morale.'

'What's that? The guttering needs replacing here?' He tried to look out of the window, lifted the blind, let it flap down again. 'Why didn't you tell me? That's going to cost an arm and a leg, and I just don't have that kind of money to spare, especially with Nicole on a spending spree.'

'Piers said he'd pay for it, and if he doesn't, the agency will. Oh, and by the way, Nicole doesn't know about the portrait yet. I thought you might like to break the news to her.'

She could see the idea sink into his mind and become a pleasant proposition. While he was mulling this over, she said, 'Of course, you might have to fend off some of your friends who'll also want their portraits painted by him, but it's not everyone who has a beautiful, pregnant wife; a project interesting enough to appeal to Piers.'

A tiresome thought struck him. 'Yes, but Lettice—'

'I'm afraid she'll be a little jealous,' said Bea, polishing off the last sandwich. 'Perhaps it will spur her on to find another sugar daddy.'

Max reddened. 'I'm not—'

'I expect you've been too soft-hearted, helping her out financially. But now that will have to stop, won't it?'

'Er, yes. I mean, I've never ... Well, only once or twice.'

Bea brushed down her skirt and stood up. 'Well, I'd better get back to work, and you'll want to give the good news to Nicole, won't you? Tell her Piers will be ringing her soon to discuss what he'd like her to wear, and so on. It's great that she's over her morning sickness now, isn't it?'

'Er, yes.'

She walked him to the front door and saw him out. Once he'd gone, she leaned against the wall, closing her eyes, breathing long and slow. *I think that went all right, didn't it, Lord? And let me say again, 'Thank you'. For getting Oliver and Zander out of trouble, for leading Cynthia to us just at the right minute. And please will you keep an eye on poor Nicole and tell me what to say to Maggie and oh dear, is she going to throw*

193

a tantrum about us giving Zander a bed for the night?

The phones downstairs kept on ringing. Cynthia had a good telephone voice, low-toned, with clear diction. She would be looking for a top job now, perhaps in one of the ministries? She'd make a good civil servant.

Maggie had not gone to help Cynthia but was crashing around in the kitchen. Oh dear.

Bea pushed herself off the wall, lifted her chin, pulled in her stomach. On with the next. Could they afford to take on more help at the agency? They were always extra busy when staff went on holiday – or were under investigation by the police – and, now that Maggie was often out all day, they could do with some help. But could they really afford it?

Wednesday evening

It was always as well to think these things through before you embarked on them.

Sandy had agreed to the after-hours meeting, as she'd known he would. After all, he needed witnesses to their collaboration as little as she did.

She left the Range Rover parked in front of a shopping centre nearby, round the corner and out of sight of his office. She had everything she needed in two large bags marked with the name of a well-known department store.

He opened the door to her himself. 'You took your time. Been shopping?'

194

'I didn't want to leave the stuff in the car. May I use your loo? You're all alone?' she said, making sure.

He nodded, turning back into the corridor leading to his office. 'First on the left. I thought you'd see sense.'

She changed into her overalls in the loo. Put on the new rubber gloves. Took the gun out. Holding it behind her, she went down the corridor into his office. He was standing with his back to her, pouring himself out a whisky.

Bang, bang, you're dead. And he was.

Her instinct was to get the hell out, but no; she'd planned to make sure he hadn't left anything on his desk to incriminate her and that she would do, even if her heart was beating too fast for comfort.

She stepped over him to get to his diary. The whisky bottle had fallen on the floor and spilled its contents; what a waste. Had the fool really imagined she was going to give way to his demands to continue their scam? She checked his diary. Good. He hadn't even noted their appointment.

If there was anything on his computer, it would lead back to Denzil and not to her.

Now came the nasty bit. She turned him over to take his wallet from his top pocket, his Blackberry and his watch. Motive for murder: theft.

One last look around. Back to the loo, remove overalls, put them and the gun back into the shopping bags. Keep the gloves on. Smear the door handles. And out goes she.

195

ELEVEN

Wednesday evening

Supper for five. Bea and Maggie, Oliver and Zander, plus Chris Cambridge, who had attached himself to Oliver's side. Chris reminded Bea of a puppy who's overjoyed to see his master again after a day spent apart.

'Did they really lock you up in a cell? How long was it before the duty solicitor arrived? Did he believe you when you said what had happened? What do you mean, "How could you tell?" Oh, you mean it was his job to believe you, but that you weren't sure that he did? Well, how did it feel to be locked up?'

Maggie was playing the non-cooperation card because Zander had been invited to supper. Maggie was sullen. Maggie was monosyllabic. Maggie said she rather thought she'd go out for supper if Bea didn't mind. Maggie had cried her eyes out when she thought Oliver was in trouble, but the moment he walked back in through the door she turned her back on him and pretended he wasn't there.

Zander behaved beautifully. Apart from slightly darker shadows under his eyes, he seemed to have come through his ordeal better than Oliver. He apologized to Bea for presenting himself in yesterday's shirt and thanked her for offering supper. He said he was supposed to collect some of his stuff from Mrs Perrot's later that evening, was waiting for a phone call to say when the police had finished with his room. He gave Maggie one long, considering look, and seeing that she didn't wish to acknowledge his presence, asked Bea if there was anything he could do for her.

Bea turned away from an almost empty freezer. 'Can you magic food out of thin air? The cupboard is bare. Shall we get a takeaway?'

'Chinese?' said Oliver, his usually well-brushed hair falling over his forehead, giving him a rakish, devil-may-care look.

'Chinese will do me,' said Chris, suspending his questioning of Oliver long enough to state a preference. 'Now, tell me in detail, don't miss anything out...'

'I hate junk food,' said Maggie, close to tears.

Bea put her arm around Maggie and held her tight. She spoke softly into her ear. 'It won't do us any harm to eat junk food for once. Oliver's safe now. One other thing; Zander had to give the police an address where he could stay tonight, so I said he could come here. Can you cope?'

Maggie shrugged. 'The bed's always made up.'

Zander found the fast-food menus they kept by Maggie's cookery books and said he'd take orders. Did they deliver? Yes, they did. Fine.

Bea started counting seats round the central table-cum-work surface in the kitchen. They had four high stools. They'd have to bring in a chair from the sitting room – or could they perhaps take everything down into the garden and eat there al fresco?

With a start, Bea remembered that she'd left Cynthia all by herself in the agency rooms, and she rushed down to see how she'd been getting on.

Cynthia was packing up for the day. 'I've done what I could. Maggie came down for a while to show me how to access the computer, but I'm afraid there was so much going on that I only had time to take messages from everybody. I said you'd ring back tomorrow.'

'Bless you. You couldn't by any chance help us out tomorrow as well, or even for the rest of the week? We're all at sixes and sevens. I hope we'll be able to get back to routine tomorrow, but we've lost so much time I don't know how we're going to manage. We'll pay you well.'

'Why not? I've got a couple of interviews on Friday, but I'm pretty free till then. Nine thirty tomorrow?' She departed, smiling.

Bea decided not to look at the stack of messages which had been left for her and went back up the stairs to find Zander on the phone, placing his takeaway order, while Chris was still bombarding Oliver with questions. Maggie, pretending she wasn't interested, was buffing up some cutlery.

198

'So what did you discover on the bad man's computer?'

Oliver exchanged glances with Zander and shrugged. 'I suppose it's all right to talk about it to you lot, but if one word of this gets out, I'm dead, understood? Mr Cambridge told us to report to the Trust office at half past seven, by which time the cleaners should have gone. In fact, we had to wait for them to leave, and it was nearer quarter to eight before we got in. Mr Cambridge then joined us, bringing his own laptop and memory sticks. Zander had his keys, of course, so we could get into the Dishonourable's room.

'Mr Cambridge sat me down at Denzil's computer and asked me to transfer all the files on to a couple of memory sticks. He gave me the password, "Kylie", which is the name of that girl in the village pub, isn't it? Anyway, it worked. I downloaded everything on to the memory sticks and started to open up the folders. At first it looked like just a whole load of porn. The folders had titles like "Maids in Waiting" and "Skirts Ahoy!". I didn't particularly want to enquire any further, but Zander insisted that he'd seen Denzil working on his computer with the screen showing spreadsheets, emails and business letters. Only there weren't any folders marked "Business" or "Staff". Every single folder had a soft porn title. Mr Cambridge said this showed Denzil's puerile sense of humour.

'He took one of the memory sticks and transferred everything to his laptop. Zander did the

199

same, using one of the office computers which is not currently in use. I stayed on Denzil's original computer.

'Mr Cambridge divided up the tasks. I was to look at the top twenty folders, Zander the bottom, while he poked around to see what had been deleted or put in the HP Gallery, was on emails and so on.

'The first three folders I opened contained soft porn, and nothing but. The next was titled "Distaff Disturbances" and bingo! It was a file for staff addresses, salaries, wages, holiday times, etcetera, both for the city office and for the one in Kensington.'

'That might be useful,' said Bea. 'I'd like a copy of that sometime.'

'Will do. "Bossy Boots!" contained a list of dates and payments to someone unknown. Not large amounts. Fifty pounds roughly once a month. Mr Cambridge guessed the payments might have been for the previous office man-ageress, who'd been very thick with the dead man. Then there were more folders of soft porn. I don't like to think,' he said, virtuously, 'of the sort of man who needs a shot of porn before he starts work in the morning.'

Bea said, 'Yes, but did you find anything for Corcorans?'

Zander nodded. 'I found it under "Shrinking Violets". I don't know why he named it that. Mr Cambridge didn't know, either. Dates and invoices covering a period of ten years. But it looks straightforward till you realize how

200

inflated the figures were.'

'But I,' said Oliver, 'found the record he'd made of kickbacks under a file marked "Discount Debs", cross-referenced to "Shrinking Violets".'

Bea mused, 'I wonder what Honoria made of it.'

Oliver shrugged. 'If she knew how he'd disguised the files. She might have thought they were all pretty pictures of girls in their underwear, which a lot of them are.'

The front doorbell rang, and Zander – who was nearest the door – went to collect their food, and pay for it.

Bea said they shouldn't discuss Trust affairs in the garden, so they ate round the kitchen table, with Maggie perched on a typing chair brought up from below.

Silence ruled for a while. Even from Chris, who Bea imagined might be making notes of everything for future use. The boys had seconds, but Bea refused.

She said, 'The more I think about it, the more I believe Honoria was the brains behind the scam. Oh, of course it was Denzil's idea to use girlie pictures as a front for his secrets, but that grubby little soul of his was surely not intelligent enough to devise the systematic fleecing of the Trust over such a long period of time. The fifty pounds he gave away every month is not sufficiently large a bribe to attract anyone at director level, so I think Mr Cambridge was right in suspecting it went to the office

201

manageress. That would be Denzil's little secret. But for the rest ... Did Mr Cambridge find anything he could use in the deleted files, or in the HP Gallery?'

Zander eyed the last spring roll as it was transferred to Chris's plate. 'He said he needed to have a go at the hard drive on the original machine, so we switched computers over. The one now sitting in Denzil's office contains a record of his current files, transferred via the memory stick, while Mr Cambridge took Denzil's original computer back to his place to spend more time on it.'

'I'd like to see him working on that,' said Oliver. 'I asked if he'd let me help him, and he said "maybe". Only then it was time to break for the night, we took a taxi back to Zander's, and the sky fell on us.'

Bea switched the kettle on to make some tea while Maggie gathered up all the empty plates and dishes. Winston the cat leaped on to the table, scenting food. Oliver picked him up to give him a cuddle. For an eighteen-year-old, Oliver had survived the day wonderfully well, but suddenly he looked exhausted. Had he slept at all the previous night? Probably not.

Bea distributed mugs of tea all round. 'Do you two want to talk about what you saw at Mrs Perrot's?'

Oliver buried his face in the cat's fur. Winston blinked but allowed himself to be caressed.

Zander shook himself back from whatever hell he'd been looking into. 'When we finished at the Trust, we helped Mr Cambridge into a taxi with his laptop, and I locked up. Oliver and I waited for another taxi. When we got to my place – to Mrs Perrot's place – we saw there were fire engines outside, two of them. And police cars. So we both got out. I said who I was, and they asked if there was anyone else living there, and I said yes, and was Mrs Perrot all right.'

He cleared his throat. 'I was really fond of her, you know? She always had a smile, could always find time to talk to people, in the shops, everywhere. She used to do the flowers at church once a month, and in her younger days she taught in the Sunday school, though they call it Junior Church nowadays. She ran the Women's Hour midweek and collected for Christian Aid. I was going to trim her privet hedge this weekend and tie back a climbing rose which had come away from its trellis.

'Her daughter went to live in Australia twenty years ago, and she's only seen her grandchildren once in all that time. There's a nephew comes around occasionally, but she told me he was a bit of a cad – that's the way she put it. "A bit of a cad." He's been three times through the divorce courts and tries to get out of paying maintenance. She doesn't – didn't – like him much. Said he was just like her brother, who apparently ... Oh well, what's the use! I'm going to miss her enormously.'

He shuddered. 'I can't bear to think of her last few minutes. If only we'd finished earlier ... but the police said it looked as if she died about nine o'clock when we were still working.'

'What do you think happened?' asked Chris.

'I don't know. A burglary that went wrong? She had some nice pieces of jewellery, and it was a big old house. Perhaps it was some passer-by, some drug addict, who thought she'd have money in the house?'

They were all quiet. Oliver yawned, cavernously.

Zander tried to smile. 'Well, it was lucky for us that Mr Cambridge could give us an alibi. We'll let the police sort it.' He looked at his watch. 'I thought they'd have contacted me by now to say when I can fetch my things. I'm desperate for a shower.'

'And a good night's sleep,' said Oliver, yawning again. 'Sorry, everyone. I'm bushed.'

Zander stood up and stretched. 'Chris, I forgot to tell your father, what with everything else that's been happening. My predecessor at the office rang me yesterday afternoon, asking me to go out to see her, somewhere in Uxbridge, I think. Said she had some information for me, wouldn't give any details. I thought she might have something useful to tell us about Denzil's little habits so I said I'd go, but then of course your father wanted us to do a spot of detective work, so I rang her back to make another appointment. She was out, so I left a message. I don't know whether it's worth following up now. With what we've found on the computer, I don't suppose it matters.'

The doorbell rang. Bea was nearest. Two plain-clothes policemen, calling for Zander. He came out of the kitchen, unafraid, looking at his watch. 'You mean I get an escort to pick up my things? Have you found out who did it yet?'

They arrested him. Formally. For the theft of Mrs Perrot's jewellery, which they'd found hidden in his toilet bag and under his mattress.

'What!' Zander blinked, took half a step back. 'But I didn't! I wouldn't!'

Bea believed him.

The police didn't. 'Come along now.'

'Mrs Abbot, believe me, I didn't!'

'I believe you,' said Bea, trying to think what this might mean.

'I've been framed!' said Zander, reaching the truth.

'Don't try that on with us, lad,' said the larger of the policemen. 'We don't go round planting jewellery. We just find it where you've hidden it.'

Bea said, 'Zander, say "no comment" to everything. I'll see what I can do about getting you a good solicitor.'

'Save your money, love,' said the larger policeman. 'He can't wriggle out of this one, no matter who he gets to give him an alibi.'

Zander gave one despairing look around and went with the policemen. Bea closed the door and leaned against it.

Excitable Chris was already on his mobile phone. 'Dad; you'll never guess what...!'

Oliver subsided on to his stool, eyes wild.

205

Suddenly he looked ten years old, a small boy wanting his mother.

Maggie mopped up tears, sniffing, urging Oliver to his feet. 'Come on; bed for you. Things will look better in the morning.'

Would they? wondered Bea.

Oliver shuffled past her to the stairs, Maggie's arm around him. He stopped on the first step, looked back at Bea. 'He was framed, wasn't he? By Honoria?'

'I don't know,' said Bea, holding back misery. 'She wouldn't kill Mrs Perrot just to get back at Zander, would she? I mean ... Surely not.' The idea settled into Bea's mind, and suddenly she was convinced that this was exactly what Honoria would do.

Oliver shook his head. He held on to the banister to help him climb the stairs. Maggie encouraged him along, saying, 'There, now. You can do it.'

Chris held his phone out to Bea. 'The man wants a word.'

She took it from him. 'Yes?'

'They say women are better judges of other women than men can ever be. Is Honoria capable of killing an old lady and framing Zander for it?'

'Yes.'

'You seem very sure of it.'

'I am now. Remember that she tried to frame him for stealing the statuette? Suppose I hadn't been able to prove he was innocent, and she insisted on calling the police? He'd have gone to prison.'

'So he would. Luckily I could provide them with an alibi for last night, though I had to go against Tommy's wishes to do so. He really doesn't want the problems at the Trust splashed all over the tabloids, but when it comes to murder ... I did hope we'd got over that piece of rough ground successfully.'

'I agree that, between you and Oliver, you can clear Zander of Mrs Perrot's murder. The theft of the jewellery is another matter because they can say he could have taken it earlier. They could even say she discovered what he was doing so he got an accomplice to kill her at a time when he had a good alibi. I need to get him a good solicitor.'

'I'll do that for you. Tell me, where do you stand on this?'

'I'm not bound to respect Lord Murchison's feelings. If it looks as if Zander is to go to prison for theft, I'll tell the police what I know.'

'Which might not help Zander.'

'It would muddy the waters – and it would make you concentrate on clearing him.'

'You have too much faith in my abilities.'

'Don't give up. I've just remembered something. Zander said he'd had a call from the previous office manageress yesterday afternoon, asking him to pay her a visit last night. He agreed, but then you asked him to help with Denzil's computer so he couldn't go. He rang her back to make his apologies, but she was out, so he left a message. I wonder now if that phone call to him was a decoy, intended to take him out on a false errand. Because if he'd gone and not found her at home, he wouldn't have had an alibi for the murder, would he?'

'This takes some thinking about. Mrs Abbot—'

'I think you might call me "Bea", don't you?'

'Very well. And I'm CJ. Tommy said he'd never seen anyone cope with Honoria as you did. I wonder if you could think yourself into her shoes, tell us what she's likely to do next.'

Bea snorted. 'As in, flattery will get you everywhere? I should hate to think myself into Honoria's mind. I don't want to get suicidally depressed.'

'You think she's suicidal? Now that's interesting. I hadn't thought of her that way.'

'Of course not. It's me who might get suicidal – oh, leave it, will you? It's been a long day, and I've got other important things on my mind apart from you and your Trust.'

He sounded amused. 'Most women retreat from confrontation, I find. Sleep on it. I'll ring you tomorrow, early.' The phone went dead.

Chris's eyes gleamed. 'Isn't this exciting? Oh, and awful, too, of course.'

Bea couldn't help laughing. Painful laughter. With tears. 'Oh, Chris! How could you?'

He patted her awkwardly on her shoulder. 'I know, I know. I'm terrible. But if I'm going to make good films one day, I need to understand how people cope with life. Cheer up. Dad'll sort it.'

Bea blew her nose. 'Of course. Thank you, Chris. You've been great.'

'Anything else I can do?'

She shook her head, saw him out into the dusk. Was it really that late? She cleared up in the kitchen, closed and locked the grilles over the windows, fed Winston, who had laid himself fatly out on the work surface. Thought over the conversation with CJ – what was his name? Was he another Christopher, perhaps?

One thing for sure: she was not, definitely not, going to try to get into Honoria's mind. That way madness lay. She went up to bed.

She prayed a bit. Was too tired to read her Bible. And against all the odds, for she hadn't thought she could, she slept.

Thursday morning

She fought herself out of a nightmare. Daylight. Birds singing. Another blue sky day.

Maggie put a cup of tea on the bedside table. Maggie was dressed but hadn't put on her war paint yet. 'Oliver won't get out of bed.'

Bea yawned, leaned on one elbow to grab her tea. 'Exhausted emotionally, I expect. He's only eighteen, after all.'

'Nearly nineteen. Should I let him be?'

Bea sipped tea. Maggie had put sugar in it. Ugh. Maybe Maggie thought sugared tea was good for shock, but Bea was shockproof after all that had happened, wasn't she? 'Yes, let him be. Did he sleep all right?'

'I could hear him tossing around every time I woke. His bed creaks.'

Bea nodded. The girl's eyes were deeply shadowed, but she'd shown her quality by getting up and getting going. Maggie wasn't eighteen any more. Maggie was five years older than Oliver and had learned a thing or two about getting through the hot spots of life. She didn't mention Zander.

Bea swallowed sugary tea and tried not to make a face at it. 'Mr Cambridge is going to get Zander a good solicitor. He wants me to think myself into Honoria's mind, find out what she'll do next.'

'Yuk,' said Maggie and went away to start breakfast. 'Sooner you than me.'

Bea got herself ready for the day while making lists in her mind as to what needed doing first, second and third. And if this or that were to happen, what she might do about it.

Oliver didn't appear at breakfast. The house seemed unusually quiet. Bea thought they were waiting for something to happen. But what could happen now?

Maggie was listless but agreed to resume her normal activities. The electrician must be appeased for having been stood up the day before, and she had to chase up some kitchen units which ought to have been delivered and hadn't. Unsmiling, Maggie took some breakfast up to Oliver, and she reported to Bea that he was awake but pretending to be asleep when she went in.

'I'll deal with him in a minute,' said Bea.

Maggie picked up her tote bag and hesitated. She didn't put her anxiety into words, but Bea did it for her. 'You're worried about Zander. Yes, I am, too. A spot of prayer might help?'

Maggie nodded, squared her shoulders, and went out to do battle with the world.

Bea finished making an enormous shopping list for food. The phones were quiet. Hadn't CJ promised to ring? Oh well; promises, promises. Miss Brook rang to say she was going to be in a little late as she'd had a poor night but was definitely on the mend ... which Bea took leave to doubt. But if Miss Brook was coming in, that would free her up for other things. Though not, of course, to look into Honoria's mind.

Cynthia arrived on the dot, and Bea spent a good hour with her, going through the systems. Cynthia was just a trifle too bright and breezy for Bea, but a godsend in view of the staff situation.

At eleven Bea made some strong coffee and took it upstairs to Oliver, who was still pretending to be asleep. The blinds were still drawn against the daylight, and she twitched them up.

'Rise and shine, my lad. We've got work to do. Because if we don't put our minds to it, Zander goes to prison.'

Oliver burrowed under the pillow.

She clinked a spoon against his mug. 'Strong coffee. A cold shower. Shave and dress. Ten minutes. Downstairs in my office, in your right mind and with that all-important memory stick

211

in your hand.'

'Dunno what you mean. What memory stick?'

'Ten minutes,' she said. 'Or I empty a bucket of cold water into your bed.'

'I'm exhausted.'

'So am I. You did well yesterday, and of course it tired you out. But you'll live. Ten minutes, right?'

She left him to it and went down to greet Miss Brook, who'd just arrived and was eyeing Cynthia rather as one might a slug found in one's lettuce. Soothing one and encouraging the other, Bea left them to work out how best to coexist and was rewarded by hearing Miss Brook graciously offering Cynthia a biscuit from her own personal tin of delicacies from Harrods.

Fifteen minutes after she'd left Oliver, he was in her office, showered, shaved, dressed and with a scowl on his face fit to shatter glass.

'To work,' she said. 'Between you and me and that illicit memory stick, we ought to be able to trace the history of Denzil's career and marriage. Mr Cambridge wants us to get inside Honoria's mind, try to work out what drives her, and above all, what she's going to do next.'

A shrug, shoulders to ear. A grunt. 'What illicit memory stick?'

'You were asked to download files from Denzil's computer on to memory sticks for Mr Cambridge and Zander to work on. You were then told to look at the first twenty files, which you did. Knowing you, you also downloaded everything else in sight: the history files, the

212

photograph albums, everything down to what music he used to play. So transfer the files from the memory stick to your own computer and search for something we can use. Anything.'

'I hadn't time to copy everything on to my own memory stick, but there was an icon I didn't recognize, and I did take a note of it because it's something I haven't come across before.'

'So; investigate.'

As he left, Bea started pacing.

Honoria. *Lady* Honoria. A title which was possibly not hers by right?

Forty plus when she married Denzil? What had she been doing before that? Had she had any business experience? Was she computer literate?

What could she have seen in Denzil the Dangerous? To Bea's mind, he was a grubby-minded little so and so, fondling teenage girls, storing mild porn on his computer, playing games with computer files to hide information from a casual eye, taking rake-offs from Corcorans. A racist.

His marriage might just have been a screen behind which he could approach young girls.

Other people might have seen a different side to him. He'd had an excellent start in life as a godson of Lord Murchison with a public school education. He'd done a good job for the Trust for some years and been promoted for it. He'd known how to manipulate the other directors when discovered. He had been, presumably, presentable. He'd had a title of sorts. He had that

213

indefinable asset: a good background.

He'd died young, of a heart attack. Funeral ... when? Soon? Would all the directors attend, in spite of what they'd discovered about him? Probably, yes. There'd be a three-line whip from Tommy, who wanted everything kept under wraps.

Why had Honoria married Denzil?

Because she could dominate him, wear the trousers, dictate the direction of events? She'd been married before – or had Bea imagined that piece of gossip?

What did Honoria want out of life? Two things, perhaps: to restore the family home, and a husband. If she'd ever loved Denzil, that love couldn't have lasted, given his propensity for young girls. Equally, he probably hadn't loved her. Maybe it had been a marriage of convenience, each accepting of the other's failings, two oddities facing the world together?

What would she have got out of it? Status.

Honoria needed money for the house. Hence the fraud. Denzil's position was not salaried, but he was able to tap into the resources of the Trust. So she'd devised the scam, and he'd carried it out. Yes, that felt right.

So ... come the dawn and Zander's enquiring mind uncovered the leak in the Trust accounts, forestalling Tommy's slower march of justice. Then Denzil died, and Honoria blackmailed the Trust into accepting her as Denzil's replacement. So far, so good. She must have been furious that a lowly employee had disrupted

214

their plans.

Bea thought back to what she knew and had observed of Honoria and concluded that she was not only a snob but also – like Denzil but even more so – a racist. Hence she'd tried first of all to bully Zander into submission when he'd visited her in the country, and then endeavoured to frame him for theft of the valuable statuette.

Both attempts to discredit Zander had failed, which must have stoked her fires of vengeance against him.

Her position at the Trust must have seemed safe enough, until the bank statements had turned up proving that Denzil had been taking back-handers. Did Honoria know who found them? Better ask Tommy what she'd been told. She may have assumed it was Zander, fuelling her hatred of him even further.

Guesswork! Bea scolded herself.

Yes, but nothing else explains why she should have taken such a terrible revenge on Zander.

If it was her, said Bea.

You know it was her. It was a woman who phoned Zander at his office, inviting him to visit her in the suburbs that evening. Oh yes, it must have been her. Believing that she'd sent him on a wild goose chase, she went to his digs and killed Mrs Perrot.

Why would she need to kill Mrs Perrot? Because ... because she wanted to punish Zander in some way, probably by framing him for theft. And then, on finding herself confronted with an elderly lady, realized she could also frame Zander for murder. It was neat; Bea had to admit it was neat. And it had worked up to a point: the point at which CJ had become involved. Bea thought it was odds-on that CJ would clear Zander, somehow or other.

So would Honoria now rest on her laurels? Unlikely. She had struck Bea as being a particularly single-minded individual. It would of course be sensible of her now to turn her mind to pastures new ... but suppose she still burned to revenge herself on someone, anyone, who had thwarted her in the past? Remember, she'd lost her only means of support.

Well, she'd dealt with Zander. Who else would she wish to vent her displeasure on?

Mm. The previous office manageress, or the youthful niece who had attracted Denzil's attention? Can't quite see why, but ... maybe. A little far-fetched, but Honoria might have resented a young girl's attempt to supplant her. If so, whatever had she thought about Kylie from the pub?

Or she might very well be angry with Bea and CJ, who'd helped Tommy find the proof of Denzil's fraudulent doings.

What? What nonsense! Bea laughed aloud. How ridiculous. Of course not.

Oliver frowned his way back into her office. 'I think I've found something.'

Late Wednesday evening

There was nothing on the news about Sandy's death. She munched her way through some nuts,

216

couldn't be bothered to cook. The washing machine whirred in the scullery. She'd cleaned her gun already and locked it away.

Phone calls from Trimmingham kept her up to date. She couldn't understand how the office boy had got off the hook for the murder, but the theft was enough to send him to jail. A brilliant stroke of hers, hiding the jewellery among his belongings. Done on the spur of the moment, but none the worse for that.

Tommy Murchison was back in hospital. Good. With him out of the way, the other directors hadn't the guts to withstand her. She'd be back at the Trust in no time at all, because they couldn't prove she'd done anything wrong, could they?

Trimmingham said Tommy had been taking advice from that pale widow, Dean or Abbot, some name like that. Said it was she who'd found the bank statements and had got Zander cleared of the murder charge. The woman had denied that Zander was her toy boy, though everyone could see he was just that.

How dare she! Didn't she realize who she was up against? She needed to be taught a lesson, and Honoria was just the person to do it.

There was someone else who needed to be taught a lesson now that Sandy was out of the picture, wasn't there? That Della Lawrence, conspiring to have her niece replace Honoria in Denzil's bed.

Honoria smiled, pushing the last of the cashew nuts into her mouth. Why not pay her a visit?

217

There wasn't much left to do for the funeral. She'd ordered some sandwiches from the pub and a couple of bottles of sherry for the funeral meats; nothing extravagant. There wouldn't be many people there. The board of directors, a few yokels, some of his so-called friends from the pub. No need to go to any great trouble for them.

And revenge was sweet.

TWELVE

Thursday noon

Bea was on her way to Oliver's office before he'd finished speaking. 'I knew you could do it. So what have you got?'

'I'm not sure yet. You know I said there was an icon I didn't recognize. Well, it was for a program I haven't used before. Steganography.'

'What?'

'It's for hiding data within pictures. The data might be text, or it might be another picture. So you could have a picture hidden within another. I looked the icon up, and now I'm downloading it from the Internet. The only thing is, I don't know which of his images he's actually hidden something in. I mean, there's dozens. Unless you can think of a short cut, I'm going to have to run the program on every single bare-assed picture on his computer to see if there's another message hidden inside it. It's going to take ages.'

'Would your guru be able to help? Presumably he saw the icon, too.' She looked at her watch. 'Which reminds me that he was supposed to ring me this morning, and he hasn't.'

Prompt on cue, the front doorbell rang. And it was him, looking greyer and less substantial than before.

'I do apologize for not having rung. I hope you can spare me a few minutes now?'

'Of course. Come into the sitting room. Coffee?'

'No need. What I've got to say is ... there's no good news. Tommy's back in hospital. The pain got too much even for him. He summoned me to his bedside and gave me power of attorney to deal with his affairs at the Trust. I arrived at the Kensington headquarters to find an extraordinary board meeting taking place. And I do mean extraordinary. Convened by the major, but with Sir Cecil in the chair. In short order they carried two motions: one, that Zander had forfeited his job by being arrested for theft; and two, that Honoria should be reinstated in her husband's place on the board of directors, since nothing can be proved against her.'

'What!'

'Yes, indeed. Both motions carried unanimously, though the major did express some qualms to me afterwards, saying that he didn't think Tommy would be a happy bunny to hear what they'd done. Honoria will officially take her seat on the board the day after the funeral.'

'But...!'

'Trimmingham declares her innocent of all charges and willing to work hard to put right the damage her husband has done. And that's that. I haven't told Tommy yet. He's not fit to hear any bad news.'

'No, I can understand that, but ... where does this leave Zander? In jail. Yet we know he didn't murder his landlady, and I'd stake my life on his not having stolen her jewellery.'

'We can clear him of the murder; true. But the thefts ... I don't know. I've got a good man working on it, but it wouldn't be the first time an innocent man's been fitted up for theft. That's out of our hands now. Honoria's another matter. I must warn you that, according to the major, she knows it was you who found the evidence of her husband's fraud. She declares there's a perfectly simple explanation for the monies that went into their joint bank accounts, and she's holding us personally responsible for his early death.'

Bea felt a cold tingle down her backbone. 'You asked me to put myself into her head, and it's given me reason to fear her. What about you?'

He washed his face with both hands. He evidently wasn't going to admit to fear. He tried out for a laugh. 'I fear that spineless board will let her get away with murder.'

'If it hasn't already,' said Bea, thinking that she could do with some caffeine, even if he didn't need any. 'Come into the kitchen. I need some coffee.'

He followed and watched while she put their newly acquired coffee machine to work. It was something Oliver had bought for her, and needed his sort of brain to operate, but she thought she'd more or less mastered it. 'It seems to me – correct me if I'm wrong – that Honoria is a very angry and vindictive woman. What she's done to Zander is appalling, but I'm wondering how many more grudges she wants to satisfy.'

'You. Me. Perhaps Tommy?'

'I was thinking more of Corcoran. A partner in crime for her husband. What is he to her?'

He pinched his nose between his finger and thumb. 'You think it might be worth asking him about her? I suppose he may be mourning the loss of his contracts with the Trust. Yes, it's worth a try. Perhaps we can get him to talk, once he accepts that no one's going to sue.'

'Then there's the question of the ex-office manager. Do you remember – I'm not sure if you were there when Zander told us? I can hardly remember which day of the week it is but it might be relevant – anyway, Zander told us she'd phoned him at work the day of Mrs Perrot's murder and asked him to call on her that evening, only of course he couldn't. Perhaps she had something to say...? It's a bit of a long shot.'

'Della something. Yes, I think you did mention it, but what with everything else that's been happening ... I'll check. Any other ideas?'

'One more. Oliver spotted a strange icon on Denzil's desktop. He thinks it's something to do with hiding text or an image inside another picture.'

'Hm, I noticed that too, but there's quite a few pictures on the computer, and so far I haven't spotted anything helpful. Perhaps Denzil downloaded the programme and didn't actually get round to using it. So unless you can come up with a clue...?'

Bea snapped. 'If you think I've got nothing better to do!'

'Understood.'

Silence. She poured out coffee for them both. He took his black, and so did she. Winston the cat plopped in through the cat flap. Spotting another cat-lover, he twined round CJ's legs and allowed himself to be lifted up to be stroked. Winking at CJ, and raising one paw in a begging position, Winston performed his usual trick of enchanting the beholder.

CJ smiled and scratched behind Winston's ears. 'I wouldn't have put you down as a cat person, Bea.'

'Winston moved in on me. People do. Maggie did. And Oliver. And if Zander hadn't been whisked off to jail last night, I suspect I'd be putting him up as well.'

'Your husband only died last year. I'm sorry.'

'Nobody moved in on me while he was alive. Not even the cat.'

'Angels and ministers of grace, defend us.'

Bea blinked. Had CJ really said that? Was he a Christian, too?

CJ put Winston down and sighed. 'Must go. Suppose we divide up the tasks? I'll tackle Corcoran, if you chase up Della. What's her second name? Zander would know. How can we find out? Ah. I know. Young Oliver copied everything from Denzil's computer on to his

223

own memory stick, didn't he?'

Bea tried not to blush. 'I'm afraid so. I don't think he's got any morals at all when it comes to computers.'

CJ was amused. 'I fear he got that from me. Well, he'll have the file on the personnel, then. Let me know how it goes?'

'I'll show you out.'

With one hand on the front door, he stopped. 'I'm inclined to back your instincts about the woman. Can you ensure someone's with you all the time from now on? Someone to guard your back, I mean.'

'To provide an alibi in case I'm accused of arson, theft or murder?'

'Precisely. And I'll see who I can get to do the same for me. Not that I think we'll need it.'

'Of course not.'

They were both lying. Bea set her back to the door once he'd gone and wondered if the day had turned colder. Perhaps she should find a jacket to wear?

She went downstairs to see how everyone was getting on and found Miss Brook and Cynthia had progressed to a good working relationship, each recognizing the professionalism of the other.

There were some matters which only Bea could deal with, and she sat down at her desk and did her best to concentrate on finding the right person for the job, no square pegs to go in round holes. And looked at the morning's post ... and yesterday's post, and tried to provide

224

answers without descending into gibberish.

Maggie rang through just the once, to ask if there was any news. There wasn't. Maggie said she'd probably be late that evening, as the electrician couldn't get back to her till five or maybe six, and did Bea realize there was nothing to eat for supper? Bea realized.

She sent a large food order through online, thinking that at least it would arrive tomorrow, and she'd worry about supper that night when the time came.

Lunchtime. She made a big tureen of soup out of lentils and some scraps of bacon, chicken stock and milk, and took hot mugs of it down to everyone, together with a platter piled high with chunks of bread and some cubes of mature Cheddar cheese. Miss Brook and Cynthia accepted the soup with gracious thanks, but declined the bread and cheese, as they were sharing a pack of sandwiches which Miss Brook had had the forethought to buy on her way in.

When she went into Oliver's office, Bea wasn't particularly surprised to find young Chris Cambridge sitting at his friend's elbow, as they processed one image of a pretty girl after another. She handed them each a mug of soup and put the bread and cheese down between them. 'Found anything yet?'

'So far, no. But I've printed off the personnel files for you.' Oliver indicated a slender file of papers on his desk. 'He's used a password, of course, on each of his folders. I'm hoping he's used the same for everything. But he might have

225

used something else as well. Anything. Any word that attracted his attention. I've tried the steganography program on three folders so far, all soft porn, using his usual password, "Kylie", and haven't found anything.' He sipped, put the mug down. 'Too hot.' He stretched, arms above his head, and yawned. 'I'm bushed.'

Chris reached for bread and cheese, never taking his eyes from the screen. In a high, false voice, he said, 'They say you soon get tired of looking at pictures of pretty girls. They lie!'

Was he trying to imitate Bea's voice? She was shocked, annoyed and only slightly amused.

Oliver laughed. Chris laughed. Bea rolled her eyes and told herself it wouldn't help matters if she cracked their heads together, which she seriously wanted to do.

Chris munched away, leaned back in his chair. With his mouth full, he said, 'There must be some way of telling which files he visited with this programme.'

Oliver rubbed his eyes. 'I'd need the hard drive to work that out. And even then I might not be able to tell you.'

Bea said, 'I know I'm an ignoramus in these matters, but do you think he'd have found it easy to use the program on a single picture in a folder that maybe contained twenty such images? Wouldn't he be more likely to use it on single jpegs on the desktop?'

Both Oliver and Chris looked at her, sat up straight, and refocused on the screen. Oliver shoved bread and cheese into his mouth with

226

one hand while controlling his mouse with the other. 'There are five. I hadn't started on them yet. Let's see...'

He brought up an image of a naked girl posing on a chaise longue, a mirror on the wall reflecting her curves. 'She's called "Rhoda the Riotous".'

Chris peered at the screen. 'I preferred "Billie the Bountiful".'

Both picked up their mugs in one hand and sipped.

'It requires another password,' said Oliver. 'It's not Kylie. Ideas, anyone?'

Bea warned them, 'If you spill soup on that keyboard, you're sunk. Why don't you try "Rhoda"?'

Oliver was peeved. 'That's just what I was going to do.'

Computer geeks hate it when a layman points out the obvious.

'There!' said Oliver and Chris together.

The doorbell rang upstairs.

Neither Chris nor Oliver were going to be torn from the computer to answer, so up went Bea, sighing to herself.

It was her daughter-in-law, fresh from the hairdressers, her blonde hair in a mass of curls around her face. Curls! They didn't suit her. Nicole was burdened with yet more shopping bags from expensive boutiques, which was going to make Max swear. She was also crying.

'Oh, my dear!' said Bea, drawing Nicole inside. 'Whatever is the matter?'

Nicole was sobbing so hard she couldn't speak. Bea stifled the uncharitable thought that her daughter-in-law could only just have started to cry, for her eyes were not at all red.

'Max said ... Oh, how could he be so deceitful?'

'That's not like Max.'

'Oh, it is. You've no idea!'

Bea had a very good idea, actually. She drew Nicole into the sitting room and sat her down. 'Would you like a box of tissues? Some coffee?'

'No, of course not.' Nicole tossed her head, making her ringlets dance. 'Oh, I'm so unhappy!' She applied a tissue of her own to one eye, and then the other.

'Are you, my dear? Can you tell me why?'

'It was all so wonderful when Max said that Piers wanted to paint me, and I told everyone and went off to the beauty salon and had my nails done and their new stylist devised this hairstyle for me, and then ... and then I rang my sister and told her the news and she said ... she said ... Oh, I can't bear it!'

'Lettice?'

'Yes, of course, Lettice. She said Max had only said that Piers was going to paint me to keep me sweet, and that of course he wouldn't be bothered with me and ... Oh, I'm so unhappy. So I went and bought this dress which I don't think I like at all really, and it was just around the corner from you, and I thought ... I thought at least you'd sympathize with me.'

'Well, I do. Of course. But Nicole, Piers really

228

is going to paint you.'

'No, why should he? Lettice's right. He never paints beautiful women, only famous people. I mean, he can charge whatever he likes. Everyone wants to be painted by Piers. He's the uttermost.'

'So he is. But he came over the other night to ask if I'd persuade you to sit for him. I thought you might be interested, so I told Max to ask you.'

'Yes, but...!' She caressed her bump. 'He doesn't paint young women, and I'm sure he wouldn't want to paint someone who's as pregnant as I am.'

'Granted, he hasn't painted beautiful women before, but he's seen something in you, pregnant as you are, that appeals to him. Something to do with showing ripeness and beauty in pregnancy. I think he's also interested in the fact that you aren't a brainless young schoolgirl, but a mature woman. He says he can make quite a statement with that.'

Nicole was hooked. She smiled. 'Ripeness and beauty in pregnancy. One in the eye for my little sister.'

'Absolutely.' Bea wondered if Nicole's strongest emotion was dislike of her sister, or love for Max. Possibly it was a tie between the two? 'So you see, Lettice wasn't speaking the truth. I expect she's green with envy.'

'I expect she is.' Nicole scrabbled in her handbag for a mirror and inspected her make-up. 'I don't look too bad, do I? I had been wondering about Botox, but...'

'Please don't. Piers specially mentioned his dislike of Botox. I think he prefers the natural look. But of course, you will have to discuss all that with him. Will you be able to sit for him soon? I think he rather wants to do it straight away. You're not being sick now, are you?'

'No, no. Or not often, anyway.' She scrabbled in her shopping bags and produced a pale blue, filmy drift of chiffon. 'Do you think this would be suitable?'

Bea put her head on one side. 'It might well be. Why don't you ring him? Ask him for an appointment to visit you and make the final arrangements.'

Nicole went to stand in front of the fireplace, looking up into the mirror. 'I'm having second thoughts about these curls, if he wants the natural look. What do you think?'

'You'll have to ask him that. Can you straighten the curls, or reproduce them at will? He might want to see you both ways before he decides.'

Nicole heaved a great sigh of relief, then peered into the mirror. 'Is that a spot coming?'

'Don't worry,' said Bea. 'Remember, he doesn't paint what he doesn't want to see.'

'No, I suppose not. "Ripeness and beauty." I really like that. So Max was telling the truth, after all.'

'I think he's trying to rid himself of Lettice for good. But she does tend to cling, doesn't she? A sign of insecurity? But now you feel well enough to accompany Max on his official engagements, she'll really have no excuse to hang around him, will she?'

'You're right there.' Nicole smiled at herself in the mirror. Then returned to business. 'I'm glad I caught you in. Max said you've been in a spot of bother. He worries so about you. I hope it wasn't anything serious?'

Bea crossed her fingers. 'Not really.' Only murder, arson and theft. Only fraud and prison.

'Well, I suppose I must be going. I haven't got my big diary with me, and I'll need that to block out the times Piers will want me to sit for him, so I'll ring him from home. And I won't even bother to ring Lettice back. Let her stew!'

'Indeed,' said Bea, helping Nicole to gather her shopping together and seeing her to the front door. 'Take care, now.'

A passing taxi whisked Nicole away, and Bea turned back into the house, to meet Oliver coming up the stairs with some papers in his hand.

'The personnel files you wanted. And here's what I found hidden in the picture of Rhoda the Riotous. It's a copy of Honoria's birth certificate, though why he should need to hide that, I don't know.'

Bea took it from him, and held it up to the light. Bridget Honour, born October 1959 – which made her fifty this year. Mother, Bridget Honour Mulligan, shop assistant. Father, the Earl of ... ah. Yes.

'She's illegitimate,' said Oliver, who had probably also been born out of wedlock.

231

'Though I can't see it matters nowadays.'

'It matters enormously to her,' said Bea, 'and explains why everyone tries not to titter when she claims to be Lady Honoria. She is the daughter of an earl, but as he wasn't married to her mother, she has no right to claim the title. I agree with you, Oliver, that it's what a person is inside that counts, but not everyone is as secure in themselves as you are. I imagine Honoria has let the fact that she's not legitimate fester inside her. I am almost, though not quite, sorry for her.'

He shrugged. 'It's disappointing. I thought we'd find something incriminating.'

'It is incriminating. She'd go a long way to prevent her illegitimacy being made common knowledge. Go on looking. If he's hidden this, he may well have hidden other things.'

'If I can keep awake.' Oliver disappeared down the stairs, passing Chris on the way up. Chris was holding a collection of empty mugs and plates. 'Where shall I put these?'

She waved him towards the kitchen, her mind on the personnel files Oliver had found for her. 'CJ wants me to look up the office manager who was there before Zander. Didn't someone say she left under a cloud, towing a schoolgirl niece behind her?'

Chris located the dishwasher and loaded the dirty plates and mugs into it.

Bea was surprised into a laugh. 'Forgive me. How nice to meet someone house-trained. I'm afraid Oliver isn't.'

Chris grinned. 'Dad said the daily woman has

enough to do without clearing up after me, so I had to learn pretty quickly. Oliver's different, though. He doesn't see why he should do any housework when he's got more important things to think about.'

Bea was both shocked and annoyed. 'And you haven't?'

'Ah, well. That's the question, isn't it? Do I give a toss about going to uni? No, I don't. I even suggested to Oliver one day that he turned up there instead of me.'

'Your father would have a fit.'

'Mm. And Oliver didn't want to do my subject, anyway.' A quick glance to check how she'd take his next words. 'You will let him go to uni one day though, won't you?'

She felt as if all the breath had been driven out of her body. Of course she'd suggested Oliver should go. And he'd refused. She hadn't tried very hard to change his mind, though, and she felt guilty about that. 'I have urged him to apply again. Really I have.'

'He thinks you'd be lost at the agency without him.'

'We'd manage. Of course we would.'

He sighed. 'It's a weird old world. There's me not giving a hoot about going, and him dying to go but thinking he owes you too much to leave you.'

'Nonsense!' said Bea, as firmly as she could. 'Anyway, I thought you'd an agreement with your father about making films.'

'Oh, that.' He was listless, now. 'I'm not that

233

interested. It's just something I thought of to rile him. It's not hard to think up something to film, and the girls all think I'm something special when I say I want to make films. I'm not really committed to it, if you see what I mean. Truth is, I'm not sure what I want to do in life. Just get through it, I suppose.'

She wanted to say that if he hadn't had an indulgent father and a moneyed background, he would have had to settle down to earning a living by now, but she refrained. She turned back to the personnel records. 'Ah, here she is. Della Lawrence. Address and telephone number. I'll give her a bell, find out why she wanted to see Zander so badly the other day.'

Chris had located Winston, or Winston had located him. Arms overflowing with black fur, Chris said, 'Do you know, I think I'm beginning to get bored?'

Bea didn't know what to say, so dialled Della's number. 'Is that Mrs Lawrence? My name's Abbot, Bea Abbot. You won't know me, but I'm a friend of Zander's.'

'Who?' A hoarse, low voice. A sixty-a-day smoker's voice.

'Zander. Alexander. The man who took over from you when you left the Trust. I believe you phoned him a couple of nights ago—'

'What? Who is that? What *is* going on?'

Bea backtracked. 'I have got the right number, haven't I? You are the Mrs Della Lawrence who worked for—?'

'Yes, yes, of course. But I never expected to

234

hear from them again, and I certainly didn't ring Zander. Why should I?'

'Mrs Lawrence, I am equally confused. Zander was rung up by someone who said they were you, asking him to visit you that evening. He agreed, but then something came up and he had to ring back to apologize and make another appointment. Only, you were out.'

'I got a message on the answerphone, apologizing, that's right. Couldn't think why. I hadn't rung him, so why did he say I had?'

Bea rubbed her forehead. 'Why, indeed. Mrs Lawrence, something rather strange appears to be going on here. Could you spare me a few minutes this evening if I came out to see you?'

'Bringing Zander?'

'No, I'm afraid ... No, that won't be possible. I'm acting for him, though. Would you mind?'

Bea could imagine the shrug down the telephone line. 'I suppose. I've only just got in, as it happens. Need to rustle something up for supper. Half seven do you? Do you know where I live?'

'Thank you, yes. I have the address.'

'Parking's difficult around here. Get in where you can.'

Bea put the phone down and reached for the A to Z.

'Can I drive you?' asked Chris. 'I'm totally at a loose end, and I've got a driving licence, just. At least, I will have after I take my test again next month. If I go home I'll only get in my

235

father's hair because he'll want me to work on an essay or make myself useful around the house or something.'

'You are quite mad,' said Bea, laughing.

Thursday, early evening

Honoria looked up the address in her A to Z. It wasn't far away, tucked into suburbia near a park. Should she go there tonight, or leave it for a couple of days? Or forget about it altogether?

No, she couldn't forget. It made Honoria mad to think how Della had schemed to introduce her little tart of a niece into the office. Della knew exactly what sort of young girl appealed to Denzil, didn't she? Sit on his knee, stroke his cheek, let him kiss and fondle her, lead him on to think she'd marry him. It was the talk of marriage which had frightened Denzil into confessing to Honoria.

No, the slut deserved to die. So how should it be done this time? The gun? Perhaps not in such a built-up area. Might alarm the neighbours.

The hammer, then. Yes; why not? Della wouldn't be expecting trouble. It would be best to change in the loo again. Her overalls had come out nice and clean, and she'd bought a pack of thin rubber gloves to wear. Her shoes had been splashed with blood last time, and she'd have to clean them. She'd considered throwing them away, but they were good shoes, had cost a lot, and comfortable, stylish shoes were hard to find. Perhaps she'd throw them away after this

236

next one?

No, better wait till she'd finished off the lot.
She decided to cook a frozen meal for herself
in the microwave and then get moving.

THIRTEEN

Thursday evening

As a driver, Chris liked to cut in, in front of others. He talked too much, gestured too much, and thought it funny when other drivers made rude gestures at him.

Bea resolved that she'd drive on the way back.

'How many driving lessons have you had?' She clutched at the door handle as they rounded a corner a trifle wide.

'What? Dunno. Lost count. It's practice that I need. Dad won't take me out any more, so I'm really grateful to you for letting me come out this evening. I asked Oliver if he'd come out with me, but he says his nerves aren't up to it. I asked Maggie, too, but she says she's in the same boat as me.'

His cheerfulness remained undented as he squeaked between a bus and a Volvo. Bea kept her eyes closed for a count of five, telling herself that fools led charmed lives. Which didn't help much.

When she opened her eyes again, he was peering out of the side window, when he should have been looking at oncoming traffic. 'Is this the road?'

Bea croaked, 'Didn't you...?' She cleared her throat and tried again. 'Didn't you hear the satnav say to take the next road on the left? Della said parking's difficult here, so we should get in where you can.' She couldn't stand his driving any longer. He eyed up a potential parking space like a boxer squaring up to an opponent in the ring. She told herself not to kill his self-confidence by offering to park the car for him. She closed her eyes. Sent up an arrow prayer. *Dear Lord, a spot of help here?*

Finally, he hauled on the handbrake and turned off the ignition. 'There, that didn't go too badly, did it?'

Her hands were shaking as she checked her watch. She'd estimated the journey would take forty minutes, and they'd done it in twenty-one and a half. A very long twenty-one and a half. 'We're a little early. Let's sit in the car for a few minutes.' She wasn't sure her legs would hold her up if she got out straight away.

He beamed at her. 'I hope you'll let me drive you often. You're so calm.'

'Thank you,' said Bea, hoping her voice didn't wobble.

He sighed, still smiling. 'I can see why Oliver's latched on to you. I wish you were my mother.'

Bea raised her eyebrows. 'You've got a very satisfactory father. Oliver hasn't got anyone.'

'I know, I know. I doubt if my mother would have been much good as a driving instructor, even if she'd lived. I was a surprise to both of them as they'd married late and hadn't expected to have children. She was totally wrapped up in her research, the ancient Sumerians, you know. She didn't have any maternal instincts, handed me over to nannies and then bundled me off to boarding school. I mean, I was terribly sorry when she died of course, but it did mean I could live at home with Dad and go to school locally. At least he cares what happens to me.' He shot her a look to see how well this had gone down.

She took it with a pinch of salt. 'Does the grieving motherless child bit go down well with the girlfriends?'

'Works a treat.' Another grin. 'Truth to tell, I really haven't much to complain about, have I?'

'No, you haven't.' She unhooked her seat belt and got out of the car, holding on to the door till she was upright and sure she could stand unaided. 'Shall we try to find Della's now?'

He got out with one lissom movement, yawned, slammed the car door – ouch! – and peered along a street of houses which all looked exactly alike.

Bea checked her A to Z. 'It's the next road on the right.' And it was, though indistinguishable from the first one except to those who lived there.

These houses were all three-bedroomed semi-ds, bow-fronted, many with loft extensions. Almost all had converted the front gardens into hardstanding for cars, shut off from the pavement by elaborate ironwork gates topped with gilded finials.

'Indian territory,' said Chris, hefting her bunch of keys and looking around with a knowledge-able air. 'The first thing they do when they buy a house out here is to get their car off the road, so they don't have to pay when the Car Parking Zones arrive. It's a disgrace, I think, because it means that the people who usually park here can't; but I don't suppose householders would agree with me.'

Bea led the way along Della's road, checking house numbers. Della's had neither loft con-version nor ironwork gates. Her house was not exactly shabby, but it might soon become so. The front garden had been paved over recently, and there was a scooter on it, chained to a block of concrete. Was the scooter Della's? Or her husband's? Or possibly the niece's?

There was an old-fashioned display of stained glass in the upper part of the front door, echoed by that in the window bay. Original glass, circa nineteen twenty. Rather charming.

The woman who opened the door to them was probably in her early fifties. Fifty-four and flir-tatious, was Bea's thought. Heavy smoking had ruined her complexion and roughened her voice, but her figure was still good though it might not continue to be so for much longer. Crow's feet, no Botox. A good bra. Hair dyed mid-brown to conceal the grey. She looked like she wore clothes from the charity shop and TK Maxx, which announced that she still had an interest in fashion and the opposite sex.

'Mrs Lawrence? I'm Bea Abbot, and this is young Chris, who was kind enough to drive me out here.'

'Come along in.' Della looked both ways down the road. 'A neighbour said she's taken in a parcel for me, though I wasn't expecting anything. I wonder what it can be. An early birthday present, perhaps. She said she'd only be a jiffy, but I suppose she's been held up. You can never rely on anyone when they say they'll do something, can you?'

'True,' said Chris, beaming as he wiped his feet thoroughly on the door mat.

Della laughed, taken in by his ready charm. 'Oh, well. Not everyone's careless about time. Come on through.' She led the way into the sitting room, which seemed dark by contrast with the bright evening sunshine outside. A brown leatherette three-piece suite, a glass-topped coffee table, four Spanish dolls, two in Japanese costume and two china pixies on the mantelpiece. Above the picture rail someone had fitted shelving, which was crowded with more holiday souvenirs, mostly dolls, some still their cellophane packaging. On the coffee table was a mess of tabloid newspapers, *Hello* and *OK* magazines.

'You've lived here long?' asked Bea, making conversation. The ripe smell of fish and chips mingled with that of cigarette smoke and a cheap wine which had probably come from a cardboard box.

'It was my husband's aunt's house, which he

inherited, and we've been here ever since. Barring holidays abroad, of course. We did enjoy our holidays.' She sighed and looked fondly around at her souvenirs. 'He passed on some years back, but there's no point in getting down in the dumps about it, is there? Tea or coffee? Something stronger?' She waved them to seats. The leatherette groaned under Chris's weight, and he pulled a comical face.

'No, thanks. I don't want to put you to any trouble,' said Bea. 'You were working for the Trust then?'

'I was, and if I say so myself, I ran that office efficiently, even the major said he couldn't have done it better.'

'The major. I met him at lunch the other day.'

'Oh, he's all right,' said Della, lighting up, giving a little cough, and pushing newspapers around to find an ashtray. 'No harm in him.'

'Nor in Sir Cecil?'

The woman's complexion darkened, she gave a hoarse laugh, and shook her head. 'Randy old whatsit. Mind you, when I was missing my old man, I could always, you know, pass the time of day with him. If you see what I mean.'

In other words, Cecil had had her over his desk when they both felt like it.

'And Mr Trimmingham?'

A shrug. 'I never really got to know him. He joined us only a short while before I left.'

'You worked mostly for Denzil?'

Della stubbed out her half-smoked cigarette with a vicious twist. 'What's this all about? I

243

heard he'd popped his clogs. I slaved for that man all those years and went out on a limb to cover for him when he forgot things, and then he turned round and got me the sack, fitted me up, would you believe? I'd never have thought it of him, but there it was: not "thank you very much" but "thank you, and you're fired"!'

'Two-faced, was he? After all you'd done for him?'

The woman's lips tightened. Perhaps she thought she'd said too much already? 'Dunno about that.' She lit another cigarette. 'So what's all this about, then?'

'A strange phone call, which was supposed to bring Zander out here to see you on Tuesday night.'

'I'm always out on Tuesday nights, seeing my aunt that lives over in Greenford. I take her shopping to Tesco's and she pays for the taxi. So I wasn't here. I got back about nine, I suppose, didn't bother with the answerphone then, got the message next morning, thought someone got the wrong number.'

'I think someone wanted Zander out of the way that evening, wanted to make sure he'd come out here to see you. Someone who knew you were always out on Tuesdays. How long have you been going out on Tuesday nights?'

'For ever. A couple of years. No, more than that. Ever since my aunt had her hip replacement.'

'Everyone knew about it at work?'

'Of course they did because I always went off

244

early on Tuesdays, to make sure I could get her done and dusted by nine, which is when she goes to bed. So what gives with Zander? Nice lad, I thought. Quiet. Well spoken. He didn't have anything to do with the way I was forced out.'

'Forced out?'

'In a manner of speaking.' She stared off into space, then made up her mind to Tell All. 'Denzil's gone now, so what does it matter? Milly pushed him too hard, saying she might be pregnant. I told her, I said to take it gently. His sort takes fright, and we were doing all right as we were, weren't we, with him giving her nice presents, and popping the odd fifty in an envelope for me every now and then. But Milly wanted a ring on her finger, she wanted to be the Honourable Mrs though I told her his sort don't divorce their wives just for a bit on the side.'

'Do you know what he did? I can hardly believe it, even now. He fitted me up with some notes he took out of the petty-cash box, marked them up with his initials, and "found" them in my handbag. I tell you, you could have knocked me down and out, I wasn't able to do anything but stare. He got Cecil and the major in to show them the notes in my handbag, and I couldn't think of anything to say, not a word – though I thought of plenty afterwards, you can be sure of that!

'He put me and Milly in a cab and sent us home, and he rang me that night to say I'd better not ever talk about anything that had happened, or he'd have me prosecuted. But now he's dead, well ... It doesn't matter now, does it?'

She lit another cigarette from the stub of the one in her hand. A couple of rings flashed on her fingers. She had a gold chain around her neck which must have cost a bob or two, as well. And a good watch. The fifty-pound tips had come in handy.

She blew out smoke. 'I've got another job now, not so far away though not the high class the other one was. I don't want my new employers to know I was fired. I told them my boss had been making advances to me and had got me the sack when I said "no". They believed me, said I should sue, but I said I couldn't be bothered, that I was sorry for the old trout.'

'And Milly?'

A shrug. 'Got herself a job at the Three Feathers, barmaid, down the road. She moved in with me a couple of years ago when her mother got herself a new boyfriend and he – that is, the new boyfriend – started touching her up, Milly, that is. Which wasn't at all what she wanted, nor her mother, neither. And I could do with the company.

'That's her scooter outside. She leaves it here when she's at work because she's had it knocked over in the car park at the pub a couple of times. So I usually go along there for a quick one before they close, help her clear up – the landlord says he'll give me a job in the bar any time, which is a laugh, really, though I don't mind helping out now and then for the odd tenner –

and then I walk back with her. It's not far.'

She looked at her watch. 'Where's that woman with my parcel? I wanted to get to the pub earlier today because they've got a quiz on, and they get a good crowd in on quiz nights.'

She stood up, signalling they should leave. Bea wanted to ask more questions but Della was fidgeting, evidently anxious to see the back of them.

Once out in the evening air, Bea was abstracted, thinking over what they'd learned. Della's niece sounded exactly like young Kylie from the pub near Denzil's home. Chris began to whistle, strolling along with his hands in his pockets. Irritating boy!

They rounded the corner to see a couple of louts peering in through the windows of Bea's car. After the satnav, no doubt. They scattered when they saw Bea and Chris.

Bea said, 'My fault. I usually take the satnav out and hide it.'

'What?' said Chris, feeling in his pockets. 'I did give you the keys, didn't I?'

'No,' said Bea, suddenly anxious. 'You were tossing them around in your hand when we walked along to Della's.'

He delved into his pockets, talking the while. 'I put them in my right-hand jeans pocket, I know I did. That's where I always keep keys.' He produced a bunch of keys, but they were not Bea's. 'Those are mine for home.' He tried three other pockets, without success. It was a warm night, and he wasn't wearing a jacket.

Bea tried to contain impatience. If he'd lost her keys, how would they get home tonight? If they left the car where it was, wouldn't it be vandalized before dark, the satnav taken through smashed windows? And if she abandoned the car and took a taxi home, did she have enough cash on her to pay the driver, and how was she to get back into her house? She supposed she could phone Oliver to wait up for her – if he hadn't gone out for the evening, which he often did. Or Maggie.

'I remember now,' said Chris. 'I put them on the arm of the chair in which I was sitting at Della's. Remember how it squeaked when I sat down? Reminded me of a Whoopee cushion.'

Bea gritted her teeth. 'Run back and see if she's still at the house and not gone out to the pub yet. I'll stay with the car.' She wasn't running anywhere.

'Cool,' he said, and to give him his due, he did break into a run, disappeared round the corner.

And then returned. 'What number house was it?'

Bea contained annoyance with an effort and told him. 'One forty-two.' He disappeared again. Bea leaned against the car, angry with herself rather than with him. What had she been thinking of to entrust her keys to him? He had all the charm in the world and no common sense. No wonder Oliver wouldn't sit in a car with him.

Two hooded youths passed by on the other side of the road, and she felt herself to be under scrutiny. Ah, a woman of uncertain age, all alone, and stranded in darkest suburbia. If she took out her mobile phone to summon help, they'd want to take it off her, leap on her in a trice. They'd probably want her handbag, too.

If only she had a second key to her car, but it was ... where? In her mind's eye, she could see it hanging up on a hook in the end cupboard in the kitchen.

She was a walking invitation to muggers. Satnav, plus mobile phone, plus credit cards. This was a quiet road. It was too late for young children to be out, the breadwinners were all home from their offices, television programmes were well into their soaps. Should she go and knock on the nearest front door and ask for sanctuary?

She told herself it was ridiculous; she was panicking for nothing.

Dear Lord, I'd be grateful for some advice here. And protection. Those boys ... No, I must not prejudge all young people who wear hoods. They are not all criminals. I'm sure they're not. Only, I must admit to feeling afraid. Could you send a white knight on a charger to rescue me, please?

She looked at her watch. Chris was taking his time, wasn't he?

He came galloping round the corner and came to a halt beside her, breathing hard. 'Whew. Out of ... condition. She's out. I rang and rang. The hall light's on, and I thought I heard someone moving inside, but no. Probably a cat. She's left

249

the light on in the hall as a security measure while she's out. Shall I go down to the pub – if I can find it – and ask for her?'

Bea hadn't noticed any sign of a cat in Della's house, but what did she know about it?

The two young hoodies passed by on the opposite side of the road again.

Chris saw them, too. His fists clenched. 'I don't think we should stay here, do you? If I hadn't let the battery on my mobile run down, I'd call Dad to help us out. What do you think?'

With an ear-shattering roar, a sleek, powerful motorbike turned the corner and ran up the drive of a house opposite, before cutting off its engine. Two helmeted, leather-clad figures descended into the silence. The hoodies stopped in mid-slouch.

Bea knew a white knight on a charger when she saw one. Crossing the road, she said, 'Could you help me, please? We're stranded and...' She looked at the hoodies and then back at the black-clad figures. Her heart was beating so hard she could almost feel it, but she'd prayed and these people had arrived prompt on cue, so let's have a little trust in God, right?

The black-clad bikers took off their helmets to reveal one middle-aged, coffee-coloured man with a spreading girth and kindly eyes, and a blonde, teenage girl. Fake blonde, but pretty with it.

'Oy, you! Young Darren! Jojo!' The biker shouted at the hoodies, who hesitated but came forward. 'Been worrying this lady?'

'No, never. Not us. You know us.'

'So I do.' He turned back to Bea. 'They're harmless, most of the time. But need an eye kept on them. Run out of petrol, have you?'

Bea explained that they'd called on someone in the next road, had left the car keys there by mistake, that the lady had probably gone down to the pub where her niece worked of an evening, but they didn't know exactly where the Three Feathers might be.

'Is that all?' He resumed his helmet. 'Here, take my daughter's helmet and hop on the back.' To his daughter, 'You look after this lady's son, right. Oh, and Darren – and you, Jojo. You keep an eye on the lady's car, right?'

Bea gulped. She was wearing lightweight trousers rather than a tight skirt, true. But her pretty sandals were not the most suitable for riding a bike. Well, what must be, must be. She'd never been on a motorbike in her life before. Should she send Chris, who would relish the opportunity? But no, the nice biker had offered her a ride, and she would do it if it killed her ... which she sincerely hoped it wouldn't.

Chris was already eyeing up the teenaged blonde. What was it with men and teenaged blondes? First Denzil and now Chris!

The biker was already back on his steed, giving it a kick start. Bea put the helmet on, slung her handbag over her back and managed to get her leg over the pillion of the bike without hurting herself. She seemed to remember that passengers held tight to something behind them.

251

Yes, there it was. And the other hand went on the belt round his body? Yes, that felt right.

Goodness me! Her head nearly snapped off as the bike was turned and roared off. The biker yelled something at her, and hoping she'd interpreted correctly, she yelled back, 'The Feathers'. He seemed to know where the pub was. It was probably the only one for miles.

It wasn't that far off. They passed Della's house in a whirr and a whizz, turned sharply left, and then right, and finally panted to a stop outside a hostelry which looked as if it had grown out of the earth, it was so low and ancient. The car park was packed, and yes, there was a sign outside advertising a Quiz Nite. 'Nite' as in 'nit' with an 'e'. Oh, well. Why not, if it made people stop and stare?

The biker kept his machine growling away. Bea got off, with some difficulty, and said, 'That was wonderful.' And meant it.

The biker removed one of his huge gauntlets and tipped up his helmet while killing his engine. 'Busy in there, quiz nights. I'll come in with you, make sure you don't get stranded. What does this woman look like?'

'Della's a fifytish brunette with a fine bust. Mid-brown hair, good-looking in a way. Her niece serves behind the bar, and she's a young blonde. I think she's called Milly.'

He nodded. 'I think I know who you mean. Della smokes like a chimney, always complaining because she can't smoke inside the pub any more. Milly's newish, that right?'

'That's right. You're very kind.'

'George.'

'Bea.'

He led the way into the public bar – there was a 'snug' which had once been a separate domain, but the whole ground floor was now a series of interconnecting rooms. Pillars here and there upheld the ceiling, and the floor was now of tile and now of wood – what you could see of it. The place was, indeed, crowded. And noisy.

George bent over to shout in Bea's ear. 'Can you see her?'

Bea scanned the crowd. Shook her head.

George pushed his way through the crowd along the back wall till they got to the end by the toilets. The noise was unbearable. The quiz-master was in full swing, using a mike and getting the laughs.

No Della. Perhaps she was in the loo? Bea signalled she was going to check, and he nodded. There were a couple of people in the toilets. Bea waited till both were out. No Della.

She went back to George, who was standing with his arms folded, looking dour. He approached his mouth to her ear. 'No luck?'

She shouted back. 'She *said* she was coming. Was looking forward to it. She might be helping out behind the bar?'

'Hang on to me, and I'll push.'

Push he did, and they eventually ended up at the bar, with a dozen men and women all holding out their hands to pay or give orders. No blondie. No Della. They shook their heads at one another. George signalled he was going to work round to another section of the bar, and Bea followed, grimly holding on to his belt.

In the next section, the press of people eased up. And an unmistakeable Milly was serving behind the bar. No Della, but they could easily have missed her in the crowd.

George pushed Bea under arms and around shoulders till she was at the bar, with him jammed up against her back. Milly was a tousle-headed poppet, almost naturally blonde, with a plunging neckline and a pert manner.

'Milly!' yelled George. The girl laughed and said, 'You wait your turn, you!'

She was quick and deft and able to attend to them quickly enough. 'Milly,' said George, 'I'll have a pint in a minute, but first, this lady left her keys in your aunt's house by mistake. Do you know where she is?'

'Haven't seen her tonight,' said Milly, rapidly polishing glasses. 'She said she was coming in, never misses a quiz night. Truth to tell, I was beginning to wonder where she was. She always rings me if she can't make it, and the landlord's expecting her to help out at closing time, as usual.' She switched her eyes to a rough lad at George's side. 'Yes, sir? What can I get you ... apart from what you're looking at?'

The lad laughed, and so did one or two others. Bea and George withdrew to the back wall.

'I don't like it,' said Bea. 'I wonder if something's happened, if she's fallen and hurt herself or something. She was expecting a neighbour

254

who'd taken in a parcel for her, but she was quite definite that she was coming on here afterwards. Chris – that's the boy who drove me over – he went and rang her bell but no one came to the door.'

'Back on the bike, luv. Let's investigate.'

Dead sober, unlike everyone else in the pub, they got back on the bike and went tearing back through the quiet streets to Della's house. The daylight was fading, and the occasional street lamps were beginning to glow. As Chris had said, there was a light on in the hall at Della's, but all the other rooms were dark and no curtains had been drawn. George pressed the bell. They could hear it ringing inside, but no one came to the door.

Bea pressed her face to the bay window, but though she could see the furniture clearly enough, there was no Della. Wait a minute, was that another light at the back?

She jerked back her head. 'George, I'm a bit worried. The door into the hall from the sitting room is not quite shut, and I think I can see a sort of flickering glow through it.'

He pushed open the letter box and yelled, 'Della, are you there?' And swore. 'You're right.'

'Fire?' said Bea, feeling around in her handbag for her mobile.

George already had his out and was summoning the fire brigade.

'Should we break in?' asked Bea.

He chewed his lower lip. 'If we do, the fire

255

will go whoosh through the house. Ditto if we break a window.'

'But if she's lying there unconscious...'

'I know.' He took a step back, eyed up the windows of the bay. 'I could break just one pane and open up, but ... No, I can't. She's got locks on all the windows.' He stamped around, cursing.

'We should alert the neighbours,' suggested Bea, stepping through a spindly hedge to reach next door's bell.

'Fire, dammit. I hate fires.'

'Ditto.' Bea hung on next door's bell, and eventually a tired looking young woman came to the door while a man's voice told her to send whoever it was selling things away.

The woman said, 'We don't buy at the door.'

'Neither do I,' said Bea. 'Just to let you know your next-door neighbour's house is on fire, and we think she's still in there.'

'What's that to do with the price of bread?' But she relayed the information to the man inside, and he came out to join them. George said the fire brigade was on its way, and they couldn't do anything till it came.

The fire brigade arrived and took over. The front door was broken in, and the fire did indeed go whoosh, but was sharply contained by the men.

The chief fireman reported, 'Not much of a fire. Luckily all the upstairs doors were shut and there were no windows open, so it hardly got going. We found her in the kitchen. A heavy smoker, what? They can be so careless. Sorry, luv, is she some relation?'

Bea asked, 'Is she all right?' Silly question, of course she wasn't.

'Fell and hit her head, looks like. The ambulance is on its way.'

The police dead-heated with the ambulance.

George informed the police that Della's niece, who shared the house with her aunt, was working at the Three Feathers pub and ought to be informed of what had happened.

They nodded. A police car peeled off to collect the girl. Meanwhile, neighbours twitched curtains or came out to stare, arms folded across chests in the evening air. Dog walkers appeared, as if by osmosis, and met to gossip by the lamp posts. Eventually Milly arrived in the police car, only to see her aunt being carried off on a stretcher. Still alive, but only just.

Milly, crying, wanted to go with her aunt, but the police and fire brigade detained her with questions. 'Your aunt was a heavy smoker? Did she have any heart trouble, or could she have tripped over something...?'

Milly seemed genuinely upset about her aunt. She said she couldn't think straight, didn't know anything except that she had to go with Della to the hospital. Bea pulled out one of her business cards and wrote on the back.

'Milly, you don't know me, but we came to see your aunt earlier. Can you find somewhere else to stay tonight?'

'What? What do you mean? Oh, because the

back of the house...? Oh, poor aunt! She does love her house. The police said they'll secure the back door, and there's not much damage except to the kitchen. Oh, and I suppose the smoke and the water ... Oh, whatever will I do?'

'Can you stay at the pub?'

'I suppose so. Yes, I promised to ring them, let them know what's happened. I had to leave them with all the clearing up to do, you see.'

The police and the firemen said she should go in the ambulance. There'd be more questions on the morrow though it looked open and shut: heavy smoker loses her balance, starts a fire as she falls and hits her head. Finally Milly got into the ambulance and it drove off.

'And if you believe that,' muttered Bea to herself, 'you'll believe anything.'

Bea and George gave their names and addresses to the police and retired to George's house, where they found Chris flirting with the teen-aged daughter and were regaled with cups of tea.

Wearily, Bea got out her mobile phone to contact Oliver.

Thursday evening

Honoria hummed to herself as she drove back home. Another good job well done.

She'd noticed the back alleyway as she drove up to Della's house. Taken the bag containing the overalls and hammer down the alley, changed there behind ragged high hedges and

258

fences which concealed her from view. Counted houses along till she got to Della's, forced open the back gate – a rickety affair – trod up the garden path, tried the kitchen door and found it unlocked.

The woman had been lighting a cigarette in the kitchen – filthy habit – and turned to see the hammer descending.

There'd been a lot of blood. Unfortunately more had got on her shoes. Well, there was nothing for it. They'd have to be disposed of now. In the river, perhaps? Burned? A pity that the young one hadn't been there as well, but one down and one to go, as you might say. Oh, and she must get round to Kylie as well some day.

But not just yet. Get the funeral over first.

FOURTEEN

Late Thursday night

Bea rang home to ask Oliver for help. There was no reply to her landline. She tried his mobile with more success and gave him the bad news. 'You'll have to bring my other keys out by taxi. Take some money from petty cash to pay for it, and leave an IOU. I'll settle up with you in the morning.'

He said, 'Hold on a mo,' while he consulted someone in the room with him. He was at CJ's house. Of course. After a couple of minutes he got back to her. 'Mr Cambridge is going to ferry me out to you, but we'll have to make a detour back home first, to get your other keys. What's the address?'

She gave it to him and glanced at her watch. It was getting late, and she was flagging. How long would it take for them to get her other keys and drive out here?

George the biker had been marvellous up to that point, but now Bea found keeping the conversation going was a strain. To her mixed horror and amusement, he inched along the sofa on which they were sitting to press his thigh against hers. His wife didn't seem to notice. Chris was occupied in teasing the blonde daughter, and altogether Bea felt it was way past her bedtime.

Eventually CJ and Oliver arrived. Bea was so tired by that time that she could have fallen on their shoulders and wept. But she didn't, of course. She thanked George and his wife, promised to keep in touch to let them know what transpired, and left them her card.

During their farewells, Bea noticed Oliver shooting dark glances at her and Chris. What was going on there? He seemed to be angry with both of them. Could Oliver be jealous of Chris? How absurd!

Oliver said he would retrieve Bea's car and drive her home in it, but Chris invoked his seniority – he was one month older than Oliver – and insisted that Bea go with his father. Bea thought this was probably to avoid a rollicking from CJ but was too weary to care.

George insisted on seeing them down to their cars. Although the two young hoodies were nowhere to be seen, rather to her surprise Bea found her car still intact. CJ had parked his a little way back. As they reached CJ's car, George enveloped Bea in a hug and gave her a smacking great kiss. 'Soon as I laid eyes on you,' said George, 'I thought to myself, there's a girl I'd like to buy a pint for.'

'Er, thank you,' said Bea, shaken. 'You really have been marvellous. I don't know what I'd have done without you. And my love to your wife.' She got into CJ's car, not knowing whether to laugh or cry. He drove off, smooth as silk. Looking as grim as young Oliver.

She sniffed, found her handkerchief, blew her nose. 'I gather there's more bad news?'

'You first.'

'Well...' Should she skate over Chris losing her bunch of keys? No, he'd have to know because they were still in Della's house somewhere. 'Well, we had a chat with Della, who certainly did not make the phone call enticing Zander out here on the night of the murder. I think, if she'd been a blonde, she might have flirted with Denzil. But no, of course not. He only went for very young blondes, didn't he? Anyway...' She talked herself out, finishing up with, 'but there can't be any connection with Mrs Perrot's murder, can there?'

He didn't bother to say she was being stupid, but one raised eyebrow did the trick.

She sighed. 'All right. It's pretty obvious that there is a connection, though it's probably a different police authority out here from the Kensington one, and unless we drop them a hint, they'll treat the two murders as separate cases. Look, we can't keep on pretending we don't know what's behind all this, because bodies are beginning to build up in the morgue, and if I'm right, then young Milly's next in line. I know we have no proof and that this is all circumstantial, but do we hang on till every single blonde chick that Denzil's cast eyes on wakes up dead one morning? I don't think Tommy's embargo on going public can hold.'

'Tommy's very ill.'

Her voice rose, despite her best effort at keeping it down. 'I know. And the Trust was started by one of his ancestors and we should all respect that, shouldn't we? Even if the institution is now totally out of date and its directors are corrupt? Ancestors are pretty useless allies when we come up against modern murderers, aren't they?' She grimaced. 'Sorry. Overtired. But what else can we do now but tell the truth?'

'Sandy Corcoran's body was found this morning when the cleaners went into his office. A shotgun had been fired at the back of his head.'

It was all too much for Bea. She shifted her seat belt into a more comfortable position, leaned back and closed her eyes. 'That does it. Count me out for the rest of the night. Let me know when we get home, will you?'

Friday morning

Bea forced herself to get out of bed and tottered over to the window to draw back the curtains. And blenched. Too much sun, too bright, too early.

It was half an hour after her usual time to get up, and she didn't care if she was late. There were days when it was allowable to sleep on for a while.

She decided that the greenish tint under her eyes needed attention. And wasn't it time for a visit to the beauty salon? Her hair looked life-

263

less. She discovered a grease spot on the front of the blouse she'd put on and had to discard it. Her tights laddered.

If it's going to be one of those days, Lord, would you kindly take extra care of me? The way I feel now, I'm liable to walk into doors and trip over paving stones. As for solving murders and soothing ruffled feelings ... is Oliver really jealous of Chris's charm? Oh dear. Please, Lord; give me the right words to say.

She made it downstairs, holding on to the banister and telling herself that today surely couldn't hold anything worse than yesterday.

The house was unnaturally quiet. No TV, no radio on. No clashing of pans in the kitchen. When Maggie was in the kitchen, she surrounded herself by noise, so she must have gone out already. Bea checked the time by her watch and found a gap on her wrist. She'd forgotten to put it on. The day had indeed started badly.

As she turned into the kitchen her ears caught murmured conversation and the susurrus of frying, which her nose informed her meant spicy sausages and bacon.

Oliver was sitting at the table, spooning cereal into his mouth with an air of great concentration. Opposite him lounged Chris, peeling an orange while chatting to Maggie, who was being polite. What was Chris doing here?

And Zander!

Wearing one of Maggie's aprons, Zander was distributing sausages, bacon and fried bread from a frying pan. Zander here? Zander doing

264

the cooking? And Maggie letting him do it? Wonders would never cease.

Bea slid on to a kitchen stool, reaching for the orange juice.

'Morning,' said Oliver, keeping his eyes on his plate.

'Good morning!' Chris, ultra-cheerful.

'How are you?' asked Maggie, without a smile.

Bea said 'Bewildered.'

Zander hovered. 'A soft boiled egg? Or perhaps poached? The cupboard was bare so I went out for supplies. Hope you don't mind.'

Bea braced herself. 'The lot, please, Zander. And may I say how delighted I am to see you?'

He replaced the pan on the stove and picked up one of her hands to kiss it. 'I am deep in your debt, Mrs Abbot. I shall never forget what you've done for me.'

Maggie looked at her watch. She was still not smiling, and she had dressed all in black today. So unlike her. 'I'm out early today, connecting with the electrician who swore he'd make it yesterday but didn't. In case you're wondering, Mrs Abbot, Zander was released last night. He spent the night here, but he has been told he can collect his things from his landlady's today. Under supervision, of course.'

Zander said, 'One of the churchwardens has offered me a room, and I'm moving in there this afternoon. One sausage or two, Mrs Abbot?'

'Two,' said Bea. This kissing business must be catching. First George the biker last night and

265

now Zander. While the only person she really wanted to be kissed by was long dead and gone. Oh, Hamilton; how I miss you!

Oliver was avoiding her eye. Chris was trying to catch hers.

She considered Chris's far-too-cheerful face. 'Have you spent the night here, too, Chris?'

'No, no. Oliver dropped me off at home last night, but Dad was in such a bad mood that I thought it best to make myself scarce this morning. Besides, I'm dying to know what happens next.'

Bea stifled a yawn. Milly was next on the list, she thought, but she decided not to say so. The less Chris was around her at the moment, the better. 'Back to work for us. I'm afraid you'll find us rather dull, today.'

Did Oliver shoot her a grateful look? What was going on there?

Zander served her up a plateful of cholesterol-inducing sausage, bacon, fried bread, mushrooms, tomatoes and eggs. Absolutely fabulous! She ate with concentration while everyone else stayed respectfully silent.

Putting her knife and fork together on her empty plate, she said, 'Mmm. Now, tell me, Zander; what happened?'

He switched on their new coffee machine which made a wonderfully strong cuppa if you could get it to work. Even Maggie hadn't always been able to operate it. Needless to say, it performed perfectly for Zander. 'They went on and on at me for a while, then left me to "consider my position". I wasn't worried because I knew you were on the case. Prayed a bit. You know. Counted up to a thousand and started again. Then about half past seven they opened the door and said I could go. Just like that.

'I made a fuss until they explained. Apparently they'd found a neighbour who'd seen someone – a stranger – going into the house about eight thirty. A white person wearing some kind of overalls, the type you use for decorating. Also, the forensic people had found footprints in blood traipsing up the stairs, and those footprints were no match to my shoes. Smaller, in fact. This proved someone else had been in the house after she was killed and that that someone was not me.

'They'd also found traces of blood on those things of Mrs Perrot's that had been hidden in my belongings. They'd already checked my hands and my shoes and taken my fingerprints and DNA and goodness knows what else, so they knew I'd no blood on me. Conclusion: I hadn't done it, and they'd have to let me go. They didn't like it, of course. It would have been so much more convenient if they could have proved it was me, but they couldn't.'

'Did you tell them whose computer it was you'd been working on?'

He shook his head. 'I was going to if they went on at me much longer. I asked God what I should do, and He said not to bother as He'd got it all in hand ... which wasn't much help because He might have wanted me to stick it out. I really

267

wasn't sure. Anyway, it turned out that He was right. So, no. I didn't say anything. Mind you, I'm not sure that the police ought to be kept in the dark.'

'Me, neither,' sighed Bea, taking a slice of toast and spreading butter and marmalade on it. 'You and Oliver promised to keep mum, but I've warned CJ that enough is enough. I'll have another word with him about it today.'

Zander poured out cups of mega-strength coffee and handed them around. 'I'll shove the stuff in the dishwasher and get out of your hair. Shall I strip the bed?'

Maggie still didn't look at him. 'Zander, you'll leave us your new address? And what about a job? You know the Trust doesn't want you back.'

'I could fight them,' said Zander, sweeping dirty dishes into the dishwasher with economical, graceful movements. 'But I don't think I'd ever be comfortable working for them again.'

Bea murmured, '"Leaving the world to darkness and to Thee." That's a quote from Thomas Gray, I think. I agree that it's the easiest course of action for you to take, Zander, but is it the right one? If all the good people abandon the Trust, what will happen to it? Isn't it worth fighting for?'

Zander grinned, 'Now, now; Mrs Abbot. You had me go back there once, and look what happened. Do I really need to be arrested three days in a row?'

'You heard Sandy Corcoran's been found

268

dead?'

No, they hadn't known. None of them. Big eyes all round.

'How "dead"?' asked Oliver, frowning.

'Shotgun to the back of the head.'

'No fire?' asked Chris. Everyone looked at him, and he raised both hands in apology. 'Just asking.'

'I don't know,' said Bea, 'and I'm not sure it's any of our business now. Let CJ sort it out.'

They were restless, not wanting to accept that it was over but unwilling to question her further. Maggie stood up, pushed her stool under the table. 'Suppose Zander takes over my job here in reception? I'm out most days, anyway. Plus, he can cook.' Now that was a generous offer for Maggie to make, in view of all that passed between them.

Zander, laughing, shook his head.

Bea also shook her head. 'Maggie, that was a really nice thought, but...' She didn't know how to put it, but Zander could earn more than a receptionist, however good.

Zander said, 'Maggie, you're the best. But I hate working where I can't see the sky out of the window. I know, I'm odd that way. That's why I like...' He swallowed. 'I *liked* working at the Trust. And before, when I worked just off the High Street, my desk was right by the window. I'll have to put an ad in the paper, "Anything considered above street level".'

He was making a joke of it, but he was serious, none the less. Or perhaps not. One never knew

269

with Zander. He wasn't always transparent.

Maggie shrugged, still not meeting anyone's eye. 'Well, if that's what you want ... I'm off out for the day.' She withdrew in good order.

Chris leaned across the table to pour Bea out some more coffee. 'Now what can you find for me to do today? Anything considered. Vacuuming, for instance. I like to sit and watch a robot vacuum cleaner at work. Shall I polish all the shoes in the household? I'm not terribly good at it, but anything to stop me having to go back home for a lecture.'

Bea laughed, as he'd intended she should. 'Let me see. How about watering the pots in the garden at the back here? Maggie usually does it, but she's been somewhat distracted of late.' And don't mention Milly, or he'll be haring out to the pub to question her, and goodness knows how the police would view his interference.

Chris beamed and went to wrestle with the back-door keys. Zander had to help him get out. Oliver had his stone face on, so Bea beckoned him to follow her into the sitting room.

'Oliver, my dear boy. What is it?'

'Nothing. Absolutely nothing. Is there anything special you'd like me to do today? Groom Winston? Cook a roast dinner?'

Ah. So he *was* jealous of Chris, whose easy charm beguiled everyone, right up to the point when they realized he was a lightweight. Oliver, on the other hand, was no lightweight. He was dependable, resourceful and had his own brand of charm which was not like Chris's at all. She

270

could see that he might envy his friend, who must seem to have everything that he'd lost: a caring parent, a moneyed background, a university place.

Oliver was so uptight he twanged. How to reassure him?

Bea sat down and patted the seat beside her. 'I've been meaning to talk to you about Chris. I know you two are great friends, and I can see that you'd like me to keep him around, maybe even give him a job, but really Oliver ... I don't quite know how to put this ... He's so charming that one has to laugh, but he's not exactly, well, reliable, is he?'

Oliver didn't meet her eyes, but he did relax one notch. 'I suppose not.'

'You ought to have warned me about his driving. Oh, Oliver, I'm not sure how we got there without an accident!' She laughed, so that he could laugh with her.

He twitched a smile, but no more.

She said, 'I had to tell his father that we got stranded because Chris lost my keys at Della's, and I suppose if the police need to interview us about it, then I'll have to tell them, too. But his losing my keys made things very difficult for me. Not,' she put her hand over his, 'that I blame you for his carelessness, but perhaps in future if he offers to do something for me, well, I don't want to hurt his feelings but you might just drop me a word of advice, shake your head at me when he's not looking, or something? Then I'd know not to trust him to do – whatever it is.'

271

He twitched another smile. 'Do you think he'll know how to turn the hosepipe on without soaking himself?'

'Probably not, but I didn't think it would matter.'

He heaved a great sigh. 'He's one of my oldest friends, my best friend really. He's terribly clever. All that fun stuff, it's all on top. And yes, he does play the cack-handed idiot on occasion and to a certain extent it's true. He is careless. But he can master anything he puts his mind to, speaks French and German like a native, always been brilliant that way. And he can add up a column of figures faster than I can think.'

'So what is he going to make of his life? Is he going to be any good at making films?'

'He might be. He's produced some intriguing footage, but from one moment to the next he loses interest.'

'Is he going to last the course at university? It didn't sound like it to me. And by the way, he was on at me, practically accusing me of preventing you from going to university.'

He reddened, shuffled his feet. 'He knows I won't leave you in the lurch.'

So Oliver did want to go, after all? It was right and proper that he should, of course, even if the prospect was so dismaying it almost made her cry. She'd manage, somehow. Her heart thudded, but she told it to behave. Perhaps if she did break down and cry, he'd promise not to leave her? But no, she mustn't do that. However painful it might be, she must let him go.

272

'You wouldn't be leaving me in the lurch, Oliver. This gap year of yours has been wonderful from my point of view. I don't know how we'd have managed without you, but now you've got us straight again, we'll be just fine. Miss Brook is a marvel, Maggie's spreading her wings as a project manager, and yes, we'll be looking around for another full-time person to join us, of course. And I expect I shall ask you to help us out in the holidays.'

'Really?' She could see him getting all excited. Oh dear, he really did want to go.

She produced a smile, somehow. 'Of course. Now, how do we go about getting you there? Have you got a place this autumn?'

More shuffling of feet. 'Yes, I ... Mr Cambridge made sure they realized that I'd missed taking up my place last year for a good reason, and yes, they have said I could start this autumn but ... I'm still not sure. He wants me to join the police, go to Hendon, be a specialist in computers like him. The money would be good.'

How dare CJ! The interfering so-and-so. Well, two can play at that game. 'Whatever you choose is all right by me. The police?' A shrug. 'But ... just a thought. You could always join the police later on. Why narrow your options now? Get a degree behind you, and you can do anything, go anywhere. As for money, if you're going to take my name, I can see you through university.'

This time he met her eyes. 'I'd like that. Mr Cambridge offered to sponsor me, too, but

273

there's Chris to consider. I worry about him.'

He kept his eyes on her, wanting her to offer ... what? She frowned. 'What is it you want me to do? Be a mother to Chris?'

He flushed. 'I don't know. He always denies it, but he has missed out, not having had a mother around. His father's always been a bit, well, distant.'

'You think Chris needs someone to scold him when he's careless, make sure he changes his underwear and ask if he's got a handkerchief and keys before he goes out?' She started to laugh, but Oliver didn't.

'Yes, I think that's about it. If I go to uni, will you look after him for me?'

She lifted both hands in helpless fashion. 'You'll be the death of me, Oliver. I can't possibly promise that. Anyway, he'll be off to university again himself in the autumn, won't he?'

'I suppose.' Meaning Oliver wasn't at all sure that Chris would.

A ring at the front door, a murmur in the hall, and Zander poked his head around the door. 'Someone for you, Mrs Abbot. I've stripped the bed and put the sheets in the washing machine, so I'll be off now. Right?'

Max, Bea's self-important Member of Parliament son, pushed past Zander into the room. 'What's he doing here? And who is he, anyway? He hasn't actually been sleeping here, has he? Oh, Mother! What have you got yourself into now?' Max was in a state, tie at half mast,

274

perspiration on his forehead.

What did they say ... Horses sweat, men perspire. Max was sweating. Oh dear; now what? Politics, Lettice or Nicole?

Oliver murmured, 'Excuse me,' and slid out of the room, then came back in to say, 'Oh, forgot to tell you. I got another couple of pictures deciphered. The first said, "Times, two two one." The second is a copy of a letter to a solicitor, asking him to hold the deeds of the Manor, which are in his name. He actually owned the Manor, not her. As for "Times, two two one", I'll see if I can track the reference down now, if you don't want me for anything else.'

Bea brought her mind back from Max, focused on Oliver, wondered what the multiplication table had got to do with the price of bread, nodded permission, and made herself smile at Max. 'Lovely to see you, Max. Coffee?'

'No, no. I've no time for coffee. So, who was that strange man?'

She considered telling him that Zander had just been released from prison and had nowhere to stay, but decided against it. In her sweetest tone, she said, 'A friend of Maggie's needed a bed for the night. He's moving on today. What's worrying you, then? Some political crisis?'

'Nothing to concern you although, well, it will all be in the papers soon and it's a great compliment to me, but ... No, it isn't that. Mother, you've got to help me! Lettice—'

'Ah, it's Lettice, is it? In a strop because her sister's being painted by Piers?'

275

He took out a handkerchief and dried his forehead. 'That's it. Wants me to arrange for Piers to paint her as well, but he refuses. You've got to help me, mother. If she doesn't get what she wants I'll never hear the end of it.'

'It's not a good idea to bed two sisters at one and the same time.'

'I didn't!' His protest was overdone. More perspiration. He went to the French windows at the back and threw them wide open. 'It's so hot in here. Why don't you get a ceiling fan? Which reminds me that Piers says he can't use his studio to paint Nicole because it's too hot in this heatwave, and the light in our flat's no good, so he'll have to do it here. I said you'd be glad to help.'

'You might have asked me first.'

'Well, yes. But I know you like Nicole and at least you'll be some protection for her from ... Well, you know what I mean.'

'You mean you want me to fend off Lettice for you? Oh, Max. I thought you'd got rid of her ages ago.'

'I did. Of course I did. But she's not so easy to discourage, and what with Nicole being sick all the time, well ... And there didn't seem any harm in letting her tag on for official functions, after all, it's all in the family. And it was difficult to say no. Besides, she's got a really good brain, Lettice. And a flair for politics.'

'Then let her stand for parliament herself.'

'She would have, if only it didn't take so long to get in, especially for a woman.'

'I thought your party was keen to promote women.'

'Some of them seem to think she's a bit, well, threatening.'

Bea could understand that. Lettice was a bright-eyed blonde with a titanium core. Flirtatious and glamorous. And the darling of her wealthy parents. Yes, she'd frighten men off. She certainly frightened Max, even as she tempted him into sleeping with her. He was a rabbit to her snake, no contest.

She decided to put the boot in. 'If the tabloids were to get to hear you were sleeping with her while your wife's pregnant...'

'Mother! Don't even think it! Besides, I didn't. Haven't. Honestly.' More perspiration. 'But she says that if I do this one thing for her, she'll leave me alone. And Piers refuses. Mother, you've got to make him change his mind.'

'What makes you think I can do that? Or that I should? Grow up, Max, and tell Lettice to do the same. It's about time she found someone else to sink her claws into because from now on you're going to be the ideal husband and father, aren't you?'

'Of course, of course. You know I'm devoted to Nicole.'

'Well, then. I'll speak to Piers – oh, not about Lettice – but about the possibility of his painting Nicole here. I'm not sure it's a good idea for all sorts of reasons, not least because we're extremely busy at the agency at the moment. Which reminds me I ought to be at work downstairs by now.'

The front doorbell pealed, long and hard. Not an ordinary visitor's tentative ring. An official-sounding peal, one intending to be answered. Bea shot to her feet. She knew the peal of doom when she heard it, and this was undoubtedly it. CJ? The police? Or both?

Friday morning

Honoria hummed as she set the washing machine going. The hammer lay in a bowl of warm water, liberally treated with Dettol. Her shoes – a pity, but sacrifices had to be made – were on a bonfire in the kitchen garden. The gloves she'd disposed of in a litter bin on the way home. Nothing remained to link her with the murder.

Goodbye dear Della, inefficient office manageress and leech. No more fifty-pound notes will be coming your way, dear.

It was amusing to speculate how much damage the fire would have done to Della's place. Such a heavy smoker deserved to die by fire. To be accurate, to die by fire after she'd been hammered to death.

Zander was safely locked up in prison, and the charity was hers to do what she liked with.

She'd never realized how exciting life could be till she started taking out those who wronged her. How dull things were going to be when she'd finally come to the end of her list! Not yet, though. She was enjoying herself too much to stop now.

278

FIFTEEN

Friday morning

Bea went to the door to let in not one but three people; CJ came first, looking even frailer than before. Behind him toiled along two policemen in plain clothes, holding up their IDs and giving her their names – neither of which registered with her. Now what was Max going to say to this visitation?

'Do come in,' she said, ushering her visitors inside. Max was still standing by the hearth, legs apart, waiting to continue their discussion. Well, tough. 'Sorry, Max. Business. You had a meeting to go to, I believe?'

'What, what? Oh –' a quick glance at his watch – 'I suppose so. Ring you later. Don't forget to speak to Piers about ... you know what, will you?'

'Of course not, dear.' She saw him out, mentally shook herself to attention, gave a passing thought to wondering what Chris was up to – surely not still watering the garden? – and returned to the sitting room.

'DI Warner.' Thickset, fiftyish, rubicund complexion, small bright eyes. A man who smiled without meaning it. A smooth front; a man of authority. Not to be trifled with. He glanced at CJ, who as usual was effacing himself. 'May we have a word in private?'

'Is it about the attack on Mrs Lawrence last night?'

They nodded.

'In that case, you will probably want to hear what Mr Cambridge has to say as well,' said Bea.

Both policemen transferred their eyes to CJ, who was looking out of the window, probably thinking about Tommy and the Trust. Probably not wondering if the sun was going to be with them all day.

'Mr Cambridge?' said the DI. 'Ah. Saves us a journey.' Again came that flicker of a smile.

Bea realized they thought that CJ was Chris, who they would indeed need to speak to about the previous evening's entertainment. 'Well, actually,' she began, and then shook her head. 'Coffee first, explanations later. Or tea? If we've got enough milk, that is.' Any excuse to get away and think what she ought and ought not to be saying. First and foremost, how to convince them that Milly needed protection?

'No, thank you,' said the DI, and he took a seat, unasked. As did his sidekick.

Bea hesitated, and then did likewise. She said, 'How is Mrs Lawrence? I ought to have rung the hospital to find out this morning, but—'

'I'm afraid she didn't make it.'

Silence. And in the silence, Bea heard the faint

280

swish of water from the hosepipe in the garden outside.

'That's bad,' said Bea, glancing over at CJ, who kept his station by the window, divorcing himself from their conversation. *One down and one to go. CJ, this can't go on.*

'Now, could you tell me how you came to be calling on Mrs Lawrence so late last night?'

'Late? It wasn't late. We got there about seven forty-five, I suppose. Give or take a few minutes.'

The DI had a notebook out. 'It says here that you were with a Mr George Bundell when he reported the fire at coming up to half past nine.'

Bea crossed one knee over the other, leaned back in her chair. She looked at CJ's back, which continued to be uninformative.

'Mrs Abbot?' The DI was going to insist on answers, and of course he was right to do so. This was no burglary that had gone wrong. This was murder.

Bea sighed. 'I'm sorry, CJ, but they've got to know what's been going on.'

He shook his head, and said in a voice that didn't rise above a murmur, 'Tommy's dying.'

'I dare say,' said Bea, 'but Mrs Lawrence is dead and so is Mrs Perrot, Zander and Oliver have spent time in police cells, and this has gone way beyond a joke. And what about Milly? Now you may have promised Tommy to keep quiet whatever happens, but I haven't.'

'Discretion,' he said, still in that thread of a voice. 'For the benefit of all concerned.'

'Murder!' said Bea. 'Milly's next, remember.'

Silence.

The DI hadn't missed a word of this. 'Shall we start at the beginning?' No smiles now.

'Heavens above,' said Bea, tried beyond endurance, 'I don't know where to begin, and I suspect CJ doesn't, either. With her birth certificate, perhaps?'

CJ swung round to stare at Bea. 'You've found her birth certificate? Where?'

'Where Denzil the dirty-minded left it, of course. On his computer. You'd have found it yourself if you hadn't been doing so much hospital visiting.' Bea switched back to the DI. 'And before you ask who Denzil is, and what he's got to do with this, all I can say is, ask CJ, not me. This is his story, and I've only been dragged into it right at the end.'

The DI leaned back in his chair. Against all the odds, it seemed that he really might be enjoying this, for there was a flicker of amusement in his eyes and a twitch at the corner of his mouth. 'I expect that at some point one or other of you will say something which makes sense. Am I to understand that you two have been withholding essential information from the police?'

'Oh, not just me,' said Bea. 'Zander and Oliver and the whole caboodle, I wouldn't wonder. And Tommy, of course. Lord Murchison. He's ninety plus and probably in intensive care at the moment, so I shouldn't think you'll be allowed to question him today, or tomorrow. Your best bet, from what I've gathered of the

282

man, is to hold a seance and try to get through to him after he's dead.'

The DI laughed, genuinely amused, but his sidekick went red in the face and looked as if he'd rather like to hit someone.

Bea got to her feet. 'Sorry about that. But this has gone far enough. CJ, if you don't start talking, I will. Meantime, I need caffeine. I've already had two strong cups this morning, but just for once I'm going over my limit. Coffee all round?'

This time the DI nodded, though his sidekick shook his head. Bea stormed out to the kitchen and tried to switch on the new coffee machine. Needless to say, it refused to cooperate. She picked it up and dropped it back on the work surface. It said 'Glop!' fizzed, and died.

Bea screamed, fairly silently. A mouse squeak.

Chris came through the kitchen door, wearing Winston around his neck rather like a feather boa. 'Ah, coffee?'

Bea eyed him with dislike. 'I hope you don't get bitten. I haven't given Winston his flea medication for a while.'

'He don't mind me, and I don't mind him,' said Chris, reaching past her to switch this and press that. The machine obligingly burped into life. 'Lucky I went out to get some milk. I saw you hadn't got any. Oh, and some ginger-nut biscuits, too. I like dunking them in coffee, don't you?'

She struggled with a desire to bop him one over his head. 'I hope you remembered to turn off the hosepipe in the garden or we'll be flood-ed. Oh, and thank you for the milk. I'm grate-ful.' She didn't sound grateful, and she knew it. She tried to soften her tone. 'Your father's here and so are the police. Della Lawrence didn't make it.'

'Really?' He was more excited than depressed by the news. 'That's one up for Oliver. He said you could do with another murder as it boosted the coffers nicely. Where is he, anyway?'

'Investigating,' said Bea. 'And no, I don't know what and I don't know where.'

Leaving her to gather mugs, milk and sugar together, Chris drifted off into the sitting room, from which came the quiet murmur of CJ telling the police some, if not all, of what had been happening. Bea followed, kneeing open the door with some difficulty and depositing the tray on the low table before the settee. Chris was now sitting in her chair, sharing a bag of crisps with Winston.

Bea poured coffee and handed it round, while CJ murmured to a close. 'So you see, there's absolutely no proof that we can offer you. We can prove that neither Zander nor young Oliver killed Mrs Perrot, but any ideas that we might have as to who might have been responsible are only that; ideas.'

The DI was spellbound but not stupid. 'Tell me, Mr Cambridge, why you went to see Mrs Lawrence last night.'

Chris blew into the empty crisp packet, held the mouth closed with one hand and exploded it with the other. Everyone jumped but him. Winston treated him to a look which in a human being would have meant 'Oh, grow up!' and jumped down to the floor, tail waving.

'That was me,' said Chris, 'not my father. I went with Mrs Abbot to find out why Mrs Lawrence had phoned Zander the day of Mrs Perrot's murder. But she hadn't. Phoned him, I mean. At least, that's what she said, and I believed her – didn't you, Mrs Abbot?'

He transferred his smile back to the DI. 'By the way, did you find the keys I left at her house? I mean, that's why we went back, because I'd left them by my chair. Or in my chair. Whichever. We knew she was expecting to meet up with her niece at the pub so Mrs Abbot went off to the Feathers to see if she could find her there, but she couldn't. So she came back and looked through the window. And that's when Mrs Abbot saw the fire and called the police and fire brigade.'

The inspector was stone-faced. 'I'm sure that if we find the keys, you'll get them back in due course.' He turned to Bea. 'So what did Mrs Lawrence tell you?'

'Not much,' said Bea. 'She gave us some background about the way she'd lost her job at the Trust, saying she'd been framed by Denzil because her niece had been getting ideas about becoming his second wife.'

'Dear me,' said CJ. 'But that's hearsay, isn't it, Inspector?'

The DI sipped his coffee, added sugar and

milk. Took his time about it. 'What you're all saying is that you think you know who is responsible for the murders of Mrs Perrot and Mrs Lawrence, but you can't prove anything, and so therefore you won't tell me who it is?'

'I'll tell you, Inspector,' said Bea. 'Because I don't think it's just two murders that we're looking at. What about Sandy Corcoran? She's done him in, too, hasn't she? Oh, and if you don't look sharp, Della Lawrence's niece will probably be next on the list.'

'Sandy – Corcoran? Who's he?' The inspector treated her to a long stare.

'A builder. Mixed up in a scam Denzil was running at the Trust. Found dead in his office yesterday morning.'

The DI put down his coffee cup, got out his mobile and, walking over to the French windows at the back, pressed numbers and spoke into it.

Chris rubbed his hands together. 'What a girl! Now you've done it!'

'I hope so,' said Bea. 'Sorry, CJ, but this woman has got to be stopped.'

Oliver let himself into the room. He grinned at Bea and waved some sheets of paper in the air. 'Eureka!'

'The Internet triumphs, I assume?' said Bea. 'What have you found?'

The inspector shut off his mobile and rejoined them, with the air of one squaring up for a fight. 'I've just been hearing about the Corcoran murder. So how does that tie up with what you've been telling me, and who –' looking at Oliver – 'are you?'

'Oliver is my right hand,' said Bea. 'He's an expert on computers and what they can do, trained by CJ. He's already found Honoria's birth certificate, which proves she had no right to the title she's been claiming. What else, Oliver?'

'And just who is this Honoria?' The inspector was beginning to lose his temper.

'The woman who aims to take over Lord Murchison's Trust,' said CJ.

'Your murderer,' said Bea.

Oliver was smiling. 'Three times at least.' He addressed the inspector. 'I've just been checking on the Internet. Bridget Honour Mulligan – known to us as Lady Honoria – has been married twice. The first time to a Sidney Watts-Long, with whom she was in partnership as a dog breeder – Staffordshire bull terriers, as you might have guessed. On February first, two thousand and one, Sidney was found dead in bed with a young girl beside him, also dead. Shot at point blank range. Apparently he'd been having an affair with the girl for some months. Naturally suspicion fell on his wife, but they couldn't break her alibi for the night, which was given her by ... Sandy Corcoran!'

'This begins to make sense,' said Bea.

'The one who's just been found murdered?' asked the inspector, faint but pursuing.

'According to *The Times*, dated February second, he swore she'd been dining out with him that evening, that he'd accompanied her back to her house to pick up some literature, and that they'd found the couple dead together. The murder was eventually put down to a burglary which had gone wrong, since Sidney's mobile phone and laptop had gone missing.'

'What was that name again?' said the inspector.

Oliver continued. 'I'll let you have a copy of the report. At some point Denzil must have wondered if he might be next for the high jump, because he's gone to a lot of trouble to hide clues to her background in girlie pictures on his computer.'

Oliver distributed papers all round. 'I imagine that she paid off her debt to Corcoran after she married Denzil, by getting him to channel the Trust's building work through the man who'd given her an alibi for her first husband's death – and, incidentally, providing herself with a nice line in kickbacks. Once Zander had pulled the plug on that project, she realized that had to stop. Corcoran must have got restive, seeing his cash flow dry up. And so she silenced him.'

Everyone else was silenced, too.

At length Bea said, 'This is a very dangerous woman. If you're right, Oliver – and I'm sure you are – then everything starts with the fact that she's illegitimate and resents it. She wants to be accepted as her father's daughter, as a member of the nobility. After that she requires the status of being married and money to keep her ancestral home going. If anyone threatens what she's

288

got, she switches into revenge mode.

'Zander exposed Denzil, which threatened both her income and her partner in crime. Denzil dies, and she faces financial ruin. So she lashes out at those she thinks responsible. She couldn't get at Zander himself, so framed him for Mrs Perrot's murder. Mrs Perrot was elderly and frail and expendable. Sandy Corcoran was always a threat and only kept sweet with the money from the Trust; when that ended, he had to be taken out. Della and her niece threatened her position as Denzil's wife. Even though Denzil was dead and the women were no longer a threat, Honoria felt insulted by what they'd done. So Della had to be eliminated.

'Now what about her niece, Inspector? I think she must be next on the list. She proposed to stay at the pub where she's been doing evening work. Now that her aunt's dead, how long is she going to be safe? She doesn't even know she's in danger. And she is, isn't she? As I see it, Honoria thinks she can murder with impunity. She enjoys it!'

The inspector closed his mouth with a snap. 'What pub?'

'The Three Feathers. George the biker can tell you where it is exactly.'

'We shall look into it, of course. Also, we'll need to take a look at that computer of yours.'

'Not our computer,' said Bea. 'What you mean is that you need Oliver's memory stick, which I am sure he will be happy to give you.' She didn't think he'd be at all happy about it, but

289

needs must. 'Oliver?'

'I'll get it for you.'

She glared at him, meaning that he was not play any tricks, such as substituting his memory stick for another one. He smiled angelically and slid out of the room, meaning ... what? That he was prepared to do as she'd asked? Hmph. Maybe. He could be a tricky Dicky at times.

She gathered the empty cups together and put them on the tray. 'Before anyone else asks, was Denzil's death entirely due to natural causes? It was lucky for her that he died when he did, wasn't it? Granted that he had a heart condition; I'm beginning to wonder if she frightened him to death.'

The inspector got to his feet, looking a lot less smooth than when he'd arrived. 'We'll have to make some enquiries and get back to you.'

'Don't forget my keys,' said Chris. 'I left them on the arm of the chair I was sitting in, so they may have dropped down to the floor, or at the side of the cushion.'

'They're not his keys, Inspector,' said Bea. 'They're mine. A transponder for the car, house keys, and keys to the agency in the basement. I hope you find them soon as it is extremely inconvenient to be without them.'

'I'll bear it in mind,' said the inspector. He followed Bea as far as the door and stood there, making it clear he wasn't moving till he'd got Oliver's memory stick. Up the stairs came Oliver, still wearing his innocent face.

'Careful with it,' he said and handed it over.

'I'll give you a receipt for it.'

They all waited while a receipt was written out and handed over. Bea saw the policemen out and drew in a deep breath. Whatever next!

None of the men had bothered to take the coffee cups out to the kitchen. Naturally. Bea had thought Chris might, but no, he was busy teasing Winston with the crackly ball he'd made of his crisp packet. CJ stopped her as she went to pick up the tray.

'I wonder if you could spare me a few minutes...' It was a command, not a suggestion. She raised her eyebrows but seated herself again.

CJ said, 'I'm sure you realize how difficult this is for Tommy. His life's work falling apart, the Trust damaged by fraud and left at the mercy of an unprincipled woman and Denzil's appointee, Trimmingham. Tommy's mind is still clear. He has refused to take the morphine he needs to kill the pain, so that he can make one last try to right the situation.'

Now what? Playing the sympathy card won't get you anywhere, CJ.

He interlocked his fingers, leaning forward to make his point. 'He has formed the highest opinion of your abilities, and he would like to appoint you chair of the board of directors for the Trust, starting today.'

'What?' She almost laughed. Then realized he was in earnest. 'Me? No, no. That's ridiculous. Impossible!'

'Why should it be so impossible? You have an excellent business brain; you know how to deal with rogues such as Trimmingham and Sir Cecil. You could sort out the problems there in no time, and of course you would receive an excellent remuneration for your trouble.'

Bea blinked. 'CJ, I appreciate the compliment, but I have a full-time job here. This business does not run itself. As it is, I have spent far too long away from my desk trying to salvage your beloved Trust, and I expect to find all sorts of problems when I get back to my computer. Butlers will have been sent for interview as nannies and au pairs, estate managers will be parading as chefs, and aged aunts will have been escorted to the wrong terminal at Heathrow. You have no idea ... Well, why should you have? I'm sorry, but you are looking at the wrong person to help you out of the mess. And incidentally, why don't you do it yourself?'

He blenched. 'No, I'm afraid that would be impossible, conflict of interests, my work for the police ... No.'

A tiny worm of an idea inserted itself into the back of Bea's head. No, she couldn't do it, but did she know someone who might be suitable? Someone with a good brain and a manipulative mind? Someone at a loose end? No, of course not. Ridiculous idea.

'Yes?' he said, latching on to her sudden stillness.

She shook her head. 'No. Really. I'm flattered, but ... no.'

He stood up. 'Tommy will be disappointed. He's convinced you're the only person to stop

Honoria in her tracks. Will you please think about his offer? Seriously? You could always appoint a manager to run the agency for you, and you would be influencing the lives of thousands of people for good – not just the occasional schoolgirl who needs escorting across London.'

Bea shook her head. In one way it was tempting, yes. But Tommy only wanted her because she'd stood up to Honoria. What he really needed was a businessman or woman with a core of steel. Someone as tough as Honoria but on the side of the angels. And at that point Bea smiled to herself, because the person she'd thought of to fill the gap wasn't necessarily on the side of the angels. Far from it. So much for silly ideas! She shook her head, more at herself than in reply to CJ's offer.

CJ was watching her. 'Very well. But will you do one thing for Tommy? Would you meet the directors of the Trust this afternoon and make them see why Honoria cannot possibly be allowed to get involved? They'll listen to you. Show them the birth certificate and the report from *The Times*. Tell them about Sandy Corcoran. Link it all up for them.'

'Why don't you?'

'I have ... another appointment. Hm, yes.' A glance at the clock. 'In fact, I'm due to meet with Counsel shortly, on another matter entirely. A difficult case with all sorts of interesting ramifications. I really ought to be on my way there now. Take young Oliver with you; let him

293

show them how he discovered what Denzil had hidden. He'll enjoy that. Three o'clock at their offices, say?'

Before she could start making excuses, he'd managed to glide out of the room. They heard the front door open and close. He had gone.

Oliver grinned. 'Well, why not?'

Chris looked at the clock on the mantelpiece. 'What's for lunch?'

Bea tried to control her temper. 'What CJ wants is tantamount to waving a red rag in front of a bull. It would focus Honoria's attention on us. She'd be here, seeking revenge, within hours, armed with a gun or cricket bat or whatever weapon she's toting around nowadays. Do you want to be slaughtered in your beds?'

Oliver stopped smiling. 'No, but we could take precautions.'

'I could doss down here overnight,' offered Chris.

The doorbell rang, and Bea went to see who it was, saying, 'None of you are taking her seriously. This is not a game to her, though it might be to you.'

She opened the door to Piers, her ex, who was carrying an artist's portfolio, and who dived into the house as if the devil were after him ... which in a way he was. Or rather, she. For chasing him up the steps came Lettice, Nicole's blonde bombshell of a younger sister, who was either the bane or beauty of Max's life, though neither he nor anyone else seemed to know which. Lettice's blonde mop was almost dishevelled as she tottered along on her high heels, eeling into the hall as Bea closed the door behind Piers.

'There you are, you naughty man! You can't escape me, you know!'

Piers shuddered. He reminded Bea of a cornered fox. 'Get rid of her, Bea!' He shot into the sitting room, leaving his ex-wife to deal with the problem.

'Sorry,' said Bea, standing solidly in front of Lettice. 'I have a business meeting here today.'

Lettice went on tiptoe in her heels to peer over Bea's shoulder. 'Is my sister here yet? She said she was coming. Piers wants to do some preliminary sketches of us.'

'No, she isn't and I'm sorry, but I really am very busy—'

The doorbell rang again. Before she could prevent her, Lettice opened the door, and there was Nicole, with an armful of dresses and plastic bags.

'There you are!' said Lettice, triumphant. 'Now we can get this sorted out.' She pulled her sister into the hall and shoved her, squeaking, into the sitting room.

Piers was getting the boys to move the dining room table away from the windows which overlooked the road. Of course, the light would be better there than at the other end of the room.

'Lettice, I told you—' Nicole was bleating, already wilting under attack.

'Two for the price of one,' said Lettice, complacently. 'Piers will do a twin portrait of us, right?'

'Wrong!' said Piers. He was wearing a starched white shirt over jeans but looked very far from cool. 'Bea, can't you—'

Oliver and Chris could see a storm brewing and edged towards the door. Oliver said, 'I've got another picture to look at.' And made his escape, closely followed by Chris.

The doorbell rang again. Nicole collapsed on to the settee, still surrounded by her bags of clothing, and began to cry. Lettice seized one end of the dining table and began to push it further from the window. Piers said, 'Stop!' But she took no notice, pinning him up against the fireplace.

'Right!' Piers said. 'That's torn it, good and proper. I don't often lose my temper, but ... sit over there, and I'll do a sketch of you that you won't want to show to anyone!'

Bea threw up her hands and went to answer the door. It was a van delivering the food order she'd given the day before, and which needed to be attended to straight away. Frozen food in the freezer, perishables in the fridge, groceries in the cupboards, fresh vegetables and fruit here and there ... something left out for lunch and tonight's supper.

She'd rather hoped that Chris might have come up to assist her, but no; he'd disappeared downstairs with Oliver to look at more pictures of pretty girls. If she called him up to help her, he'd be sure to drop or break something, to make the point that this sort of thing was way beneath his dignity.

The phone rang and she answered it. CJ, saying that the board of directors were expecting her at two thirty that afternoon, not three.

Bea sighed to herself. Did those awful old men really think she could pull rabbits out of a hat for them? Surely not.

All had quietened down next door. Bea couldn't think why they weren't all still shouting or weeping. She opened the door into the sitting room and went in, to see Piers tear a sheet off his sketch pad.

'There,' he said. 'And much good may it do you.'

Standing behind Lettice, Bea saw he'd sketched the girl as a harpy, with huge, greedy eyes and fingernails extended into talons. Her hair writhed around her head like a bundle of snakes. Bea snorted, trying not to laugh. Piers had got Lettice exactly right.

'Piers; I didn't know you did caricatures.'

'I don't,' he said, still in a savage temper. 'I only draw what I see.' He looked down on Nicole who was still gently weeping, surrounded by a pile of dresses and bags which she hadn't bothered to set aside.

She looked back up at him. 'I'm so sorry. I know I look a mess.' She tried to smile, and suddenly his eyes sharpened. He got out a tiny camera and started snapping away. 'Stay just like that. Keep smiling if you can. Don't bother to wipe away the tears.'

Lettice was transfixed by the caricature of herself. She made as if to tear it up but desisted.

Perhaps she'd never realized before how she appeared to other people? Bea caught Lettice's arm. 'We need to talk. Come down to my office.'

Friday noon.

She could trust Trimmingham to keep her in the picture. She'd recognized him for what he was as soon as she'd met him and had known he'd fit perfectly into her plans for the Trust. And he had. He'd helped Denzil to get rid of the Della creature when the fluffy little niece had grown tiresome. He'd tried to stifle Zander and failed, but that was the only black mark against him – so far.

He'd nominated her for Denzil's position, and she knew he wouldn't oppose her in trying for the top job.

She couldn't understand why he was losing his nerve. So Tommy wanted the board to meet that afternoon? What could he possibly do to change things? Wasn't he still in hospital, anyway? Whether he came out or not, his day was over. The king is dead, long live the queen.

Trimmingham was uneasy about the meeting because the toy boy's Sugar Mummy was going to be there? What was her name again? Dean? Prior? Abbot.

Well, if Mrs Abbot wanted to cross swords with her, then Mrs Abbot was going to get the shock of her life. Honoria wasn't going to let that pale creature stand in her way.

298

Should she attend the meeting? She had an appointment with the solicitor that afternoon, which she really ought to keep. But if Trimmingham really was worried, then perhaps she should reschedule and go up to town? She couldn't make up her mind.

SIXTEEN

Friday noon

'Now,' said Bea, pushing Lettice into the big chair opposite her desk. 'Let's talk.'

Lettice shuddered. She'd made no demur when taken downstairs. Was she still in shock? Once more she made as if to crumple up the caricature, then stopped. She didn't cry. That wasn't her scene.

Bea said, 'If you'll take my advice, you'll get him to sign and date that. Then frame it. Hang it in your office to terrify wrongdoers.'

'What office? I have no office.'

'You haven't a job, either. Or an income. Or a husband. Or prospects. Right?'

Lettice's mouth twisted. 'You've noticed? I need ... I don't know what I need.'

'You need a job with prospects. Good prospects. Sorting out a load of stupid, shifty men who've made a mess of running a Trust that benefits hundreds of people. The sort of job which leads to an MBE, if you do it properly.'

'Oh, and pie in the sky to you, too.'

Bea contained her temper with an effort. She swivelled her chair to look out of the window.

She'd seen her husband do that a thousand times when he needed to think something through. Or pray. So now she prayed, too. *Dear Lord, what I'm about to do may be quite the wrong thing. It might be the last straw to break the Trust, or it might ... She has got the right attitude, hasn't she? She's bright and forceful and very like Honoria in some ways. But not, hopefully ... Oh, I do hope I'm not doing the wrong thing.*

She listened for a moment or two, but heard only the whirr of the fan, stirring the hot air in the office. *Please give me some sort of sign, if what I'm going to do is wrong. It might be the saving of her. Please?*

Nothing happened, except that Winston stalked into the room, sniffed all round Lettice's legs, and jumped on to her lap.

Winston didn't usually favour strangers with his company. Winston had shown a predisposition for young Chris's company earlier that day, and that had been surprising enough. And now he was on Lettice's lap?

Even more interesting, Lettice's face had softened, and she was scratching behind Winston's ears.

She said, 'I always wanted a cat, but my father said...' Her voice trailed away. 'Nicole's allergic, you see.'

Oh. Bea considered Winston's behaviour and thought that, on balance, it indicated Lettice was not altogether the out-and-out villainess she'd been painted. Maybe.

'Lettice, I've been asked to sort out a Trust

301

which has been run by a group of well-connected but inefficient men. One of them has been fiddling the books, and another has probably been corrupted into going along with the fraud. The fiddler has died and a most inappropriate person wants to take over. Being a bunch of lily-livered whatsits they haven't enough sense to fend her off.

'They need to bring in some fresh blood, a qualified accountant for a start. Someone has been suggested for that position but they're baulking at the cost, which is really stupid of them ... but then they are stupid, most of them. They also need a new broom; a facilitator, someone who can drag them into the new century, someone to knock their heads together and get the Trust back on a sensible footing.

'I've been offered the job but can't take it on because I've my work cut out for me here, so the position is up for grabs. They have a meeting this afternoon that I've been invited to attend, principally to see off the challenge from the fiddler's wife. Would you care to accompany me?'

Lettice's eyes were sharp. She considered what had been said and what had not been said. 'I have a business degree but never used it.'

'You're also tough enough to deal with a load of dithering directors, at least two of whom might be eligible as husbands. One of them even has a title.'

Red flared in her cheeks. 'Do you think I'm that shallow?'

Bea, too, flushed. Yes, she had thought it. 'I apologize. I shouldn't have said that.'

Lettice went to look out into the garden. 'What you're saying is that you'll nominate me for an interesting job if I give up Max.'

Silence. Yes, that's what Bea had meant.

Lettice said, 'I don't suppose you'll believe me, but I really love Max.'

'He's not yours.'

'You've never liked me, have you?'

Silence. No, Bea hadn't. 'I didn't realize you really loved him. I thought – well, never mind.'

'You thought I was a silly, spoilt child latching on to someone else's husband for kicks. Perhaps I am. But he's ... There's something about him. I can't keep my hands off him. And yes, I acknowledge that he won't leave Nicole. I thought he might, but he won't. Not now. So I suppose you're right, and I ought to rethink my position.'

Bea cleared her throat. 'Talking of straying hands, there's a pair of them at the Trust.'

Lettice turned back into the room. 'I know how to deal with straying hands.'

'I'm sure you do. Can you also keep the owner of said straying hands on the straight and narrow? And would you mind sticking to the straight and narrow yourself?'

Lettice considered this, wearing a slight frown.

Bea waited. Prayed a little. *Lord, am I doing the right thing? Surely she'll turn it down if I'm wrong? I'd never thought of her as being a white knight, riding to the rescue of the home-*

303

less, but maybe she's never thought of herself that way, either. Maybe this is a turning point for her? But if I'm wrong ... heavens, what a disaster for all concerned.

Lettice's eyes focused on Bea. 'No one's ever thought I could be a force for good before. What makes you think I can do it?'

'They need someone tough enough to knock their heads together.' Bea gestured to the caricature, now resting on her desk. 'That side of you – it's right up your street. Max has always said you've a sharp mind. Of course, they may not like you. You may not like them. I suggest you accompany me to a meeting this afternoon, and we'll take it from there.'

Lettice looked down at what she was wearing. A blouse, knotted at her midriff, and cut-off jeans. 'I can't go dressed like this.'

Bea looked at her watch. 'No, of course not. I'll have to change, too. Nearly twelve, and there's a lot to be done. I have to make copies of everything we're going to use this afternoon and drop some into the police before we go to the meeting.'

'I could help – if you'll let me.'

Bea approved. 'Thank you. I'll give you a quick run-down of what's been happening as we go through the paperwork. Then I've got to sort out some lunch and see what's going on in the office. I suggest we meet at the charity just before two thirty.'

Friday afternoon

As Bea and Oliver walked up the steps to the
Trust's offices, Lettice descended from a taxi.
Both women were now wearing grey-striped
business suits. It didn't look as if Lettice was
wearing anything but a bra under her jacket, but
Bea certainly was. Both wore high heels and
carried briefcases.

Oliver, who ought perhaps to have considered
shaving, wore a black shirt and matching black
jeans. He was carrying his laptop.

The meeting was to be held in the room which
doubled as the Trust's dining room, but there
were far more people present than on the occasion of Bea's previous visit. She counted six
men on either side, with the major at the head of
the table in the place previously occupied by
Lord Murchison. The men were all in their
sixties and seventies, all wearing dark clothes
and downbeat expressions.

Not one woman was represented on the board.

The major fussed around, finding extra chairs
for Lettice and Oliver. 'Lettice, is it? Mrs Abbot
asked if she might bring a colleague. And ...
Oliver, is it? Delighted.'

Lettice gave no sign of the nerves which were
afflicting Bea. Oliver, of course, was enjoying
himself. Lettice and Oliver were given chairs on
either side of Bea, but a little away from the
table. Lettice crossed one knee over the other
and, as one man, the men all switched their eyes
that way. Lettice had nice legs and knew it, but

she didn't allow the knowledge to show on her face. Having caught their attention, she uncrossed her legs and pulled her chair closer to the table so the men could no longer see her knees. Pulling a pad and pencil from her briefcase, she turned slightly towards Bea, the very picture of an efficient PA.

The major introduced Bea, saying that unfortunately Lord Murchison was still in hospital, but he had asked that they give Mrs Abbot the courtesy of, etcetera, as she had some important information for them, which they should all consider very seriously, blah, blah.

He then introduced the board of directors to Bea. She recognized Sir Cecil of the straying hands, Mr Trimmingham the solicitor, and the man who looked rather like him but had a different surname. Birds of a feather, presumably. Smooth and possibly not all that honest.

By their body language she could tell that not one of them wanted her to be there, and that they were not at all interested in what she had to say. Their minds were made up. Mr Trimmingham and his ilk had seen to that. Honoria had been taken to their hearts, full stop.

Bea decided there was no point in being sweetly reasonable. 'Gentlemen,' she began, 'I bring you messages from the dead. To be precise, from the Honourable Denzil, your fellow director and architect of the scheme which defrauded you of nigh on a million pounds.' She turned to Lettice. 'Do you have the exact figure there?'

Lettice read it out in a businesslike voice. Several men, who hadn't been properly briefed as to the amount the Trust had lost, winced.

'Yes, gentlemen,' said Bea, 'that appears to be the sum he got away with. He did this by arrangement with Sandy Corcoran, a builder, who overcharged the Trust and then deposited a kickback in Denzil and Honoria's joint account once a month. You would, of course, like proof of that. Lettice?'

Bea turned to Lettice, who retrieved a bundle of paper from her briefcase. They had arranged that Lettice should have as much of the limelight as possible. Now she went round the table, saying, 'These are copies of the fraudster's bank statements over the last six months.' She distributed several pages to each person. Some of the men gave the statements a quick glance, but others studied them intently.

'As you can see,' said Bea, 'Large cheques were deposited in the bank account about the twentieth of each month, only to disappear by the twenty-ninth. The account was a joint one, operated by Denzil and Honoria. We have Denzil's chequebooks and stubs. According to his chequebook, he didn't withdraw these monies from the account, so I think we can safely assume that his wife did. This would indicate to me that she knew exactly what was going on.'

'No, no,' said someone. 'It's far more likely he transferred the funds to an offshore account somewhere.'

'Perhaps so,' said Bea. 'In which case, she'll have some difficulty in getting hold of the money now he's dead, won't she? Meanwhile, I have some messages which he left for you on his computer.'

'What messages?' asked Mr Trimmingham. 'There were none.'

'Oh, did you check?' said Bea. 'Well, they were very cleverly hidden in what appeared to be routine pin-up pictures of young girls. My assistant here will show you what he's found. He's also run off copies of the messages for each of you to read. Oliver...?'

She sat down, handing the floor over to Oliver.

'He concealed his messages by a method known as steganography, which involves hiding information within an electronically stored image without noticeably affecting that image. I had to try to open each picture with the decoding program in turn, guessing at the passwords until the program let me see the information.'

He turned the computer so they could all see the image of a pretty girl and tapped on his keyboard. Something else then appeared on the screen. 'You can see what he'd hidden in the picture – another image. This turned out to be a birth certificate for his wife.'

'I have a copy for each of you,' said Lettice, going round the table again. Some of the men were riveted by her back view, but she took no notice. When all had copies, she returned to her seat. By and large, the men gave the birth certificate sharp attention. Only Mr Trimmingham took one glance at it and looked away. He'd known all about it beforehand?

'As you can see,' said Lettice, 'she was registered at birth as Bridget Honour Mulligan. Although her father bore an ancient title, her parents were not married, and therefore she is not entitled to call herself "Lady Honoria".'

'Of course,' said Bea, 'anyone can call themselves what they like. Princess or Duchess or Elvis Presley. It is up to us whether or not we go along with it. The second piece of information which Oliver discovered was a letter requesting his solicitor to keep the deeds to the Manor, which are in his name. Not hers, you understand. In his name. The third picture contained a reference to a report in *The Times* newspaper dated the second of February two thousand and one. Oliver downloaded the relevant part, and Lettice has copies for each of you.'

Lettice started to distribute more papers. 'You will see that on the first of February that year, Honoria Mulligan found her first husband and his mistress dead. Naturally she fell under suspicion and would have been charged with murder ... except that she was given an alibi by a man named Sandy Corcoran.'

'Ouch,' said someone, softly.

Someone else cleared his throat. 'The same Corcoran who...? Oh.'

This time they all read with concentration. Even Trimmingham.

Bea continued, 'Soon after Denzil's marriage,

309

his computer records show that he'd begun to steer contracts to Corcorans. It is difficult to avoid the conclusion that this was by way of pay-off for services rendered.'

Someone choked. Sir Cecil Waite, he of the straying hands. He reached for one of the carafes of water laid out on the table. The chink of bottle against glass sounded loud in the silence.

'And the next picture, Oliver?'

'I couldn't make out what it was at first.' He tapped the keyboard and turned the screen so that they could all see. 'It's a gun certificate, made out to Honoria. It's dated a month before her first husband was shot dead. It's for a double-barrelled shotgun. Pellets, not bullets. Close to, it has a devastating effect.'

'Oh, and by the way,' said Lettice, 'you will be interested to hear that Sandy Corcoran was found dead of shotgun wounds in his office a couple of days ago. We must suppose that he'd become a threat to Honoria since she wasn't going to be able to continue sending contracts his way even though he'd covered for her when her first husband had been killed.'

Several mouths dropped open and stayed that way.

'And then of course,' said Bea, 'there was the murder of your ex-office manageress two nights ago. Honoria must have been furious when Della Lawrence's niece started making eyes at Denzil. Which of you helped to frame Della so that she got the sack? I'm sure the police will be

310

very interested to interview you about it.'

A gaping silence. Trimmingham's hand shook as he in turn poured himself a glass of water.

'Is there any more?' asked the major.

Oliver grinned. 'One last thing, yes. As you know, the deeds to the Manor are in his name, not hers. I found a copy of a letter to his solicitors, dated six weeks ago. Only a couple of lines, confirming changes to his will. Five pounds to his wife, and everything else to the Trust.' He turned the screen so that they could all see.

'What!'

'That's—'

'Order! Order!'

Trimmingham's face was puce. Sir Cecil gobbled and choked on his glass of water.

The major rose to his feet. 'Have you run off copies of that letter?'

Lettice distributed more copies. A dozen heads were bent over them. Finally the major sighed. 'If this is genuine—'

Trimmingham snorted. 'It's not witnessed. It gives notice of intent, but not of fact. He probably never carried through his intentions. Why, if this were proved in court, Honoria would lose the Manor.'

'Yes, but the Trust would get it. We could sell the Manor and claw back ... How much?' said a soldierly man who hadn't spoken before.

'If all this paperwork were proved in court,' said the legal eagle, 'then Honoria would lose more than the house. It looks to me like an attempt to railroad her into jail.'

'Perfectly appalling!' bleated a man who was twisting a device on his hearing aid. 'If this were to come out, even if nothing could be proved—'

'Exactly,' said Bea, signalling to Oliver to close up his laptop. 'If this got into the tabloids, who knows how much damage it would do to the Trust? Gentlemen, I think you've had a very lucky escape. Copies of all these papers have been sent to the police, and they will no doubt act upon them.'

'Fortunately,' said Lettice, smiling brilliantly at the men, 'Honoria is not currently a director of the Trust, and as Denzil is dead, there will be no need to drag any of you into this sordid affair. I shudder to think what might have happened if she'd been appointed to the board of directors and then arrested for murder. As it is, the Trust is now the fortunate owner of a most desirable Grade I manor house in beautiful countryside, well within reach of London. It should fetch a bomb, don't you think?'

Mr Trimmingham lost all the colour in his face and Sir Cecil choked, but most faces relaxed into a relieved smile.

'Luckily,' said Lettice, 'Lord Murchison fore-saw the need to bring new blood into the charity some time ago, and he's asked Mrs Abbot here to consider joining you.'

'I very much regret,' said Bea, 'I am not in a position to accept his very flattering offer, and indeed I really must be going as I have another appointment this afternoon. However, if you take my advice, I suggest you adopt Lord Murchison's earlier suggestion of bringing in a professional man to manage your finances. It will cost you something, but the days are gone when you can leave that side of the business to amateurs; you've seen what happens when you do. You might also like to reinstate Zander as your office manager and recompense him for what Honoria has put him through lately. I understand that he put your interests before his. Not a bad reference.

'And gentlemen –' here she smiled at each of them in turn – 'I can't help noticing that you haven't yet appointed any women to your board; apart from Honoria, that is. Women are notoriously good at the practicalities of life and charity work appeals to their nurturing side. Perhaps at some point you might like to look for a younger businesswoman or two to join you.'

Prompt on cue, all eyes switched to Lettice, who appeared impervious to their gaze as she shut her briefcase. Glancing at her watch, she said, 'Well, if there are any more questions...? Otherwise...?'

The major stuttered, 'We need to c–consider what action we should take most carefully, b–but I think I speak for all of us when I say that we appreciate your c–coming today.'

The soldierly one addressed his next-door neighbour in a voice intended to be confidential, but which everyone could hear. 'She seems to have an excellent grasp of the matter. What's her

313

background, eh? What?'

It was Lettice's chance to make her pitch, and she took it. 'Business degree, King's College, London. Two years working for a headhunter, based here in the City. After that I spent some time studying the political system in America, and since my return to London I've been working as a researcher in the House of Commons. I have no particular ambition to stand for Parliament, though it has been suggested that I do so. I am currently looking for an opportunity to work in a company where my talent for organization would be appreciated.' She treated them to a smile, looking into the eyes of each one of them in turn, and followed Bea and Oliver to the door.

Down the stairs they went, in silence. Once down in the hall, Bea and Oliver paused as Lettice exclaimed and dived into her handbag for her mobile, which had been set to vibrate. She noted who the call was from and killed it.

A door opened above them, and they could hear someone else speaking on his mobile. Mr Trimmingham? He didn't see them, concentrating on his phone call. 'Honoria, something's come up...'

Oliver held the front door open as they passed out into the sunshine.

'What are the odds they'll take me?' said Lettice.

Bea shrugged. 'Depends on how scared they are. I suppose they're even now discussing you. Some will be all for having a woman on board,

314

some will be against it. But the modernizers should win, I think. Knowing them, it will take several days for them to act. Then they'll make you an offer, which I suggest you refuse – at first. They'll up the offer. You'll refuse again, but express some doubts about doing so. Eventually you'll agree. I think you'll be very good for them.'

Oliver said, 'I suppose I'd better drop by the police station to make sure they've found the letter about the will. Won't Honoria be mad when she finds out!'

'That thought does not aid digestion. Oliver, I want you to be really careful for the next couple of days, till the police catch up with her. They've got all the information we've managed to get together, and perhaps they'll question her today, but it's more likely that they'll take some time to evaluate the evidence. We must drop the deadlock on the front door at the house, always remember to switch on the alarm, and never go out at night alone.'

'Sure,' said Oliver, buoyantly.

He might remember, and he might not. Bea began to calculate how long it was likely to take before the police arrested Honoria, even they could be convinced that she was their man. Woman. Whatever.

Lettice was wearing an abstracted expression. She caught Bea's arm. 'A moment.'

Oliver lengthened his stride. 'See you back at the ranch.' And disappeared.

Lettice put her arm through Bea's as they

315

followed him at a slower pace. 'I suppose I'm safe for the moment, since Honoria doesn't know where I live. But ... I was just thinking. If I get the job, and make a success of it, then Piers would paint me, wouldn't he?'

Bea fought down impatience. What was it with these two sisters? Sibling rivalry at its worst. 'He does paint the great and the good, yes. You understand that I have no influence there.'

Lettice gave her an old-fashioned look. In many ways she was far more acute than her sister. 'You don't know what it's like, being brought up in the shadow of a beautiful older sister.'

Bea smiled, said nothing. They both seemed to think the other sister had blighted their lives.

'I enjoyed dominating that meeting. You're right; I could make a success of that job. If I don't get it, though, would you be prepared to help me get something else?'

'I could look around.'

Lettice looked off to one side. 'If you did ... if I did get a good job ... and Nicole produces a healthy baby, I promise I'll give Max up. I'll even give you his letters to destroy.'

Bea felt her heart go thud. So Max had been stupid enough to put pen to paper? Of course – be still my heart – the letters might not be incriminating, they might be absolutely innocent in intent. But in the hands of someone who wished him ill they'd be lethal.

'Thank you, Lettice.' What else could she say?

Friday afternoon

It was lucky she hadn't been driving when Trimmingham rang, or she'd have crashed the car. She'd just left the solicitors, trying to come to terms with the fact that Denzil's last will had cut the ground from under her feet. Talk about shock! She'd staggered out of his office, leaned against the wall, breathing hard, when her mobile had gone off. Trimmingham giving her the bad news.

One moment she'd been on top of everything, and the next ... It felt as if the earth had shaken and tumbled her off her wall. Humpty Dumpty sat on a wall. Humpty Dumpty had a great fall.

The mobile dropped out of her hand. A passer-by picked it up for her, asked if she were all right. She stared at him, trying to focus. No, she wasn't all right. She could hardly see straight. Was she having a stroke? Her vision cleared. She took back her mobile, straightened herself up.

What to do now? How much was lost?

The police had found incriminating evidence on Denzil's computer? She didn't understand. She'd erased all the pretty pictures, hadn't she? So how...? That fool Trimmingham must have misunderstood. But right or wrong, the Abbot woman had placed the Trust beyond her reach and, what was even worse, had said Honoria had no right to call herself 'Lady'.

She got herself back to the Range Rover and

317

locked herself in. Began to think.

If she denied everything ... what evidence did they have to connect her with Sandy's death, or Della's?

Her overalls! They were in the washing machine but she hadn't yet turned it on. The gun had been cleaned, of course. She always cleaned a gun once she'd used it. Gloves? Thrown away. She couldn't for the moment remember where she'd thrown them. The hammer was wrapped in plastic, waiting to be soaked in water and Dettol.

She put her head down on the steering wheel and gasped for breath.

Could she rescue them before the police got to her? She was only a couple of miles from home. Yes, it would be worth trying that. And then what. Flight? It tore her apart to think of leaving the Manor, for which she'd done so much, made so many sacrifices.

She hit the steering wheel with her fist. If she couldn't live at the Manor, no one else would. Suppose...?

Yes. The cleaner wouldn't have finished yet. Suppose...

She smiled. She began to plan what she should do when she got home. And after that, she'd pay a visit to the interfering Mrs Abbot.

SEVENTEEN

Friday evening

Back home, Bea didn't know what to do first. She must warn Maggie to be careful, see what problems might be lurking downstairs for the agency, organize something for supper, restrain herself from ringing up the police every five minutes to see if they'd arrested Honoria yet.

A series of images kept flashing through her head. First was that of a taffy-headed girl lying on the floor with her head beaten in. That would be Milly, Della's niece, who had narrowly missed being killed the previous night. Or was it young Kylie from the pub near Honoria's home? Both had given Honoria cause to wish them harm.

Then came another image, even more disturbing. Nicole, reading a love letter from Max to her sister. Another image, even worse: Nicole, reclining on Bea's couch, surrounded by shopping, weeping, while Honoria crept up behind her, arm raised to strike.

Bea held her head in both hands and shook it. She closed her eyes. She was overtired, overimaginative. Over the hill. Too old for this lark.

319

She reached for the phone and dialled the local police station. Was told DI Warner was not available. She asked if he'd gone out to arrest someone and was given the brush off. Of course they wouldn't be able to tell her that, even if it were true.

She paced the floor. Stood in front of the portrait which Piers had painted of her beloved husband, and stared at it. The man in the picture stared back at her; a kindly, intelligent, loving and caring gaze.

But he was long gone, and she was on her own.

She went down the stairs to the agency rooms. Cynthia and Miss Brook were packing up for the day. She tried to smile, to behave normally. Wanted to scream.

'How are you managing? I shouldn't have left you alone all day, but...'

'That's all right, Mrs Abbot. We quite understand,' said Miss Brook. 'There was a little problem this afternoon when Cynthia was due to attend an interview in the City, but she decided against going so that we could keep on top of things here.'

With a shock, Bea remembered that Cynthia had said she was looking for another job and had some interviews lined up. Without thinking it through, Bea said, 'I'm extremely glad to hear you didn't go, Cynthia. Instead, I wonder if you would consider a full-time job here? I know it's not as glamorous as working for some city magnate, but...'

'I was hoping you'd ask,' said Cynthia. 'I like finding the right jobs for people and making people's lives so much easier. And it's only a hop and a skip from the little flat that my cousin wants me to share with her, and not much further from my niece, the one who's expecting soon. I'd as soon not work in the City, come to think of it, with all their scandalous goings on, pension funds going missing and everyone getting bonuses that they've no right to in my book.'

Miss Brook inclined her head by way of approval. 'I was telling Cynthia that there's a nice little cafe across the road where we could have our lunches when the weather gets cooler, very near the library, and there's more than enough work for the two of us to do. In fact, when Mr Oliver goes to university, I'm wondering whether we could perhaps take on a part-timer, someone who can spell us for holidays. It's no use saying that Maggie can fill in, because she doesn't find the computer compatible with her nature, and she's certainly more use going out and about and dealing with workmen than she is here, forgetting to save documents and leaving the filing in a mess.

'We've talked it over, Cynthia and I, and we've decided we'll continue working in this room so that if we have to consult, we can do so with ease. We'll leave Oliver's room for Maggie to spread herself out in. And if we do get a temp in at any time, then we can easily make room for her in here as well.'

'You have it all arranged,' said Bea, laughing because everything was falling into place, and at the same time wanting to cry at the thought of Oliver leaving. Had he really discussed leaving with Miss Brook already? She pulled her mouth back into a smile. 'Cynthia, shall we have a quiet word in my office, start the paperwork?'

And explain it all to Oliver as soon as possible.

'Is that the police station? Has Detective Inspector Warner returned yet? No? Oh. Will you tell him I called? Mrs Abbot. Yes, I rang earlier.'

She put down the phone, tried another number. 'Is that The Feathers pub? Would it be possible to speak to Milly? I believe she may be staying with you because of the fire at—'

'Who is this?' A woman's voice, middle-aged and smoky. The landlady?

'It's Mrs Abbot here. I called on her aunt last night. We – that is, my companion and I, a neighbour from the next road – called the fire brigade and the police.'

'She's back there, at the house now. With the police. My husband's gone with her because she's wrecked, poor kid. He'll bring her back here soon. Who shall I say called?'

'Mrs Abbot. Did the police warn her that she might be in danger, too? That whoever killed her aunt might be after her as well?'

'Really? Whatever for?'

'We think she and her aunt may have upset

322

someone at the Trust where she used to work. You know what happened to Della, and I'm worried the same thing might happen to Milly. The police haven't said anything to you about it?'

'Not a thing. Are you sure?'

'Yes, I'm sure. The police are going to arrest the woman responsible, but until they do, would it be possible for you to keep an eye on Milly?'

'There was a man at the Trust that she liked, but he died.'

'Yes. But his wife is on the warpath. It would be awful if something were to happen to Milly, too.'

'I'll have a word with my husband about it. Who did you say you are?'

'Mrs Abbot. I'll give you my phone number, just in case. Do you have a pen?'

Next was Kylie. Except she didn't have a phone number for Kylie. What was the name of the pub she'd worked at? Bea couldn't remember that, either. She told herself to hold it together. She was not going to go to pieces. No.

Think, woman! Oliver took us to the pub which was at the bottom of the hill, within spitting distance of the manor. She could visualize its frontage, but for the life of her, couldn't remember its name. The Chequers? No. Cross Keys? No.

She went round the house, closing and locking windows in spite of the heat. She closed and locked the grilles which had been fitted over the windows overlooking the garden at the back.

She double-locked the front door and set the alarm, which she didn't normally do till after dark.

It was still very hot. Sultry, almost. What should she cook for supper? If anything?

Where was Oliver? She went downstairs. The agency rooms were empty. So where was he?

And where was Maggie? Had something happened to them? Had Honoria caught up with them somewhere? Because if so, there was no point in preparing supper for three. What a stupid, stupid thought!

She was wittering like an old woman, jumping at shadows.

Someone tried the front door. Someone with a key. The relief! It must be Oliver or Maggie. *Thank the Lord.*

It was both.

'Why's the front door double-locked?' said Oliver. The alarm went off, and he killed it. He laughed. 'Overdoing it a bit, aren't we?'

Bea tried to laugh, too. 'I expect so. Just taking precautions. Maggie, are you all right?'

'I suppose.' The girl was avoiding Bea's eye. Unusually subdued.

Bea decided not to probe. 'How did it go today? Did the electrician turn up?'

'Oh. Him. Yes, eventually. I think I'll have a shower. I'm a ball of sweat.' She went off up the stairs without a backward look.

Oliver was already in the kitchen, searching for a cold drink. 'I dropped the stuff off at the police station. The DI was there, and we had a good chat. I gave him the stuff, like you said. What's for supper?'

Bea bit back the words, *They told me he was out!* She said, 'Something light, I think. Chicken breasts, salad, baked potatoes.' She started to prepare the food. Her hands were trembling.

'Not afraid of Honoria, are you?' Oliver up-ended an empty carton of orange juice. 'They'll get her long before she can think about reveng-ing herself on us. It makes me laugh to think how Denzil scuppered all her plans.'

'She does frighten me, and if you've any sense at all – which I doubt – then you'd be frighten-ed, too.'

'They're on to her now.'

'There's many a slip.'

Bea cut herself, slicing tomatoes, and ran her hand under the tap. The cold water stung. Oliver wasn't watching. He had his mobile out, was leaving the room.

Bea closed her eyes, tried to still the jitters. *Dear Lord, I know there's no sense in panicking. My imagination's running away with me, that's all. I hope. Could you give us a little extra attention this evening, please? Sorry to disturb, if you're busy with big wars and famines and all sorts of dreadful things happening all over the planet, but ... Just a passing thought. I know you can put a protective apron round a million people and we're only three ... Well, a few more than three if you count in all the other men and women who Honoria might wish to harm.*

Oliver put his head back round the door.

'Chris says is there enough supper for him as well? Then we're all going on to a party at one of his friends' house, if that's all right with you and you don't mind being left alone?' His voice changed. 'Oh. I can see you do mind. Well, that's all right. What's one more party, anyway? I'll stay.'

She found a sticking plaster and put it round her forefinger. 'Of course you must go. Maggie can keep me company.'

'She's invited, too. You don't really mind being on your own, do you? I wouldn't suggest going out if it weren't that the DI said everything was under control.'

Did she believe everything was under control? No. Every instinct said she was being hunted down at this very minute. She breathed deeply. There was absolutely no point letting fear take over. 'What was the name of the pub where we met Kylie? I'd be happier if I knew she'd been warned to stay away from dark corners.'

He shrugged. 'I'll give them ring, see if she's there, if it'll make you feel better.' His tone was so patronizing that she wanted to scream, but she didn't. She put the chicken breasts on to a baking tray and shoved them into the oven to cook. She wondered about having a slug of sherry to calm her nerves but decided against it. Went back to preparing baked potatoes and a salad.

Oliver burst back into the room. 'Guess what? There's been a fire at Honoria's! Yes, really. Four fire engines, the police, ambulances, every-

326

thing. They're all out in the garden at the back of the pub, getting an eyeful. This dry weather, all that timber framework, it must have gone up like a torch. Kylie's not at the pub, though. Got a cleaning job somewhere, helping her mum. Oh.' A change of tone. 'Didn't Kylie say her mum worked up at the Manor, cleaning?'

Bea put both hands over her heart. 'I wouldn't think she'd be cleaning this late on a Friday afternoon. But perhaps you'd better give your DI a ring, see if he knows. See if Kylie's safe.'

'Why shouldn't she be?' But he was frowning as he punched numbers ... and got no joy. He shut off his mobile. 'The DI's not available. I expect he's on his way out there.'

'Try the pub again. Explain that we're worried about Kylie, that she might be up at the Manor.'

'You said—'

'I know what I said. Just do it.'

He punched more numbers, waited for someone to pick up, which they did eventually. Bea unlocked and threw open the back door, gasping for fresh air. Winston was laid out in a shady spot in the garden but managed to lift his head when he smelled chicken being cooked.

Oliver said, 'Yes,' and, 'No, of course not,' and then his tone changed. 'Hi, Kylie. How are you doing? Great dramas at your end, I hear.' Bea could hear an excited girl's voice on the phone. Eventually Oliver glanced at Bea, eyebrows raised, and said, 'Yes, I suppose it would be worth another tenner to get the low-down, as you put it.'

Bea nodded, and Oliver settled down to listen, making appropriate soothing noises at regular intervals. Finally he said, 'Well, how about that! And yes, I'll put the money in the post to you tomorrow if you'll give me your address.' Bea handed him the back of the shopping list they kept on the notice board, and he scribbled away on it. And then shut off the phone.

'As you've gathered, Kylie's safe. The fire's out, though one engine's staying on to make sure the blaze doesn't start up again overnight. The kitchen wing is a write-off, but they were just in time to save the rest. Some of the firemen have just dropped by the pub for a spot of lubrication, and they brought Kylie back with them. She's in shock. She was on her way up there when she saw the fire and rang for help on her mobile. It's a good thing she did, because otherwise it would have swept through the whole house.'

'The police were there, and ambulances?'

'Poor old Honoria. They don't know how the fire started yet, but it seems she was sitting in her car in the stable yard, and it was caught up in the blaze. It started in the kitchen, they think. The firemen have been through the rest of the house, but there was no one else there. One body, removed by ambulance.'

'How very odd. Do they think Honoria fired the place herself?'

'What else? She must have got word that the police were on to her – through Trimmingham, I suppose – and decided to kill herself and burn

328

down her beloved Manor at the same time. I must say, it's a relief to know she's dead.'

Bea sank on to a stool. Honoria was dead? It was hard to take it in. Bea told herself she ought to be feeling a great surge of relief, but all she could think of was how unexpected it was. Now why was that? Because ... because she wouldn't have thought Honoria was the sort to commit suicide or to be careless with matches.

Bea wondered how she'd done it. Had she doused the back quarters of the Manor with petrol, and then poured it all over herself and the car? Bea shuddered. Don't think about it. Nasty.

Be thankful, she said to herself. The cloud has lifted, etcetera.

Thank you, Lord. Deep thanks.

She supposed she'd begin to feel better soon. She didn't rebound from fear as quickly as the youngsters did. Chris wandered in, sniffing the air, and Bea turned her attention back to providing supper for them all.

There was a lot of talk across the dinner table about the party. Maggie was in a sombre mood and decided not to go, but Oliver and Chris left together. Bea double-locked and put the chain on the front door, laughing at herself for shutting the stable door after the horse had bolted, but felt safer when she'd done so; and then she locked the back door as well.

She helped Maggie to clear away the supper things and start the dishwasher.

Maggie was abstracted, monosyllabic. It look-ed as if she'd begun to get ready for the party and then changed her mind. Her eyes were made up with a purple shadow that sparkled, and she'd gelled her hair into spikes, but she wasn't wearing any lipstick and had pulled on an oversize white cotton T-shirt and cut-off jeans. Of course, youngsters often did go to parties in those clothes, but Maggie went in for lurid colours and spandex when she was in party mood.

Bea made some good coffee – how many cups had she had that day? – and set one down in front of Maggie. 'Want to tell me about it?'

Maggie gave a long sigh. 'I don't know that talking's much help. I rang Zander today to see if he'd settled in all right. He said he had, though his new place didn't sound ideal to me. He asked if I wanted to go out for a drink or a walk or something and I said yes. And then I rang back to say I'd changed my mind.'

She sat on her stool, hunching over the coffee, both hands around the cup. 'Why can't things stay the same? I'm going to miss him something chronic.'

Was she referring to Zander or to Oliver's going to university?

'I know.' Bea sat next to Maggie and put her arm around the girl's shoulders.

'I mean, we were all doing all right, weren't we? He liked the work, and he's got friends here and, well, everything.'

She was talking about Oliver. Probably. 'Mm. But he's growing up. He ought to go to university. And yes, I'm going to miss him something

330

chronic, too.' It was hurting her, too ... but she knew she must let him go.

'What are we going to do without him in the agency?'

'I've offered Cynthia a full-time job, and we'll probably need to take on a part-timer as well, when Oliver's gone. He's been doing the work of three, hasn't he? We'll adapt, Maggie. You've already outgrown your original job here, anyway. You're out and about, bossing workmen around and consulting with architects. A far cry from being our receptionist. Why, one of these days you're going to need your own personal assistant to help you out.'

Maggie spluttered into a laugh. 'Go on!'

'No, really. When Oliver goes, you're to have his office as your own, and we'll employ more people as we need them.'

Maggie sniffed. 'He doesn't even know how to boil an egg.'

Bea wanted to push the box of tissues nearer to the girl but decided against it. Maggie didn't like people to see when she cried. 'I expect he'll be in a hall of residence at first. You and I will have to give him some basic lessons in cookery in the holidays. We'll keep his room for him, of course, so he'll always have a base to return to.'

'You're serious about him taking your name?'

'He needs someone in his corner for the next time he's hauled in by the police.'

'Silly! He enjoyed every minute of that.'

'In parts, yes. Not all the time. He is only eighteen, still.'

'He loves the work here.'

'No, he doesn't. He likes to be useful, but you know as well as I do that he could run the agency with one hand tied behind his back and never feel the strain. I can see the signs already. He needs to use his brains, or very soon he'll get bored. And then he'd look around for something more interesting to do, and we'd lose him completely.'

Maggie took a tissue and blew her nose, hard. 'He likes solving crimes. Couldn't we turn ourselves into a detective agency?'

'No, we couldn't. Trying to solve murders is turning my hair grey. I'm too old for it. Our domestic agency helps a great number of people to find the right jobs and generally spreads light and happiness around. Dealing with people like Honoria is another matter entirely.'

'Someone has to solve murders.'

'Someone tougher than me. Let's face it; Oliver is a high flyer, an eagle. And we are more like hedge sparrows, you and I.'

A giggle, sort of. 'There, now. And I always thought I was more of a noisy, colourful parrot.'

'And what am I?'

'A wise owl, who knows all the answers.'

Bea didn't think she knew all the answers; in fact, she thought she knew very few of them. But she rubbed Maggie's shoulders, reassuringly, then let her go. The child would survive, and so would Bea.

The phone rang. It was Max, in hectoring mode. 'Mother, I need to see you. What have you been saying to Lettice?'

'Calm down, Max. Lettice and I have been getting to know one another better, that's all.'

Heavy breathing. 'She's not picking up my calls.'

Ah, Lettice had noticed a call on her mobile as they left the charity's offices and had decided not to accept it just then. Had that call been from Max? And if so, was Lettice's decision not to take the call a good thing or not? 'She makes her own decisions.'

'You're at the bottom of this, I know. I'm coming round.'

'It's not terribly convenient. Oh well, if you must. Ring three short and one long on the bell, and I'll let you in.'

'What? What are you up to now?'

'We don't want all and sundry ringing the doorbell tonight, that's all.' She killed the call.

Maggie was feeding Winston some chicken skin left over from supper. 'I'm sure a proper detective agency would have a spyhole in the front door.'

'I expect it would.'

The phone rang again. This time it was Piers. 'Are you all right? I tried you just now, and earlier on. You were engaged both times. I want to show you the photos I took of Nicole, see what you think. I'll be round in a few minutes, right?'

'Right. Use Beethoven's Fifth on the doorbell.'

'What?'

'Three short, one long.'

Maggie looked at the clock. 'It's early. I wonder if I might go along to that party, after all.'

'Or ring Zander?'

She didn't change colour but slowly shook her head. The phone rang again. Maggie was nearest and picked it up, listened and said, 'Give three short and one long ring on the doorbell and we'll let you in.' She put the phone down, considered her make-up in the mirror.

'Who was that?'

'Policewoman. Making sure you're all right. She'll be around in five minutes.'

Oh. The dishwasher had finished its stint. Bea opened it up. She looked at the clock, looked out of the window on to the flawless evening sunshine falling across the garden. It was, of course, ridiculous to think there was anything odd about the police calling her up at that time of night to make sure she was all right.

Only, she couldn't help remembering that there had been other misleading phone calls recently. Zander had been called up by someone pretending to be Della Lawrence; a call which was supposed to have taken him out to the suburbs and leave him without an alibi when the murderer called on his landlady.

Next, Della had reported a phone call from a neighbour who had supposedly taken in a parcel for her, and that phone call had kept her at home when she'd intended to join her niece at the pub.

The doorbell rang. Three short and one long. Max? Piers? Or ... who?

Friday evening

Honoria tried to breathe deeply. For the fourth time she went over what she'd done. She'd had to take her own small car and leave Denzil's Range Rover. Another sacrifice. But at least she'd brought away the evidence with her. She'd loaded the gun again, but seeing how built-up this neighbourhood was, she'd decided against using it. Too noisy. The hammer would do the job just as well.

She'd brought the bloodstained overalls with her in a plastic bag but didn't fancy struggling to pull them on over her ordinary clothes. For some reason, her magnificent body was no longer as responsive as it had been.

Humpty Dumpty had a great fall. Oh, what a fall was there!

She'd left the Manor ablaze and Denzil's beautiful car burning like a torch, with that stupid cleaning woman's body inside it. It hurt to think of all that she'd lost, all that she'd worked for, so many years of plotting and planning. Lost because of that pale Abbot creature. If it hadn't been for her...

Well, if it was the last thing she did, she was going to put that right. No one, but no one, got the better of Honoria and lived.

She rang the doorbell, three short and one long.

EIGHTEEN

Friday evening

Maggie sang out, 'I'll get it.'

'No, don't!' Bea, on the far side of the dish-washer, was too late. The girl was already unlocking the door, undoing the chain, opening it.

The door flew back, taking Maggie with it. The girl squawked, all the breath driven out of her as she was slammed back against the wall.

Bea heard the door crash to and knew she'd guessed right. A pity she hadn't thought to set the alarm when Oliver had left. She looked around for a weapon. Couldn't see one. A knife? There was only one small paring knife easily accessible. She snatched it up, held it behind her.

Honoria powered her way through the hall, her breathing loud, her eyes turning from left and right, searching for her prey. The hall was dim as sunlight faded from the day.

'Where is she?'

Maggie dragged herself upright, holding on to her ribs. 'Who are you! Why—?'

Honoria cut her off. 'Where's the Abbot woman?'

Bea showed herself in the doorway from the kitchen as Maggie gave a thin scream.

Honoria had Maggie's right arm bent up behind her. The girl was bent over, left arm flailing.

'Let her go,' said Bea, arms at her side.

Honoria pushed Maggie ahead of her as Bea backed slowly into the kitchen.

'So you're not dead,' said Bea. 'Whose body have they found in your car?'

'The cleaning woman, of course.'

'It ought to have been Kylie, though. Right?'

'Time enough.' The woman's breathing was so loud that it filled the kitchen. She threw Maggie from her, sending the girl crashing into a cupboard. She slid to the floor next to the open dishwasher, whimpering. Honoria drew a claw hammer from the bag slung over her shoulder.

'Plenty of time for Milly, too?' said Bea.

Honoria blinked. She continued to advance.

Maggie had both hands to her head.

Bea withdrew behind the table in the centre of the kitchen. 'Maggie; can you hear me? Get out! Quick!'

Maggie seemed to be only half conscious. She made an effort to rise. Honoria lifted her arm to swipe at the girl, who drew back just in time to avoid being hit again.

'She stays down on the floor until I've finished with you.' Calculation entered her eyes. 'You, Abbot. Tie her up, and then she'll be safe.'

Bea gave a short laugh, which she hoped didn't betray the fact that she was frightened to

337

death. 'How foolish that would be. No way. So long as she's free, she's got a chance. And if you want me, you'll have to come and get me – and hope I'm not holding a gun behind my back. Where's yours, by the way?'

Honoria blinked. 'Never you mind.' She advanced into the kitchen. Bea retreated till she came up against the back door. Now the table in the middle of the room was all that stood between them, too wide for Honoria to reach across.

Maggie drew herself up into a ball of misery, holding her head with both hands. She was jammed against the dishwasher. She couldn't move any further because Honoria was between her and the hall.

Bea calculated distances. She could run out of the kitchen door – if she could wrestle it open in time – but once down in the garden, surrounded by high walls, there was no way out. However, if she could entice Honoria to follow her round the table and down into the garden, then perhaps there was a chance for Maggie to escape out of the front door. If Bea did that then she would have to take her chances down in the garden, perhaps grab a spade from the shed with which to defend herself? Except that the shed door was padlocked and the key was hanging up in a cupboard above Maggie's head. And Maggie didn't seem capable of movement.

Could Bea perhaps lure Honoria round the table so that she could jump over the lowered door of the dishwasher, grab Maggie and run for safety? Not likely. Jumping over the dishwasher plus a stunned Maggie was not really on the cards. It would take an acrobat to do that. So, think of something else.

She took a step back towards the table. Honoria took one towards it. The woman was measuring distances, smiling. Perhaps she had been concerned that Bea might dive for the back door? But if Bea wasn't taking that escape route, then she was cornered.

Bea took one more step towards Maggie, acted as if she couldn't make up her mind what to do. Honoria laughed twirling her hammer, anticipating the moment when she would strike her opponent dead.

Maggie whimpered, curled into a ball. Honoria spared her a glance. The girl's terror seemed to please Honoria, for she passed her tongue over her lips. 'I'm going to kill you both, of course. I'll do the girl first, and then you. I can give the girl a quick death, or a slow one. It's up to you. If you don't want her to suffer, I can finish her off with one blow from this hammer. I know just how to do it. But I need you to beg for it first. Do you hear me? Down on your knees and beg. You'd do that for someone you're fond of, wouldn't you? So, how fond of this girl are you, eh?'

Bea held the woman's eye with hers. 'I am very fond of her. She's not my daughter, of course. You've never had children, have you?'

'What's that to you?' She swung the hammer, round and down, hitting the table. Maggie

339

shrieked. She looked up at Bea through spread fingers. Was she trying to convey a message? If so, Bea failed to understand what it was.

Dear Lord, help! Lord, in your mercy, hear my prayer. If I have to suffer, then so be it. But Maggie's still so young. Help her! Help us! Some distraction, please!

'I have a knife here,' said Bea, showing the sharp vegetable knife which was all she'd been able to pick up in her haste. 'You usually take your victims by surprise, but as you can see, I'm forewarned and armed.' She took another step towards Maggie, crouching low on the far side of the dishwasher. Honoria was still far too near to Maggie. Far too near. With one stride she could reach the girl and kill her.

Honoria put one hand on the work surface, bending forward, eyes gleaming. She began to follow Bea round the table, away from Maggie.

She raised the hammer to kill.

Winston plopped through the cat flap into the kitchen and jumped up on to the table, causing Honoria's concentration to waver for a moment. At the same time, the doorbell rang, three short and one long...

Maggie uncurled herself. She reached into the dishwasher to retrieve a dinner plate, which she sent curving through the air like a Frisbee, to catch Honoria on her upraised arm.

With a yell, Bea threw her little knife at Honoria's face. The woman ducked and the knife failed to hit her. But now Maggie had another plate in her hand, and this time aimed for the

340

woman's arm. And hit her on the shoulder.

Honoria yelled with fury. Winston fled with a shriek of alarm.

Maggie screamed.

Bea dived for the first thing that came to hand on her side of the dishwasher, a saucer, hurling it at the woman's head.

A dinner plate. Honoria threw up her arms to protect her head.

A glass, crashing into Honoria's forehead, caused her to drop her hammer, drove her back against the cooker.

Plates, glasses, knives and forks; the two women screamed and threw, crashing plates and glassware, breaking the glass of the cupboard door above Honoria, the front doorbell chiming furiously the while.

A dinner plate curled through the air and caught Honoria on her chin. She jerked to her full height and then – had she really been knocked out? – her legs gave way and let her down, slowly, so slowly, on to the floor.

As Bea stared, panting, another plate ready to throw, she saw something odd happen to Honoria's face. It slid sideways.

Honoria lay still, at an awkward angle.

Breathing hard, Bea lowered the plate she was holding on the table. She pushed Maggie towards the door. 'Let them in, whoever ... Probably Max ... or Piers.'

Maggie scrambled for the door, while Bea cast about, trying to find where Honoria had dropped her hammer. There. Under the table. Bea kicked it to one side, got the dustpan and brush and swept it into that.

Honoria didn't move. She looked grotesque, a large, untidy middle-aged to elderly woman lying on the floor, her head propped up at an angle by the stove behind her.

Maggie returned, panting out the news of what had happened, followed closely by Max, who took in the carnage and was deeply displeased. 'What on earth's been going on here? Just look at the mess!'

Piers was on their heels. 'Bea, are you all right? What...?'

'Meet Honoria, murderess extraordinary,' said Bea. 'Don't touch her! I don't trust her an inch. Although –' she peered down at the woman on the floor, whose face definitely looked lopsided – 'do you think she's had a stroke?'

Max said, 'What on earth is going on? Who is that woman? What is all this mess? Mother? I can't leave you alone for five minutes but you get into some scrape or other.'

'Shut up,' said Bea, being tough with him for once. 'Piers, tell him to go away and pretend he hasn't seen anything. After all,' she said, heavily ironic, 'he has to be careful for his reputation as a Member of Parliament, doesn't he? He won't want to be involved in capturing a woman who's killed at least four times to my knowledge. Maggie, I'm not taking any chances that she might be faking it. Can you find something – anything – that we could use to knock her out with, if she gets up and starts on us again?'

Maggie plucked a heavy Le Creuset pan off the rack by the stove. She stood with legs apart, both hands ready to wield the pan at the first sign of movement from Honoria.

Piers had his mobile phone out. 'Police first, I think. Max, get out of here while the going's good. I'll stay to support your mother and clear up afterwards.'

Max hesitated, but to do him justice, stayed. 'Let me talk to the police. They'll take notice of me.'

Reaction setting in, Bea began to cry and laugh at the same time. 'My best cut-glass tumblers.'

Maggie was grim. She had a bruise coming up on her chin and another on her upper arm where Honoria had hit her. 'I don't think we've a single dinner plate in one piece!'

Piers shut off his phone. 'I've called the police. They're on their way. I'm told that stroke victims need to be treated straight away, or they never make a complete recovery.'

Bea and Maggie looked at him, trying to work out what he hadn't put into words. Did he mean that he'd deliberately not asked for an ambulance, so that Honoria would be deprived of treatment straight away? That he was condemning her to suffer more than she need?

Bea moved towards the landline to summon an ambulance. Piers put out his hand to stop her. Bea looked at Maggie. Maggie looked back at her.

The woman on the floor grunted, her right

343

eyelid flickered. She tried to get off the floor and failed. Her left side appeared to be dead.

Maggie lifted the Creuset pan but hesitated to strike.

Somehow, painfully, Honoria managed to get to her knees, crunching shards of glass and pottery, and then, pulling herself up by the table, holding herself there by sheer willpower, she focused her one good eye on Bea ... who seemed unable to move.

Honoria lunged forward, signalling her intention to get at Bea ... and crashed to the ground again as her once enormous strength failed her.

Maggie dropped the Creuset pan. She was shaking. Crying. 'I couldn't hit her, I couldn't.'

'No,' said Bea, regarding the fallen creature with pity and horror. 'Neither can I.'

Max got out his own mobile, clearing his throat. 'I think we should summon an ambulance, all the same. They can sedate her, do whatever is necessary.'

Piers grinned, not nicely. 'We must be seen to go through the motions, mustn't we?'

Someone called out from the hallway. CJ appeared in the doorway, taking in the wrecked kitchen, the woman on the floor. He looked at her distorted face, her right hand clutching at the table leg, her left side useless.

'Who are you?' said Max to CJ. And into the phone, 'Ambulance, please.'

'He's a friend in need,' said Bea. 'CJ, can you mop up, please? Honoria came here to kill. Her hammer's in the dustpan. I haven't touched it.

344

She hit Maggie a couple of times, but I'm perfectly all right. Or, I will be when I've had a little sit down.'

An autumn morning, noon

The church was so full that the mourners overflowed the building and some had to listen to the service outside. A famous organist played Mendelssohn; a renowned quartet offered a favourite piece of Schubert. His grandson read out a roll call of his achievements for humanity. His great-grandchildren recited a poem he used to read to them when they were little.

Outside, where Bea stood with other latecomers, leaves gently dropped to the ground, yellow on green. Dahlias blazed yellow and red in the vases left in front of gravestones.

The celebration for the dead man's life was well attended by the great and the good. News photographers' cameras flashed as the mourners left the church. Most wore black, but the general mood was reflective and even cheerful rather than sad.

CJ caught up with Bea as the crowd turned into the road leading to Tommy's ancestral home.

'I tried to save you a seat,' said CJ, 'but a cabinet minister took it.' He looked back at the church. 'Quite well done. Tommy would have given it nine out of ten.' He was wearing black today.

Bea, who never wore black, was in her best

dark-blue suit. 'Yes, sorry I was late. What wouldn't he have liked?'

'The Trout Quintet. Too obvious, too saccharine. His grandson's choice.'

'I thought you were one of the executors. Didn't you have any say?'

He grimaced. 'Why quibble at something which pleases the grandson and heir? Life's too short.'

They joined the queue entering the hall of a superb Georgian house nearby. Bea wondered if Honoria thought life was too short, nowadays. She was still being held in a prison hospital wing and was reported to be making little or no progress back to speech and mobility.

Bea spotted Piers in the distance. He didn't see Bea, and she didn't wave to him. He was talking to a pretty woman of a certain age. Botox, thought Bea, and grinned to herself. Piers had painted Tommy, Lord Murchison many years before, and it was this likeness of the old man which had appeared in many of his obituaries.

Piers's picture of Nicole had received mixed reviews in the press and had, as he'd foreseen, led to his becoming more popular than ever. No doubt the woman he was escorting today also wanted him to paint her.

Bea and CJ progressed to the hall, shook hands with the new Lord Murchison, took a glass of something each, and filtered through into the dining room, which was laid out for a buffet lunch. At the table already was Lettice, all in black, wearing a stunning hat and listening with flattering attention to a portly man who looked as if he were somebody important.

'She's doing well at the Trust,' said CJ, somehow managing to acquire plates of food while others around them hesitated to help themselves. 'Come this way. It's quieter.'

Bea followed him through a communicating door into a huge library, and thence into an Edwardian conservatory, filled with the spicy scent of chrysanthemums. There were plenty of bamboo chairs around, and he ushered her to one.

Bea was suspicious of all this attention from CJ. He wanted something from her, presumably? It wouldn't be about the Trust, for Tommy's grandson had been unanimously adopted as the new chairman, and Lettice invited to become a director. Between them they were clearing out the old guard and, with Zander back in charge of the office, they were making sure that Denzil's antics were never repeated.

'I hear you have a grandson,' said CJ. 'Exciting for you.'

'Yes,' said Bea, who did indeed find it exciting. She put her hand to her bag to bring out her latest photographs of him, and then desisted. CJ wouldn't be interested in seeing them.

She believed she might know where this conversation was going but decided not to help him along. 'Max is enjoying his new responsibilities. I believe he thought the news stories about Honoria would damage his reputation, but there ... It turned out he was the hero of the hour,

347

arriving in the nick of time to save his poor old mother and her young lodger from being attacked by a hammer-wielding assassin. So it didn't do him any harm at all.'

CJ managed not to pull a face at this. 'I trust the cheque from Tommy covered replacement of your dinner service?'

And much more, as he knew very well. 'Yes, thank you,' said Bea, who'd not only replaced the broken crockery and glasses, but also put away a tidy sum towards Oliver's university expenses. Her money anxieties had been much eased by this, and by Piers coming up trumps – for once – by giving her a cheque to cover the replacement of the guttering at the back of the house.

'So.' He cleared his throat. Was he nervous? 'The agency is going well. You have quite a word for efficiency in the business. Taking on more staff, I understand? I'm a little surprised you were late this morning.'

Here it came. He knew why she was late, of course. 'Maggie and I took Oliver to Cambridge yesterday and settled him in. I'm afraid we stayed up for hours last night, talking about him and making plans. We're both going to miss him enormously.'

CJ cleared his throat again. 'Yes, of course his departure must leave a gap in your life. And a room to spare. My son Chris was wondering—'

'I understand he's not going back to university. What's he going to do with himself?'

'I said he could drop out for a year if he won

348

some prize or other, his film project, you know? And he did. Rather to my surprise. To his, too, I believe. I don't know how long this enthusiasm for film will last, but perhaps ... There's always hope that one day he'll settle into a career. I must admit we're neither of us looking forward to living cheek by jowl this next year. So he wondered—'

'No,' said Bea.

'You don't know what I'm going to ask.'

'Yes, I do. He's already tried to move his synthesizer in. Maggie and I have talked it over, and we're both agreed it wouldn't work. That room is Oliver's and not to be touched. Oliver needs a base, somewhere that's always there for him.'

CJ thought that over. Tried the pathetic touch. 'Neither my wife nor I expected to have children, and Chris came as something of a shock to us. Then, after she died—'

'No. You'll be asking me to adopt you, next.'

He perked up. 'I wouldn't mind.'

Was he trying to flirt with her? Almost, she giggled. No, flirtation was not on her agenda. She smiled to soften her refusal. 'You're old enough to take care of yourself. As for Chris, he's a lovely lad, but he drives me insane. I'd be had up for murder within months, if he moved into our house.'

'Well, as Oliver's always saying, murder pays.'

'Oliver's gone,' said Bea, suddenly wanting to cry.

349

'The terms are short. He'll be back soon enough. So you'd better save any other murders till he's around again.'

Bea tried to smile. 'Oh, he's not going to wait for half-term. We gave him a brand new laptop, and he's hooking himself on to email. He says we're to contact him at the first sign of trouble ... though I sincerely hope it's not another murder. We've had enough of those. The Abbot Agency does not, repeat not, handle murder.'

He smiled, 'What, never?'

Bea laughed. 'Well ... hardly ever.'